THE ORPHAN MAKER'S SIN

Holly DeHerrera

Eileen, you
I pray you
will feel
God's deep
love in
your own
beautiful
story!
Love,
Holly
DeHerrera

Blackside Publishing
Colorado Springs, CO

THE ORPHAN MAKER'S SIN

Holly DeHerrera

*To my five babies both big and small, and to my husband.
You are my gifts from God and fill me with joy. You have
taught me about true love and about tears-pouring-down-
your-face laughter. I am so grateful for each and every one
of you and each and every day with you.*

"There is no pit so deep that God's love is not deeper still."

—CORRIE TEN BOOM, THE HIDING PLACE

"The wisest is the one who can forgive."

–AN ARABIC PROVERB

I IZMIR, TURKEY, 2007

The bus door groaned open to the dirty Turkish street. My feet landed on pavement, though temptation told me to run back to my safe plastic seat and glue my butt down tight. The smell of bread wrapped its arms around my shoulders, an old friend I remembered well, even after fifteen gaping years away.

His spirit wanders here. I feel it.

I pulled air into my chest and struggled to exhale in a slow, stretching stream. Looking around, I spotted the familiar sight of men pressing their foreheads to the dusty ground with only small prayer mats buffering their knees from their submission to Allah. *Must be five o'clock . . . the İkindi, the fourth holy call of the day.* But jet lag made me think the sinking sun lied. The beckoning to worship echoed from blaring minaret loudspeakers, tugging me back into another time.

The person I was to meet most likely waited at the station across the street. I snatched up my bags and sprinted across the congestion. Taxis and workers' buses jutted past, nosing into inadequate spaces, and honking—like it helped. The barrage of noise, the over-stimulus, reminded me of being six years old and lost in the grand bazaar. I swallowed. Hard.

Quit being a coward. Pull yourself together.

I gripped my luggage to regain control, my sweaty hand squeezing the faux-leather handle of my suitcase. But I kidded myself. I'd never been in control. I was just a leaf being shoved down river. Forget the facts. That I chose to come here. I bought the ticket. I made all the arrangements to begin work teaching English at the orphanage on August fifth.

I'm a leaf, plain and simple. Despite all my faith, I'm hooked to nothing.

Mom pushed me to return. Said it would bring healing. Closure. Yea, right, more like cutting into an old wound with a *döner kebab* skewer and drizzling on lemon.

I crossed the busy street dodging a white Fiat whose driver leaned out the window flashing a line of piano-key-white teeth. "Hallo. Looking for fun?" He hung his arm over the door and raised his eyebrows in an "Aren't-you-impressed-I-speak-English" expression.

Everything about me screamed, "American—magnet for creeps." I turned away, pretending not to see him. I pretended to be someone who had a clue. My pulse thumped, thick and heavy in my neck.

Outside the station stood a man with a face like one of those dried apple-head dolls. He sold pomegranates, looking like rubies displayed on burlap, out of the back of his beat-up farm truck.

"*Madame?*" The helpful salesman looked at me.

I approached and asked in my brushed-up Turkish, "*Kaç para?*"

He named the price then sliced open the red orb, revealing the encased seeds. Juice trickled down his palm and onto the ground. He placed the fruit in my hand and said, "Try, try."

And just like that I transported back again, to 210 *Gaziosmanpaşa.* Seven years old. The road splattered with tiny drops of blood and burnt pistachios.

Like hot pins poking the pads of my fingers, my hand recoiled, dropping the offering.

Like something was wrong with the first one, he grabbed another and sliced it open. More juice dribbled through his arthritic fingers. I forced mine forward, accepted the fruit, deposited the asking price onto the side of his truck-bed and turned away.

I wiped my wet hand on my skirt, caring only a little about the stain, only because the blotch reminded me of my weakness.

A man stepped into my universe, clearing his throat with a manly rumble. A Roman god with black eyebrows cocked above eyes the color of wet sand, sideburns dark against dark skin.

"Is it you?" He shoved a hand into his black jeans, then removed it right away, blinked rapidly and added, "I mean, is . . . are you Ella?"

My name spoken with his heavy accent sounded foreign and for a moment I questioned. *Am I actually here? And do I want to be?*

My rigid arm ground forward to shake his hand. He drew me toward his puckered lips. I squeezed my eyes shut because being kissed seemed ridiculous. And besides, I'd travelled all morning and my lips were chapped. His mouth brushed each side of my face, a butterfly landing and taking off too soon and his warm hands enveloped mine for a moment to steady my balance.

I opened my eyes, my cheeks flushed warm at my mistake. How could I have forgotten the typical greeting: a kiss on each cheek? I managed the first word that came to mind, *"Merhaba."*

He bit the inside of his mouth maybe to keep from laughing. The slightest wrinkles formed around his eyes. He answered with a smile. "Hello. Welcome to Izmir. I'm Murat." An undertow tugged at my feet. The ocean, within walking distance, only enhanced the sensation. A seagull swooped down and pecked at something near the farm truck.

"The *dolmuş* is there." He pointed to a beat-up van, then plucked the bags from my grip. I watched his back as he strolled to the rear of the vehicle and hefted them in. The black curls of his glossy hair dulled the brightness of his white, soccer jersey.

He turned to me and said with a question in his voice, *"Tamam?"*

Okay? No. I'm not okay. I moved my lips without the accompanying confidence and echoed, *"Tamam."* And just like that I found myself shuttled in and the door closed. As he drove, scenes flickered past in a blue-green blur.

A village scattered with gray, boxy cement homes. Women wearing *şalvar,* baggy floral pants, sitting cross-legged on flat rooftops. Phone lines slumped and zigzagged with no clear starting or ending points. Minarets jutting near hanging cliffs overlooked patchwork fields of lime-green and brassy yellow—all while the seaside teased in aqua flashes.

The sweat under my hair clip lifted away as the wind blew through the window. The Turkey I savored as a child pushed the new against the old. All of it sat in a confused pile, jewels and unremarkable rocks together in one dirty-brown palm.

Touching my arm then pointing, Murat said, "There. That's it." Aware of his fingerprints on my wrist, I rubbed the feeling away.

I checked out the painted sign for the orphanage, then inspected my cream-colored skirt smeared with crimson. Two monster-sized waves—the past and present—threatened to collapse into one another. No more pressing the surging swells back at the end of each arm.

Time's come to let them fight it out. ✍

2 THE ORPHANAGE

"So you live at the orphanage?" I picked at my gauzy broom skirt, releasing its clinging. The humidity swaddling my body reminded me of hanging my head over a pot of boiling water to exfoliate my face. I lifted dangling strands of hair off my neck and blew in my shirt hoping to stop the incessant sweating. *I'm leaving my prints everywhere. Please, Jesus, don't let me have B.O.*

"*Evet.* I do. I've lived here since I was a boy." Murat steered the vehicle through the entrance of the property. As we stopped, the brake pads squealed. He ran a dark hand through his even darker hair and then turned to face me. His focused attention with no plans to move the vehicle made me feel like a criminal in an interrogation room.

"But you're a man now. Why stay?" There. That sounded casual and confident. *Why isn't he sweating?*

"I want to help. June and Barry . . . they helped my *Anne* and me." He stopped and cleared his throat. "*Ah-ney* is Turkish word for mom."

I nodded like I already knew that.

"And when we came to live here, is what I can do to work with the kids and help work on the grass, the flowers."

"You take care of the grounds?"

Murat blinked, masking for a moment his intense eyes. "*Evet.* I take care of the grounds." His hands roamed around the steering wheel. His jaw worked the muscles on the sides of his face, like gnawing on something he couldn't make himself swallow.

"What? Is something wrong?" I asked.

"Yes. Is one of our housemothers. She's missing. Just this morning she is gone."

"Gone? I'm sorry, I don't get it. She left on her own?"

"No, she won't leave. I don't think so. She was afraid of her husband. His family."

"So she was here because of him?"

"Yes. Because of him. Her little boy, Umut, has been crying. He won't talk. Just cries."

I knew how the orphanage worked with mothers acting as caregivers to the orphans, living in the many homes scattered around the property. I didn't realize they also harbored victims of abuse. The fence skirting the property, the rickety metal gate in front, all painfully insufficient to provide any real protection. "So it could be her husband abducted her by force?"

"Yes," Murat shrugged then glanced toward the entrance, like he blamed himself. The set of his brow, that of a man driven by something greater than duty. His lips pinched together in determination. His chin curved slightly upward. A rope-like bulge on his neck twitched. His thick lashes remained half-mast, searching some invisible scene unfolding. The instinct to solve this problem kicked in. I couldn't help it, I touched his forearm.

"Tell me how I can help." I said it like I was the kind of girl who could actually fix her own issues. But then, other people's problems weren't so difficult to solve.

Murat's hands gripped the steering wheel. His eyes darted back and forth at mine. A fraction of a blink and a nod told me in the Turkish way that he was thankful, that together we'd figure this out. And just like that, purpose drove out doubt like a tidal wave sweeping away an entire shoreline of skeletons. ❧

3 GÜVENLİ BÖLGE

Murat drove through the entry marked by their sign, *Güvenli Bölge*.

"What does that mean?" I pointed.

"Safe haven." He smirked.

He continued along a curved dirt road. Olive trees lining the path were dwarfed by tall, silver-leafed Russian elms draping arms together in conspiracy, enclosing the space, making it feel hemmed in and protected.

Ironic.

Sort of like the armed Turkish "guard" who once monitored my family's apartment building, loaded with high-ranking American military men. His presence was no more useful than the fence, the locked gate, or the trees.

Murat stopped the van in front of a small house then killed the engine. He exited and I opened my door. A cluster of tanned children tugged at my shirt with their hands raised toward my face.

I wavered between "how cute" and wanting to jiggle my leg to fling off the two year old wrapped around my knee like a monkey. Being an only child hadn't prepared me well for this moment. Neither did my student teaching. Neither did my need for personal space.

I noticed Murat standing, like a Middle Eastern supermodel, near the edge of the porch. I moved toward the tiny house.

The small cottage I pegged as my new place of residence was more like an American single-story, beachfront home than the basic Turkish cement structure. Dull blue vertical shingles covered the outside. The gray screen door on the enclosed front porch swung open and out stepped a fiftyish, blond woman. She whispered in the ear of a boy nestled against her bosom as she walked toward me. Waddling like a pregnant woman, the child she protected hung on the outside of her torso.

"I'm June." She leaned in and kissed me on both cheeks. This time I was ready. She wasn't a tall, exotic man, so it wasn't the same anyway. "I'm so glad you're here. How was your trip?"

"Fine, thanks." I lied, my first reaction whenever asked questions like, "How are you?" or "How are things going?" Most people didn't mind. They actually expected not to deal with the messy details of, "No, I'm not fine. I'm a wreck."

June was shorter than I, which made her five-foot nothing, with eyes like green sea glass. Smile lines ringed her wide mouth. Her feet spread shoulder-width, her body unconsciously rocked back and forth with the small boy tucked under her chin, leaving me feeling like I was in good company not having it all together. I swayed with her, then stopped myself.

"I'm sorry I didn't meet you at the bus stop. I needed to be here . . . an unexpected . . ." June bumbled for words floating around amidst all the unknowns. "Today has not been a joyful one for little Umut here or any of us. Did Murat tell you?"

Murat stepped forward. "Yes. She knows about Pinar." The scene resembled a military debriefing with me "the rookie" taking notes. Feeling awkward and in the way, I needed something to look more legitimate. Like a clipboard. Or maybe a child.

Relief eased June's tightened lip and jaw. She added, "Thank you for understanding, Ella. Later we'll settle you in and get to know each other properly." The woman rubbed Umut's back in a slow, circular motion, his eyes a dull, brown canvas, like a puppy backed into a corner with no escape. "The truth is, I hardly know where to begin. Pinar has been here only a short time, just three months. If she left on her own accord it would be less distressing." June studied Umut. "But, no. I'm thinking she was taken."

"Is there any security on the grounds?" I scanned the property. *Surely there must be something to keep any lunatic from sauntering in and stealing people.*

"No, not really. Aside from the front gate. But the surrounding wall is easy enough to climb if a person wants to."

"Have you spoken with the other children?" I resisted a pressing urge to criticize. My fingertips smoothed my eyebrows flat.

Murat scratched the side of his head, leaving his hair rumpled and sticking out at an odd angle. "Yes, it must have happened after they left for school. They said she was there in the morning and wasn't upset."

June piped up, "Umut, here, is Pinar's only biological son. He's her youngest, just four. The only one who doesn't attend the local school. I'm thinking he would have been there and seen . . . he keeps asking where his *Anne*, his mom, is. Anyway, I'd like to start searching. Murat, can you and Ella drive to Pinar's old neighborhood?"

In one second flat a storm cloud darkened Murat's face. He shook his head as his arms clamped against his chest. "Is not a good idea. She's a girl."

Say what? Heat prickled through my lips. "I'd be happy to go, June. Thanks for asking." My chin shot out toward Murat.

"Ella, you cannot handle this problem. Pinar's husband. . ." Murat squinted at me, "He might be there."

Does he think I'm an infant instead of a grown woman? "I don't care about that." *Liar.*

He eyed me, perhaps assessing whether, if the situation warrant it, I could at least fight like a girl. I swallowed, my throat dry like swigging a cup full of sand. Somehow this battle seemed important. The first of many.

Murat offered a curt nod, then said, "*Tamam*. I won't take you inside. You will help with Pinar, if we find her."

I took the words as a personal challenge; after all, I came for a reason. And not just for myself.

"Sure," I said, adrenaline cramped my stomach a little. "Have the police been notified?"

"No. That would not help," Murat said.

June explained, "They are still married, you see? Pinar's husband needs only call her unfaithful and he'd be a hero for willingly taking her back home."

I cringed at the thought. "And abuse, if there is evidence of that, can't that be dealt with at least?"

"Pinar has never been willing," June said, apology edging her words. "She doesn't believe she deserves better. And she's too

afraid of him to say anything to the police."

I couldn't think of a thing to say. What could be done then? Frustration, my companion since seven years old, constricted my throat. I followed Murat to the van.

And moments later we were driving on a ribbon of paved road paralleling the coastline. The aqua waters of the Aegean Sea glittered in the afternoon light. I considered how contradictory the setting so often is. When tragedy is at play. Like a blazing sunrise the morning after your father died.

"Murat." I pulled my gaze from the blue-green sea and turned to face him. "Can I ask you something?"

"Sure." He watched the road. His pulse thumped against the dark skin of his neck.

"Is there anything we can really do to help Pinar if she's being held captive by her husband?"

"Yes." The van hummed a background song in a minor key.

I waited for more. He didn't offer any further explanation.

"What then?" I couldn't help being a realist. Besides, we needed a plan.

"I will teach him a lesson myself." His eyes were glued to the road, but I sensed his mind envisioned something entirely different.

He's clearly not one to back away from a fight.

Respect surged up and grabbed hold of my shoulders, bidding me to follow someone else's lead—for once. Maybe vigilante justice was better anyway. Just get to the heart of things without the tangle of red tape. Punch the loser in the face and call it a day.

Murat pulled up to a run-down, cement home and shoved the gear shift into park. A high wall surrounded the small property. The drab whitewash screamed *sad*, with large chunks missing. An arched opening led to a dirt yard containing a sorry flock of chickens, more bald than feathered, pecking at gravel.

Murat squinted at the second-story home. "Stay here. I'll need you to care for Pinar if she's here. I do not want you to come in. *Tamam?*"

"*Tamam*. Okay." The feminist part of me reared its head and I told it to "shut up." My heartbeat throbbed in my chest and temple. *What if this man came out? What if he already did something terrible to the woman? What if he tried to hurt Murat?* I scrutinized the long dirt path in front of the vehicle, our escape route littered with small children playing soccer.

If Murat shared my concerns, he didn't let on. He leapt out of the van and slammed the door. I flinched thinking for sure the creepy husband officially knew of our arrival. Nothing like announcing our presence to the enemy. Murat entered the yard without a moment's hesitation.

Unfazed, Murat ascended a long flight of cement stairs running the length of the left wall to the second story of the home. The steps contained no railing whatsoever. *This is no place for a little boy to live.* I shuddered at how easily Umut could lose his footing on the crumbling steps and tumble over the side.

At the top, Murat leaned in and glanced into a window to the left of the front door. He crept toward the door gauging whether the woman was there. Whether her husband waited to pounce. And then the entrance swallowed him up. Funny how easily hope extinguishes. ❧

4 THE HUSBAND'S HOUSE

Murat's muscles acknowledged a dull ache like after a beating from his dad. The tension refused to let go no matter how many times he opened and closed his hands or rolled his head. *Why did Ella have to come along, only making the situation harder?* He ducked into the dark space Pinar once called home. Should her so-called husband dare to show his weasel-like face, Murat was sure he'd break the man's jaw.

The front room hunched in the darkness, witness to the violence. Murat struggled to make things out. His eyes adjusted and surveyed the scene. A table tossed on its side. A newspaper scattered across the floor. Glass *çay* cups shattered against the far wall, scattered in an arc below a brown, bleeding stain.

Beside the splotch, a wedding picture dangled at an odd angle by a bent straight pin. Looking closer at the photo, Murat noticed Pinar and Ahmed standing shoulder to shoulder under an arched entryway. Only—Pinar's head was missing. A jagged hole the size of a man's finger replaced her face.

Sick. Father, why do you give us the freedom to make our own poison?

Drenched in quiet, the situation didn't look promising. A small bedroom flanked the living room to the left. Murat leaned in to find it empty and trashed.

Lord, please.

He couldn't handle finding the young mother dead. His throat ached, thick and sore from swallowing his anger over and over without success. Hearing a shuffle then a sucking in of breath moved him to the box-like kitchen on the opposite side of the living area.

Cowering in the corner crouched a terrified shadow of a woman. Pinar. She squinted at Murat like she struggled to remember him, to assess whether he was friend or enemy, her eyes smeared with black eye makeup. A bluish-purple bruise glared on her right

cheek. She stared at the floor, her knees pressed against her chest like a baby. She hummed low and haunted without uttering anything intelligible.

"Pinar." Murat knelt in front of her to make eye contact.

Pinar snapped her head back, like an abused child, unsure of who to trust.

"Pinar. It's Murat. I'm taking you home."

Her eyes darted around the room perhaps expecting an ambush. She shuffled her butt back with a scrambling of her bare feet.

Determining the woman incapable of responding, let alone walking, Murat scooped Pinar into his arms. He expected a fight, but she remained limp. A rag doll.

He carried her out of the house and maneuvered his way down the steps to the van. Ella's eyes widened as they approached, but she didn't delay. She sprang out and opened the back passenger door. Murat settled Pinar into the seat. Like a scared little girl trying to be brave, Ella jutted her chin up and snapped a quick nod at Murat before jumping into the back seat beside Pinar. She wrapped her small hand around the woman's slouched shoulder.

Ella didn't ask any questions. She didn't ask about the location of Pinar's husband. Or what happened. The scene rendered her mute. Her arm stabilized this stranger and her free hand grasped the greasy tips of her new friend's hair, smoothing them between her fingers. Ella's eyes closed. Her mouth moved. *Yes, prayer is the only thing to do right now.*

Murat guided the vehicle away snatching glances through his rear view mirror. An unexpected burning spread through his chest, like he'd held his breath the entire time and just now allowed himself to breathe in the clean, salty air.

I sat in the center of June's living room. Rust and blue wool pillows scratched my legs. How could I feel so at home and so out of place at the same time? I watched June in her small kitchenette

as she poured tea into the copper, hand-embossed Turkish teapot. Watched the rise and fall of her shoulders. Heard the slight, almost non-existent sigh before she turned to face me. She plastered on a smile. I noticed a secret sadness slink into the green of her eyes.

She placed the serving tray on the low, shiny tabletop. I leaned over and caught my reflection mirrored in the polished brass. I saw a scared child peering into a well, tossing pennies into the water. I almost smiled thinking how funny to place so much hope into wishing for things on coins—like they could hold all the terrible weight of my wishes on their thin shoulders.

I leaned back and ordered the little girl to "go away." Only grown-ups were allowed to do things like help orphans. Frightened little girls had no business here. Especially when a murderer needed confronting.

The hollow, bubbly gurgle of June pouring tea drew me back. June lifted one of the diminutive glass cups, calla lilies holding scalding water. Then she extended the tea to me, coaxing me from the place my mind ran off to. The parallel universe I kept crossing into. *But she's not here either, not really.*

I grasped the thin glass rim. I imagined the swirling steam revealed whatever this woman was not saying, giving shape to the unspoken. I lifted the cup to my mouth. The warmth spiraled up against my cheeks before I sipped the deep mahogany çay, burning my lips. I snatched the glass back then swished the scalding liquid around my mouth before swallowing. I blew out, then allowed my voice to enter the silence.

"June?"

"Hmm?" She looked up from studying the tapestry of a handwoven, wool *kilim* pillow.

"What will happen now? To Pinar, I mean."

"She will stay here. And I pray will not go back to him."

"Did you talk to her? Find out what happened?"

June rubbed her chest and answered, "Yes. But she's not talking right now."

I snatched a sugar cube and dropped it into my tea, watching it collapse beneath the heat before I stirred it into oblivion with a

tiny silver spoon. "What's to stop her husband from coming back to get *her*?"

"Nothing, I suppose. Except maybe pride."

I wished June would get to the point. "But . . ."

June appraised me, first looking at my eyes, then her gaze roamed my face. "I'm sorry, Ella. I have a lot on my mind. I don't mean to be vague." She wrapped her small hands around her glass, squeezing it. Her nails shifted from pink to white with the pressure of her grip.

I stood to leave. "I can just go."

"No, please." She lifted her hand and clutched the hem of my skirt. "I really do want to sit and visit. Get to know you a bit." June's face radiated truth, but I couldn't shake the feeling she hid something.

I sat down trying not to act like a spoiled child who wasn't getting enough attention. "Why don't you tell me about the kids?"

We spent the rest of the evening talking about the children, the preschool-aged kids to whom I'd teach English. As we discussed everything except the real problem, Umut's little face floated in the back of my mind. The feel of Pinar's dirty hair between my fingertips wouldn't go away. She sat exposed, like a duck on a wide open pond. And none of us was safe. Least of all, me. ❧

5 THE RUG SHOP

The whoosh of his breath and the whispered rustle of trees hushed Murat's tension. He couldn't help but tune into everything inside and outside of him. How could the day of Ella's arrival mark the first case of a husband coming to retrieve his wife?

The incident should have occurred long ago. He'd expected the danger. Tumbling like a glass bottle in the waves, his thoughts turned over and over. Murat had no control over Pinar being taken again. *How can I protect them all? Now I have one more person to worry about.*

Murat's thoughts flicked to the moment Pinar curled into a fetal position on the van's backseat and Ella took over. From that moment, the tentative American—a mystery of vulnerability and briars—awed him. He liked that she fought with both. Uncertainty pushed a person to lean on the only certain thing in this life: God's loving arms. At least that seemed to hold true for a woman.

Murat mounted the few steps in front of June and Barry's home to check on how Ella settled in. The woman who filled his brain like liquid, opened the front door.

"Hello, Murat," she shifted from one foot to another, then leaned in and kissed his cheeks.

Now you've got the hang of it. Why have I never felt the greeting intimate until this moment?

"How are you?" Ella asked. Already they shared a history through the ordeal with Pinar.

"I'm fine. And you?" Murat shoved his hands into his jean pockets to keep from figuring out what to do with them. "You like your room?"

"Yes, it's good. I just visited with the kids. They're sweet."

Murat noticed her rosy cheeks and her lips pulled into a smile over slightly crooked front teeth. The stress he detected the day before had melted away somewhat.

He understood. The children affected him the same way too. Loving them required no effort.

Ella tucked a stray hair behind her ear and looked at her feet. Murat took in her features again, her tight dark curls amassed into a sloppy bun, like they could be tamed. Light brown freckles scattered against her pale skin. A dragonfly darted near her shoulder.

He leaned to wave off the metallic-green insect and caught the scent of her perfume—something flowery. Standing a full head taller than Ella, Murat's height gave him the strongest urge to protect her. He retreated down a step to communicate the illusion she could take care of herself, but he knew that wasn't true. Not here.

"Well, I better get to work."

"Yeah, the grass, right?" She offered another smile and he couldn't help but answer with his.

"The grass." Words and mature brain waves hid behind the trees. He'd never been one to act awkward with the opposite sex. He focused on his job. Taking care of the kids and the women awarded him no time for romance, and no desire for it either. Why take chances when he couldn't protect and love even one more person? He'd been dealt this hand and tried not to think about how things could be different if his work wasn't so all-consuming.

"Murat, it's really pretty." She waved a hand toward the field filling the center of the property. "You underestimate what you do. I mean, this place is huge and look at all these flowers." She leaned over and shoved her nose into a pink peony bloom. "Mmmmm."

"*Teşekkür ederim.* Thank you. I'm busy, that's true. Is work I like to do. Flowers are good listeners with no problems to add. Just water, prune. Is easy. The rest. . ." She eyed him and waited for him to finish. "The rest is not so easy."

The landscaping wasn't fancy and Murat worked on it whenever his schedule allowed. The grass spread neatly, a deep blue-green. The bushes sagged with healthy, pale-pink blooms, the air thick with their aroma.

"You said you also work at a bread shop?" Ella placed a hand on his forearm, snatched it away, and then mumbled, "Sorry." Her

face flushed. All insecure, she chewed on her lower lip, chapped and red. "I've missed the bread."

Was this the same woman jet lag rendered mute, irritable, and defensive? Who mumbled only a few curt words yesterday? Had vulnerability stripped her to survival mode?

"I will bring you some, *tamam*?" Murat promised.

"That would be great. Well, Murat, I've got some things I need to do. Places to go."

"*Tamam*." He said the word 'okay,' but didn't mean it. Ella brushed past him. "Ella, where are you going?" He hardly knew the girl well enough to be overprotective so soon.

She turned back to him, the softness around her eyes giving way to minuscule lines. "Well. . . just places I remember from when I used to live here." She shifted her weight, waiting for him to say something.

What could he say without coming across all wrong? "Can I take you where you must go?"

"I don't even know exactly where I'm going. I could be gone all day. I want to wander and, at some point, go to the base." She stopped short, then added, "Since I don't really start working with the kids until tomorrow."

"It's fine. I don't have plans."

"What about the grass?"

"I'll do it later." He expected her to run the other way since he most likely acted like a possessive husband. "I promise not to bother you. Just drive and wait."

Her hesitation left him with a dull ache in his gut. Forcing his attention on any person went against his grain, let alone a woman he preferred not to alienate.

"All right. I'll grab my things." She looked down.

The slump of her shoulders and the defeat in her voice made him feel like a bully who cornered someone to get his way. He set off to pull the van around front. Yes, romance needed to be avoided. Clearly his job to protect forced that possibility back like a dam against rising flood waters. The desire left him feeling empty and alone. No, he couldn't even daydream of Ella in any way other than

a co-worker on a common mission. He'd already lost too much in this life. Better to play it safe.

So what if I just got here? I need to find answers. I've waited for fifteen years already. Standing this close to my childhood, I couldn't make myself be patient. I snatched my small purse, looped it over my neck and under my arm, and then skipped down the stairs.

First the base. *I'll wander around there and see who might know anything about former service men lost during the Gulf War.* The warm wind lifted stray curls off my neck. I pulled them up and secured them in my bun. *There. Already I'm getting down to business.*

Murat waved at me from his place near the van where he leaned against the passenger side and waited. Like he had all the time in the world. His sideburns, along with his upper lip, glistened with sweat. I forced my gaze to his eyes.

"Ready to go?"

I stifled the woman I'd become. The one who didn't like to answer questions. The one who survived just fine for years without any help from a man. I answered, "Yes. I'm ready."

I didn't get it. Turkey wasn't Saudi Arabia. More like Greece, with a little bit of Iraq thrown in for good measure.

"Why do you think I shouldn't go out alone?" *Goodness, did I just whine?*

"Because, women . . . American women are seen . . ." Murat looked away, back at the grass maybe wishing he'd chosen to hang out on the green instead of explaining the basics of Turkish etiquette to a simple girl.

"I'm dressed appropriately. No large areas of skin." I waved my broom skirt like a can-can girl. "Plus, I used to live here, remember?" *So what if I was only seven then? What difference did that make?* "I know what I'm doing."

"Just. . . it's a bad idea. You don't know the city anymore. It's grown. The taxi drivers might take you the long way."

"So I lose a little *lire* until I figure things out. I can take care of myself, Murat. I need to take care of myself." The urge to thank and strangle the same person at the same time was unfamiliar.

"I'd feel better to take you."

I spit out a spoiled huff and tried to regain my composure. Tried to remind myself I'm an adult and could be gracious and do the right and expected thing.

"All right. But some places I want to go in alone. It's weird having someone come along for everything. For . . ." I wasn't ready to explain things to Murat. To anyone, actually.

Murat's broad smile almost made me step back. "*Teşekkür ederim*, Ella. You won't even know I'm with you."

I seriously doubt that. His eyes appeared almost green like the waters by the shore tangled with seaweed.

"Ready?" I noticed his attempt to move past the conflict. He steered me with his hand on my back to the van. He opened the door, depositing me inside, then jogged around to the driver's seat.

I waited with the door ajar pretty sure I'd die of heat stroke if I closed it even for a minute. Being a passenger, shuttled around at the mercy of a stranger grated. I sighed into the thick humid air. Even small victories were hard to come by.

Murat climbed in and flashed a stunning smile. I noticed the fresh shirt clinging to his fit torso. His wet hair shone all wavy and jet black. The smell of something spicy filled the small space. "Did you take a shower?"

"No." He offered a lopsided, boyish grin. "Just a Turkish bath." He chuckled, low and confident. I swallowed my jealousy of his assurance. He wasn't even fazed by my rude request to leave me the heck alone. And I wished for the millionth time I was stronger and could be sure of even one thing for once. "So, *Madame*, where do we go?"

"How about the alley? Maybe the base later."

"The alley? I don't know this place."

"Really? That's the small street outside of the base where there

are a bunch of tiny shops. Let's see if I can remember . . . Ahmed, the copper dude. Nergiz, the rug dude."

"Rug dude?" His profile revealed small creases around his eyes, almost indiscernible if I hadn't watched like a hawk.

"Yep. He sells rugs and he's a dude. See?"

"*Tamam.* I know this place, the alley. I take you there now."

"Good. And no taking me the long way. I won't pay a *lira* over ten thousand." I enjoyed his quiet chuckle along with his presence. I mostly forgot about needing to feel in control. About privately finding answers. Maybe the answers would come in the everyday moments rather than in some big shining revelation.

The sounds of the city blew on my face, loud and unfettered, as we darted past a world of places long overhauled by progress and tourism. The vibrant music faded and grayed when I imagined my father buried under the ground, under the cement boardwalk lining the waterfront, under the pounding hooves of a horse hauling a small man and a wagon full of fruit, under tall buildings jutting into the air, beneath the wheels of this van, and under me. Like so many others I got lost in, the moment muted.

I'm stuck.

A person tethered with sandbags, in the precise moment Dad died. The moment I died, too, right along with him.

Murat cut off another driver to obtain the closest parking spot in front of the rug shop on the small street. I shot him "the look," but he was clueless he'd done anything wrong. I opened the door and tossed over my shoulder, "Back in a few minutes."

He leaned his seat back and turned up the Turkish hip-hop tune on the radio. "*Tamam.* I'm here."

Yeah, you are. And how come you have to be so distracting while you're at it?

I scanned the street for some of the other shops I remembered. The copper shop still remained just across from the rug shop, the

reddish-brown glow of the room full of various pots and platters emanating through the entry, but the restaurant we frequented was gone, replaced by a drug store with the word *Eczane* in big red modern lettering across the door frame.

I turned away, not liking the take-over of one of our favorite spots, and headed to Nergiz's rug shop, unfazed by the passage of time. When I stepped into the entrance, the coolness of the dark room wrapped around me, smelling of wool and mothballs. The same rugs rolled tight leaned against the wall, waiting to be shown off.

"*Merhaba. Nasilsinez?*" Nergiz's greeting cracked open a time capsule. On the smooth, wooden bench sat dad and mom, holding hands, eyes bright as they examined the pile of *kilims*, chattering about which runner would look perfect in the entry of their cramped, base housing.

Dad's nasal-wheezing laughter and mom's playful smack against his forearm broke the quiet. The past rolled out, a scattering of tiny, white mothballs attempting to preserve something, but only making everything smell lifeless.

It took a moment to regain my bearings in the present. I looked away from the empty bench and noticed Nergiz standing in the doorway of the side room, still young and ready to sell rugs.

At first I couldn't speak thinking I imagined the man—a trick of the place. He stepped forward looking concerned and said again, a little less sure, "*Merhaba?*"

"You're real."

"Can I help you, *Madame?*"

Get it together, woman. "Yes. I'm sorry. I was just . . ." *A lunatic? Mentally unstable?* "Nergiz?"

The man's smooth face split with a smile. "No, this is my uncle. He moved to Bursa many years past. This is where his family goes."

"Oh, well, that's good. Good for him."

As the man shifted, coins jangled in his pocket. "Can I show you rugs?" Like Vanna White, he brandished his hand toward the wall of stiff rolled rugs and walked toward them, nodding his head in encouragement. "Many beautiful rugs for a beautiful lady."

My lungs unleashed air like a balloon fizzing to the ground in a pathetic heap. "No. No rugs today, thank you. I was looking for Nergiz. Please have a good day." I turned and exited into the blinding sunlight, then remembered. I craned my head into the store's entrance, "Thank you."

My stomach cramped. Saliva pooled under my tongue at the sight of thin slices of roast lamb sliced off a vertical spit in a shop window. I walked toward the beautiful sight, my way suddenly obstructed by the hot, rancid breath of a scruffy man about twice my age.

"Yes. Can I help you, *Madame*?" He leered as his head tipped toward me, his forehead nearly touching mine.

Resisting the urge to thrust my knee into his groin, I said a firm, profound, "No." I pressed his chest away from mine.

He moved in closer, clamping his hand on my upper arm. He tugged me toward an alleyway between the rug shop and restaurant. My stomach twisted, sour and hot.

From nowhere Murat appeared and pushed his hand against my stomach. He stepped between the two of us, like the parting of the Red Sea. He lurched toward my assailant, bulldozing him away from me.

I couldn't see Murat's face, just the back of his head. I heard his angry words, though I didn't understand the fast-paced Turkish. With a shove the culprit stumbled away, a stray dog slinking into the shadows of the street.

Murat whipped around to face me. "*İyi misin*?" Unaware he spoke Turkish to me, his black brows pinched together above eyes glaring with anger and fight.

"Yes. Thank you. I'm fine."

"I should have been here sooner. I got thirsty and went to get a drink."

He wasn't angry at me at all, only himself. Like he'd failed me. Like he had anything to do with this. My throat felt warm and thick, but why? I'd forgotten the feeling of being taken care of by a man. To lay clunky burdens on capable shoulders rather than dragging them behind me like a carcass.

I placed my hand on his sun-warmed arm. "Please, don't apologize. It isn't your fault. It's mine. I'm not hurt. Just a little startled is all."

Murat squinted, scrutinizing the street in the direction the man fled. "Where would you like to go?" Sharp edges lined his voice.

"*İskender*." I pointed to the lamb roasting in the shop window. Maybe food wouldn't solve the issue vexing Murat or slow down my heart rate, but I needed a distraction, and for me eating was the easiest answer. "And then we don't have to drive someplace. Much safer."

Needing time to transition, Murat ignored my implied message about his driving. After a moment he expelled a loud puff and raked his fingers through his hair. "*Tamam. İskender* is good. But not here. I know a good place."

I clambered into the van and released a shaky breath before Murat climbed in. He glanced my way. I grinned to convey health and wholeness. Murat remained silent and sober.

He drove to a small storefront in a long line of shops, parked, and pointed to the restaurant, *Ender İskender*. We walked on the sidewalk past vendors yelling out their wares. One boy walked by then stopped and turned gingerly, pointing at the huge tower of *simit*, O-shaped bread, stacked high on a round, wooden disk balanced atop his head.

"*Siii-miiiiit. Simitçi. Taze, gevrek!*" The *simit*-seller yelled about his fresh, crisp Turkish bagels in a nasally voice despite our standing just a few feet away.

"*Hayir.* No. Thank you," I said. The young man turned and moved on, probably having heard that polite refusal thousands of times already today. His dark skin blended into the dark brown bread perched atop his crown like a gargantuan halo. An unlikely angel.

"You okay?" I ventured a sideways glance at Murat.

He looked toward the road and then at me. "Are you?"

"I'm fine." I smiled like a court jester cheering a brooding king. "But I nearly died in the van on the way over here."

Murat huffed, his mouth only lifting a little in the corners. ❧

6 MERYEM'S KITCHEN

Murat nudged his food around his plate with a fork, but didn't speak. Meryem sized up Murat as the other children chattered happily around the low table on the floor.

"Are you well, son?"

"Yes, just tired."

"What happened today with the girl?"

"Ella? Nothing. She wanted to find some old places from her childhood."

"Why have you been like this then?" She waved her hand at him to point to his demeanor.

Meryem leaned over to her littlest surrogate child, who sat perched in a chair, and spooned soup into her open, waiting mouth. She patted the child's fat fist as she gazed at Murat. This man, her only son by birth, brought her such joy. He infused a sense of purpose into her old bones.

She wasn't so ancient though—only 56 years' worth of days, worn down by a hard life. Releasing the past, like birds in search of an olive branch, took faith. When they returned with nothing in their thin beaks, it hurt. This she saw in the eyes of her son.

Yes, he'd made peace with the God of heaven and earth long ago. Jesus glowed as an ember in a once dark and angry heart. Still Murat's soul was crushed like soft wood in a vice.

Guilt and regret weighed on him. Like boulders around an ox— he couldn't embrace the light yoke the Lord offered as a free gift. She'd do almost anything to keep him from more pain. He'd endured enough.

Murat rose halfway, then kneeled and looked into Meryem's eyes. "She came out of a rug shop. A man grabbed her. I should have been there. I was there to protect her. I failed."

"Was she hurt?" Meryem's throat ached at Murat's look of defeat.

"No." His eyes clouded, dark and haunted.

"Murat, son, do you think your job is to keep everyone from any harm? Such a thought is impossible. We have learned together that God is the one who holds us in His hands. We can reach out in love in His name, but we are not God himself."

Murat shrugged not fully buying it. "I know this. But I still feel as though God has given me this mission—as a protector of those around me."

"God's missions bring freedom and hope. Not fear and defeat."

At that, Murat rose, nodded and blinked his eyes at his mother to say, "Yes." Then he said, "Do you think *Baba*'s father would be willing to see us? Could we try again?"

Meryem shook her head. "He made it clear we were cut off from the family."

"But why, *Anne*?"

She raised a hand to stop him. *Some roads lead nowhere.* "It is time to look forward. Begin planning your future. Leave the old things alone, son." Meryem sensed he had not reconciled his heart with the wisdom she shared. Since his childhood, two sides warred. His father planted violence in the heart of a peacemaker, confusing Murat with hatred.

He possessed a propensity for great love. Meryem spent many hours in the still of the early morning praying for Murat, even as the *Fajr*, the melodic vibrato of the obligatory call to prayer at dawn, quavered from a nearby minaret proclaiming worship to a god she no longer knew.

"How lost we can be." Meryem sighed, then turned toward her little one. "You are covered in soup. Did I feed you or did you feed yourself tonight? Huh?" She laughed as she lifted the child on her lap.

Murat sprawled on his bed staring at the cement ceiling, praying for wisdom.

"Who am I, Lord? What do you ask of me?" He whispered into the darkness. Soft, rhythmic snores from his adopted siblings broke the silence. Murat's thoughts churned and wandered, as they often did, to the day he turned eight. The memory of working with his *baba* in his auto repair shop wove like a snake through his mind.

Murat lay with his baba under the car listening to the man's instruction. His dad's forearm stretched across Murat's small face as he removed a bolt with thick, greasy fingers.

"Son, watch carefully. This is how you make it work. Someday you will be able to do this without my help. A man should know such things, yes?" His father made it clear Murat must take over his business when he came of age. There had never been any asking.

Murat nodded without saying a word, concentration creasing his brow. He watched intently as his father's hands flexed, unhooking the starter from the car. Murat loved to be near his dad. This was their time. When he felt most like the man his father wanted him to become. Murat was always afraid of failing, so high were the man's expectations.

"Maybe later we can play soccer?" Murat ventured.

"Maybe. But we might not have time. It is more important for you to learn the skills of a man than to play the games of a child." His father's voice rumbled. A warning.

"Yes. You're right, Baba." Disappointment burned Murat's throat. When his dad spent so much time to teach and instruct, he had no right to ask for more. He didn't need to play. Allah called him to something greater.

"Tomorrow you will do this without my help. You can prove yourself worthy then. You have watched long enough." A pause hung in the air sizzling with expectation. "You must not let me down."

Murat clamped his eyes tight to block out the image. Fear streamed liquid down his cheeks in the darkness. Holding himself together tightened the noose hold on his throat.

When will I ever feel peace? ❧

7   ANKARA, TURKEY, 1978

The smoke of the burning soft coal snaked and sagged from each chimney, filling the air. Meryem's breath disappeared in the thickness of the dense, suffocating morning smog. She pressed the scarf to her nose, the damp fabric covering her mouth blackened with gloomy soot. The beaded flowers along the edge, hand stitched by her mother, pressed like tiny orbs of ice against her cheek. A scolding, she knew well enough. Leaning to see her feet, she found the path. Even though she'd practically memorized the way, she stumbled to gain her bearings.

Stop being so weak, Meryem. Cowards never find their way, only hide in corners waiting for others to solve their problems.

Breathing became almost a chore with the pollution so dense. In comparison to the tight kitchen, her journey was an escape. Her parents lost all vision for life. Meryem could hardly stand the resignation she perceived in their eyes. She'd learned having no money did that, confirming what she must do.

Ali begged her more than once to be his wife. Her stomach twisted at the idea of his proposal, much less marriage. Marrying him was the only way her family would be taken care of.

All her *Baba* worked for, the years of toil, of being an amusement to tourists, proved fruitless. She hardly knew how it happened. They no longer possessed ten *lire* to their name. They now lived miles from the warm ocean breezes of her childhood home. Living in Ankara hemmed her in on all sides, like a rat in a box. She needed a way out, a way back to the Aegean where dreams soared in the cobalt sky.

Her stomach growled. They ate the last of the *ekmek* this morning, and her delaying already cost them dearly. *I will accept Ali's proposal and all will be well.*

Baba's words, a warning, floated on the storm-gray air. "Meryem, we will make it through this. It is better to do what is

right in the eyes of Allah than to prostitute ourselves for money. Ali is impulsive and angry. No good will come of such a union."

Her father was a romantic, maybe the reason he had nothing to show for his lifetime of work. He'd rather hold his hand open allowing the scraps to be carried off one at a time than squeeze it tight so his family wouldn't go hungry.

Her heart, a full moon in her chest, was a heavy, drab stone.

Though a fool in many ways, no kinder man lived than her *Baba*. Many of her friends' parents insisted they marry a man for the fortune he'd bring. No, *Baba* still believed in love, though it had done him no good.

She stumbled on a loose rock and mumbled a frustrated, "*Allah, Allah.*"

The call to worship blared in overlapping rounds, chiding her for her insolence. She'd heard its beckoning every day of her life. This morning the summons to prayer made her feel more alone and isolated.

What has Allah ever done for my family?

Her parents struggled to please Him, never knowing if their efforts tipped the scales enough to secure heaven. They worked and worked and she had yet to see any love returned.

She stopped the blasphemous thought. She didn't want to call down punishment, despite how much she bristled against all the trying, trying to be good enough.

The repetitive, nasally prayer unleashed a familiar guilt, cascading over her like waves crashing one after the other. *I have to do it. I will marry Ali. Go there right now. Tell him so I will be forced to keep my word. Before my courage fails. Before Baba can stop me.* ∽

8   IZMIR, 2007

After seeing the kids off to their bus, Murat hopped in the van to head to his place of work, *"Ekmek Fabrikasi."* The humid air hung heavy and hot, even at 9:00 a.m.

Murat breathed deep trying to relax. He tried to take in the scene to avoid thinking. Another dug-up street with workers all standing around looking in the hole. Vendors selling *börek* and Fanta. Old women hunched over with flowered head-scarves wrapped tight under their chins. More cars than a person could count dodging, weaving around the obstacles in a chaotic flow.

Try as he might, Murat couldn't discharge his frustration. His father's legacy stuck to him like a bad smell, and more than that, something hidden out of reach that he couldn't decipher. Why did the remembrance of working with his father come with such fear? What did it mean? So much of his past veiled the rest of the story— in truth, he wasn't sure if he even wanted the full picture. The parts he remembered weren't good. *What are you protecting me from, God?* And why the incessant guilt?

He remembered his father as a harsh, angry man—very much living out the Koran's command, *"Oh ye who believe, fight the unbelievers,"* Sura 9:123. The thought of being like him in that way haunted Murat.

He tried to have grace for the fact his father did what he felt Allah called him to do, as the leader of his home—still that didn't justify the violence. Murat squinted as he determined to talk to his mother more about the memory. Maybe then things would make more sense.

Murat pulled up to the bread store, cutting off the driver in the right lane—reminding him of Ella's reaction to his aggressive driving. He smiled, knowing she was right. Driving in Turkey demanded taking control or being pushed right off the road. Survival.

Mustafa's canary hung in a rickety cage just inside the entrance of the bread shop. The creature greeted him with the usual screech.

Murat poked a finger into the cage to stroke the bird's yellow wing. "Hello, J.R.," then he yelled out, "I'm here. I hope you've made all the bread so I have some time to relax today."

The simple store contained only a small table with two chairs placed to the left. A stainless steel counter stretched the length of the back wall where customers picked up their bread each day. Behind the counter in the center of the wall stood an entrance. The opening emanated heat. A soft orange glowed from the large wood-burning oven inside.

Murat found comfort in the smell of wheat and yeast. Scanning the shelves, he noticed his boss had been busy. The racks held stacks of the bulbous loaves of golden *ekmek*, and several piles of stretched, pillowy *pide*, some as long as three meters, made mostly for restaurants. Stepping through the entrance to the open-hearth stone oven, Murat spotted the man with whom he spent every weekday.

Mustafa, the heavy-set owner of the store, removed a loaf of *ekmek* from the traditional oven's arced mouth using a long, flat wooden paddle. He noticed Murat and grinned at his employee, a large smear of flour smudged the baker's round cheek.

"Murat, my friend. Come, let's sit a minute before starting." Mustafa led Murat to the small table he used for his meals.

"Looks like you could use a break already." Murat stepped forward and offered the man a hug.

"Well, yes, of course. I don't get to sleep all morning as you do. Remember I am here before the sun rises." Mustafa plucked a pack of Camel cigarettes from his apron pocket and lit one. The man took a deep drag, turned his head to the side, and exhaled away from Murat.

"Yes, you are always sure to remind me of it." Murat chuckled as he reached for the *çay* and hunk of bread Mustafa set before him on the table. "You are good to me, Mustafa. How will I ever repay you?"

"Just keep coming. I don't like to work all day alone. You are like the son I never had."

"But you have two sons."

"Yes, but they are idiots," Mustafa said without laughing. "They want nothing to do with a simple bread maker. Those boys forget where they came from. Now they are too good for me." Mustafa rubbed his hands across his brow as if to remove the fatigue and memory of his boys' last visit.

Murat stayed quiet. Mustafa didn't often speak of his sons, but he'd once shared their story. The two boys left home together to pursue business and did well for themselves. They owned banks all across Turkey and their success went to their heads.

On their rare visits to their father, they sped off with women partying every night. They mocked Mustafa for his provincial store and "old-fashioned" lifestyle. Afterward, Mustafa was somber for days until Murat drew him out of his depression. The cycle saddened Murat who wished he could protect Mustafa from enduring his sons' disrespect over and over again. *Oh, how I long to have a father like Mustafa. Those men don't realize what they turned their backs on.*

To change the tone, Murat told Mustafa about Ella. How she arrived to help at the orphanage. How Ella seemed hand-chosen by God for the position to teach the children. Often, Murat spoke to Mustafa subtly about the love of God and hoped at some point, Mustafa considered what he shared in the privacy of the small bakery.

"So, she is pretty then, huh?" Mustafa nudged Murat's shoulder with a red-faced grin, completely missing the underlying message.

"Yes, very pretty. That's beside the point, friend. She's here to help the children."

"Hmm . . . ," Mustafa added with a sly smile, "What about you? You need help too. You are not married yet. What if she has been brought by your God for you too? Wouldn't that be something?" He punctuated the last sentence with a friendly slap on Murat's shoulder.

Blood rushed into Murat's face. The man would latch onto the idea and run with it. "You have a wild imagination, bread man. She is far too pretty for this fool."

"I don't doubt that. Ha." Mustafa's belly bounced as he rose to his feet and cleared the çay cups. Still laughing, he moved with Murat to the oven and set to work placing loaves of dough on the floured, wooden paddles. Sliding them into the wood-fired, stone oven, he waited to pull out the puffy flatbread with the paddle. "No better bread in Izmir than ours, huh, my friend?" Mustafa said with pride as he patted Murat on the back.

"No. No better bread than ours." Murat wiped the sweat beading on his brow from standing in front of the blazing-hot embers on a warm morning.

His mind bounced back to the memory stalking him, of his father pretending to care about him, pretending to make him part of his life. *How could I have been such a weakling to follow after such a man, a man who treated my Anne as he did?* Thinking of the abuse always made Murat feel as though he played a part in the violence of his father. Like his own hand slapped heavily against his mother's face.

Still, a mystery surrounded his father and his death. Perhaps that explained the ever-present dread. Murat needed to know more; even if the truth killed him. No more pretending. Then maybe the past would disappear altogether and Murat could imagine a future for himself that held more than paying penance. Like tepid water trapped away from the ocean, unable to wash out. Maybe then the invisible iron bars would vanish and he'd find himself free. Really free. For once.

The flames of the wood-burning oven danced on his face as he shoved the long paddle into the opening to retrieve another tender loaf. Mustafa hummed an aimless tune and, without realizing it, brought Murat's mind back from that dark place he often visited.

9   ANKARA, TURKEY, 1981

The heaviness of her life limped along, dragging her in a heap behind it. Meryem leaned her chest over the metal balcony railing and wondered for a moment whether flesh smacking hard against the ground would even hurt in comparison. Then it would be over.

The loveless marriage.

The disappointment flickering in her father's eyes.

The regret of failing to live up to everyone's standards.

This marital arrangement released poverty's grip on their lives, giving way to an even worse state: hopelessness. Meryem tried and tried. She couldn't figure out how to make everyone happy. Would her parents rather live day to day not knowing where the next meal came from? The arrangement allowed them a room of their own, enough food, and comfort in the small, sufficient space in the lower level apartment.

Meryem suspected, however, the only reason her parents agreed to the setup was to keep an eye on her ever-distant, increasingly violent husband. She wondered herself where he spent his days. The money came in, not always consistently, yet they never lacked the essentials. But peace? She'd never felt that with Ali.

Sure he provided for her. And what more did she want? The love her parents held for one another showed that life needn't be just about survival. Just about having enough. Maybe something more existed. Maybe a person could live on mere love.

Thinking she heard the front door's soft click, Meryem tiptoed into the living room. The apartment held few sentimental knickknacks—it hardly even felt like a home—just bare, off-white walls, a cold table with four chairs, and a tiny kitchen. No color graced the space, save the tiny black sea urchin her father gave her as a girl following their only family vacation. Failing to bring comfort in the hollow place, this reminder only made her aware of what she lost.

Meryem moved toward the front door wondering if Ali had returned home, then glanced into the bedroom. She saw him lying face-first in the bed, his wet boots still on, dripping on the shiny tile, a small pool forming.

"Ali?" Meryem's voice faltered fearing she might wake him. Even though the two lived as almost strangers, she couldn't deny he provided for her family.

The man turned his face to the side peering at her with one eye. "Meryem."

She couldn't help but notice he said her name with no feeling or expectation. The world stole something deep inside him and replaced it with a cavern.

"Are you all right?"

"Yes, and why shouldn't I be?"

Meryem stooped just a fraction at his irritated response. She knew he didn't think it her place to question anything he did. She backed up quietly to leave when he spoke again.

"Will you bring me some bread? Some tea? I haven't eaten yet today."

"Yes. Sure." Meryem walked swiftly to the kitchen and pulled out a *sahan*, the two-handled skillet for frying eggs, and started the gas stove. The tick, tick, then hiss broke into her melancholy. A low, blue flame danced on the surface. Quietly she placed the pan on the burner, poured olive oil in and cracked two eggs. She enjoyed the sizzle. Some noise, any noise, was preferable to the terrible quiet of their home.

While the eggs cooked, she tore off a hunk of the golden, pillowy *ekmek* her father picked up from the bread stand just a block away. She grabbed a plate and slid the eggs on, added the bread, and a few green-black olives. Meryem poured a thin stream of tea from the top kettle of the *çaydanlık*. The liquid glowed a rich copper in his tulip-shaped glass. With the food and tea in hand she re-entered the bedroom, placing them on the side table.

"*Efendi*," she used the term of respect, honor. "Here you are. Why not sit up?"

Ali pushed himself onto his elbows and examined the plate, a curl of steam lifted off the eggs. He glanced at her face and closed his dark eyes tight. When he opened them she thought she spotted a shallow rim of tears.

He blinked and pressed his thumbs against his eyelids then shoved himself to a sitting position. Perhaps she'd imagined it. She couldn't remember the last time Ali responded to her gestures. No, she stirred only anger in the man.

"*Teşekkür ederim.*" With his eyes down he shoveled the food into his mouth.

"You're welcome." Meryem extended a bridge over the vast sea stretching between them. "I missed you," she lied.

He considered her with an astonishing tenderness. Meryem couldn't bear to maintain his gaze. She didn't pretend he truly cared about her. She never understood why he even married her. Maybe because it was proper to have a wife to take care of a man's home. It certainly hadn't been because he preferred her company to anyone else's.

No, her life took on a sad sort of separateness and independence from the man who promised to care for her, to lead her. She lived her life day in and day out the same way, as a maid for an American family stationed at the Air Force base. She didn't love the work, but her job filled her time, distracting her from the emptiness of her routine.

Ali never approved. But after seeing the money she earned, he stopped nagging her to quit. Every cent she earned went into their savings toward the dream of moving to the seaside town of Izmir. Her husband once shared his hope of living in a home on the coast, owning a boat, and fishing for a living in the deep Aegean waters. As she surveyed his defeated expression and the slump of his shoulders, Meryem wondered if he even remembered his wish. She held onto the dream—her only life preserver in sight.

Ali finished his plate and set it on the floor then looked at her again. He appeared to want to say something, but didn't. He reached his rough hand across to hers. His thumb rubbed her

palm. She didn't move and knew her hand must feel like a limp rag. She had no idea how to react.

She accepted the distance. Now he appeared to want to pull her close again. And he did. Embraced her full up against his chest. Meryem heard his heart beating thick and slow against her ear. She smelled his sweat mingled with diesel gas. Ali pushed her back just enough to look into her eyes.

"Meryem?" He paused.

She waited. Something about his tone told her he extended a lifeline.

"Let's leave this place. I know you are unhappy and we have enough." He buried his face in her neck. "We can have a life. Start over."

Wondering what he meant, Meryem couldn't help squealing anyway. After all this time delaying, it didn't matter why he wanted to leave. Was he running away from something rather than toward the dream they laid out so long ago?

All Meryem thought of was the warm sea water rushing over her feet, washing her, making her new. The ocean held a time capsule of happiness for her.

Meryem pressed a kiss against her husband's cheek. "Thank you." She couldn't prevent her tears from wetting the pillow. She pressed her eyes closed to stop them from overtaking her.

Ali muttered something unintelligible into her hair then turned and covered her body with his. Drawing her into him. Pressing back the shadows with words of love and hope.

Meryem ignored the darkness swallowing up the room, choosing only to listen to her husband's breath after he rolled onto his side, one arm slumped across her chest, and the far-off whisper of waves drawing her home. ❧

1 O IZMIR, TURKEY, 2007

I watched the angle of sunlight as it glided over the windowsill. The first call to prayer lifted through the air like pleading or sadness. "*Allahu ekber.*" My bizarre dreams last night left me feeling strange this morning, off kilter, and freaked out.

In one dream I saw burnt pistachios on the road in front of my home. Instead of the dream playing out the way that terrible day happened, I watched in horror as children darted from all directions, grabbing at the nuts, and cracking them open to eat. I chased them and scolded them. They laughed and scurried away.

How am I actually here again?

Glowing fingertips of sunlight fanned across my room, spread across my blankets, landing on my palm. Closing my fingers around the light didn't work. Hope was like that—powerful, but unable to grab on to. That's where faith kicked in, only I lacked in that department. When leaving the U.S., I imagined myself so different. So full of grace and wizened by time, and distance, and forgiveness.

I spent my growing-up days clinging to my daddy's faith—to the words he said so often. "Trust Him, Ella. No matter what. Nothing is too hard or big or scary for him. He is God, you know."

But today I possessed a secondhand faith, infused like osmosis, and the source had been gone so very long that the power waned, flickered, and eluded.

Holding on to the sun's rays are impossible.

"Ella?" June's voice muffled through my closed door.

"Yes. I'm up." I tried to sound vibrant.

"Barry's here. Once you're up and about, you can come meet him."

"Sure. Just give me a sec." Why bother adding something like, *I'm just finishing up my Bible time.* June was on to me.

By the time I hauled myself out of bed, pulled my tangled hair through a scrunchy, and ate a glob of toothpaste to cover my

morning breath, I broke into a sweat. I eased out the front door toward the commotion: a pack of children mauling a tall, bearded man.

"Ella. Come meet Barry." June's face appeared tired, like she'd tried to hold everything together for a while and could finally hand the boulder of worry to her husband.

I stepped forward and extended my hand to greet him. "Nice to meet you."

He grinned while struggling to receive my grip. "You too, Ella. I know June is so glad you're here. And I'm thankful she will have you to help."

"Me too." *How much help have I actually been? Why is June holding back whatever she's carrying?* I resisted the urge to ask Barry where he'd been. *Why wasn't he here when I arrived?* Nobody explained, so I kept my mouth shut. Despite the joyful squint of soft skin around his eyes, dark shadows underlined them.

"Church in the courtyard at ten, should you care to join us," Barry invited.

"Sure. That'd be great."

"We thought you could lead, you know, since you're new and everyone's eager to get to know you."

A panic attack reared its head. I wouldn't describe myself as a people person, even though I came to Turkey to work with that species. More like a little-people person. Speaking in front of adults equated to walking a high wire with sharp spears jutting from the ground.

"Actually, I . . . "

Barry chuckled and patted my back. "Only joking. I'd never do such a thing."

June stepped in and linked her arm through her husband's. "Yeah, you would."

The two strolled toward the house, June's head resting against her husband's shoulder.

Murat watched as Ella fidgeted and repositioned herself over and over. Her discomfort practically screamed, "Get me out of here."

Umut climbed into her lap as if invited and plugged his mouth with a wet thumb, and Ella actually relaxed. Not just her body. Her eyes calmed and her movements stilled.

She's made for this. Like the missing piece of herself clicked into place. A strange thought. No wonder she wanted this job despite her obvious issues with Turkey in general.

Murat wondered where Umut's mother was and looked toward her home. All of the children under her care gathered. Pinar sat at a distance bent on staying separate and isolated. So strange how some people pushed away anything good and wandered toward the very thing that caused the most pain. Like a moth to a bright light.

Barry's loud voice broke in, "God doesn't say our lives will always be easy."

Murat knew that firsthand. With lulls here and there, the landscape never had been smooth. Not for him. Not for *Anne*. Most of all her. Murat noticed Barry staring at Ella and wondered what he'd missed. Ella held Barry's scrutiny, then dropped her gaze.

"But He walks with us. He never leaves us. And his love is always deeper." Sometimes the things Barry said seemed like theoretical truths—ones Murat believed, but in day-to-day life, he didn't know how to integrate.

Murat wished his life had been different. That he'd had a dad who loved him, loved his mother. Despite his fixed purpose here, he stirred with a desire to escape. Maybe go someplace where liabilities weren't living, breathing children or mothers needing protecting. Maybe then he'd find a woman to love.

The time swept by. Soon everyone stood, gathered their belongings, and talked and laughed together. Murat looked at Ella who hadn't moved. She talked to Umut and played a game with his hands. The boy giggled and covered his face then started the game again.

Umut caught his mother staring at him, lines of worry pressing her eyebrows low like storm clouds. Pinar turned her gaze away quickly and sprung up to leave.

That's when Murat noticed him. A man, peering through the trees, standing behind the cement wall enclosing the grounds. He appeared to be watching Ella. Or maybe it was Umut. Murat craned to gain a better view. As soon as he did, the man ducked and disappeared.

Murat jogged over to the spot hoping something might give him a clue. Leaning over the wall Murat looked at the sidewalk on the other side of the perimeter hoping to spot someone sprinting off and maybe catch a better look at the man.

But nobody ran down the road, just folks heading to the market and children kicking a soccer ball on the dirt road.

Murat noticed a few broken branches on a low myrtle bush lining the wall and he figured that was the spot where the stranger lurked, watching. Beside the small shrub lay a rumpled newspaper with jobs circled in blue ink.

I popped another salty, green olive in my mouth. Murat creamed Barry again, dribbling the soccer ball past him down the open rectangular grassy area clearly designed for the sport. He even pelted it between the older man's feet, catching the ball on the other side.

He has skill, that's for sure.

I tried hard not to notice the way his shirt stuck to his lower back, showing off his form. I forced my eyes to the angular almost Aztec-style design of the *kilim* rug spread under an elm tree. Focused on the colors, shapes dancing across the wool. Focused on something other than him.

He's a distraction, that's all.

I grabbed another olive and chomped on it, like doing so ground up my thoughts and made them disappear. The ball pelted me in the side.

In a moment, like a glistening angel, he appeared, leaning over, looking right into the windows of my soul, whispering a deep, "Pardon."

I handed the ball to him and giggled like a groupie. *What's the man trying to do? I need to keep my eyes on the prize.* The point of my time here? The children. Redeeming the past and something or other about forgiveness.

With a swift move of his left foot, Barry hooked the ball into the air behind him then grabbed Murat in a tackle and yelled, "Take it to the goal, boys."

"What?" Murat hollered, red-faced but amused. "Cheating? I thought I could expect more from a man of God."

"That's what you get for thinking." Barry gasped for breath as Murat ripped free, sprinted the field's length, stole the ball from a gangly youth, and kicked it from the far end of the field into the goal.

Murat raised his hands above his head whooping out a victory yell. At this Barry fell onto the rug occupied by June and offered her a boyish grin. I noticed June imploring him with eyes that screamed for him to quit. But quit what? She didn't look mad. Was it concern?

The boys on Murat's team tackled him. Murat yelled out, "See that? Cheaters are never prosperity."

Barry threw his head back and belly laughed. I wondered if it was because of Murat's wording of the proverb or that Barry was scolded by one of the people he'd spent years mentoring. "Good game, Murat. Good game."

A group of teenage girls sat on the sidelines and gawked at Murat. The man turned heads, not just mine. The revelation calmed me—I tended to overthink things. I simply experienced a normal reaction to a good-looking man.

The idea of standing amongst a throng of admirers gave me a strange twist in my stomach. I brushed invisible crumbs from my skirt. Why did it feel like he should belong to me? Like I had any claim on the man?

My weakness ticked me off. What sort of bimbo flew all the way across the Atlantic only to find a boyfriend in one week flat?

"He is full of heart, my son," one of the ladies near me commented proudly.

I looked over at the woman and noticed her watching Murat too. I gagged on my olive, took an eternity to clear my throat before croaking out, "You . . . you're Murat's mother?" I couldn't believe this. What could be worse than being caught staring by his mom?

"Yes. Is me." She grinned, her round face creasing only around her eyes.

"Oh, I didn't know." Those were the only words I managed.

"Yes, of course. I am Meryem." She said her name elongated and slow and slightly louder than necessary, *Muh-ryah-a-muh.*

"So nice to meet you."

Why am I sweating so much? I touched my fingertips to my upper lip to swipe away the moisture.

"Murat say to me you live here when you young." The woman reclined on her side and propped her head on her hand. Her T-shirt stretched over a rounded belly. Her white teeth stood out on her full, tanned face as she grinned at me.

Must be used to the attention her son receives. She probably heard, "What a beautiful son," his whole life.

"Yes, I lived here about fifteen years ago when my father was in the service."

"Then why you come back?" The words came out clipped. Strong.

Uncomfortable on a whole new level, I cleared my throat to ensure my sentences came out even. "My father. He died when I was seven. That's when we left Izmir, my mother and I, and returned to my Mom's hometown in America."

"Then this must be both sweet and terrible return, yes?" Her manner softened and she looked as though she understood. The change in tone threw me off-kilter.

"Yes. Exactly." I looked away, unable to bear her gentle probing any longer. *Like Murat's eyes, full of feeling and depth.* "Thank you. You're kind."

I remembered the obvious: this woman was no stranger to suffering. Surely living at the orphanage proved that to be true. I wondered about her story. About Murat's.

Meryem snatched up another olive and popped it in her mouth. Her face turned to Murat and her chewing slowed. Her smile drooped and eyes squinted. The change occurred as smoothly as the brakes on a worker's bus, bodies swaying to keep from tumbling. I turned away too. Back to my relative isolation on my rug on the sidelines. ❧

I I PINAR'S HOUSE

He'd done it for three months, bringing bread to the woman. Still Murat couldn't help but think he threw crumbs at a dead bird so unresponsive was Pinar. The house was quiet as usual, as he walked toward the open front door—no squeals of happy children, no clothes flapping and billowing in the wind—just empty quiet.

Stepping into the dark home Murat made his presence known as he always did by ringing the small copper bell hanging outside the doorway. A fly buzzed around his head. Murat swatted it away.

He squinted his eyes to adjust to the darkness of the home. "Pinar. It's Murat. I've brought you bread."

No response.

Murat set the bread on the small space beside the sink. Every home at the orphanage looked the same: one large living room and dining space as you walked in the door. Straight ahead against the far wall stood the counter with a sink and refrigerator. One small room stood to the right of the living room, for the surrogate mother, and another larger room with bunks for all the kids. Beyond that, each woman decorated the space as she chose.

Pinar, however, did nothing to create an atmosphere of home. The starkness of the room only highlighted to Murat the difference between his home and Pinar's.

Umut stuck in Murat's mind as he considered what the small child's life must be like. The youngest boy of the family possessed no frame of reference to know what a loving family looked like. Ironic, since Umut's name meant "hope." Invariably the boy sought him out on Sundays and clung tightly like a shadow seeking light.

Determining Pinar must not be around, Murat turned to leave and that's when he heard her call.

"Murat? Is that you?" Her voice fragile as a brittle branch.

Concern pressed against his chest. The frail voice came from the bedroom so he pressed his ear to the door and spoke, "Yes. It is me. Do you have a problem, Pinar?"

"Yes, please come in."

Murat hesitated wondering how it might look for him to enter the bedroom of a woman close enough to his age to be dangerous. His fear for Pinar won out. The door grated out a squeak as he pushed it open. Murat saw nothing but a rumpled pile of blankets on the bed, Pinar's small frame curled in a ball right in the center. She peeked at him, a frightened animal.

"What is it, Pinar? Are you hurt? Can I help you?"

"No. Please, don't leave me. I am not hurt. I can't get up."

Murat stepped closer and kneeled beside the bed to determine what the problem might be. That's when he smelled it, the foul odor of day-old alcohol. Pinar shoved herself up on one elbow, her nightgown slipping off her shoulder, her breasts dangerously close to complete exposure. She looked at her bosom then at Murat, offering a fragile smile, reaching her hand out to his.

"Murat, you saved me. Please stay here with me. I could make you a happy man. I know how to please a man. I am so alone here. Umut adores you. It would be perfect." This she said half begging and half breathless and seductive.

Murat sprung to his feet and backed away shaking his head. "Pinar, you should be ashamed. You've been given a second chance here. A new life could be yours, but you continue to throw it away. And what of the kids? Don't you even care that they need you and deserve better than to be ignored?"

Pinar scrambled to her knees. The blankets slipped down around her, her nightgown unbuttoned and open in the center. She no longer looked the temptress—no, a pitiful creature full of darkness. Her eyes, dark empty caves, gaping with need.

Murat darted out the door leaving her alone. As he headed along the path toward June and Barry's home, he heard her low, pathetic cries. He would not let her continue to press the life she knew so well on the children in her care. ✍

12 BARRY'S COTTAGE

Murat rapped on the door to June and Barry's home. His knuckles ached from the brusque action. Impatience fueled his desire to have Pinar dealt with quickly. He refused to allow the same old evil most of these kids once experienced to seep like poison through the inadequate stone walls surrounding the property.

He pictured the kids in Pinar's home watching her, learning from her, or seeing her choices as the only way. No, she'd only perpetuate the ugliness. Taking a deep breath Murat lifted his hand to deliver a louder knock when Barry opened the door.

"Murat. What a nice surprise. How are you? Come in." Barry grabbed Murat's hand and pulled him into a hug. Murat noticed bruises on the insides of both of Barry's arms.

"Is everything good?" Murat's angry tone sounded like the question was an accusation. For a while he'd noticed his mentor slowing down, thinning out. He figured the workload could drain any man. Himself included. Now he considered far worse possibilities.

"Yes. All is well. Couldn't be better."

Stepping inside Murat noticed June's weak greeting. She avoided looking him in the eyes, turning her back as she braced herself in the kitchen. Concern filled the space in Murat's chest. He looked between June's hunched shoulders to Barry as if the truth would appear like text scrolling across his forehead.

Maybe I'm reading into things again.

The elusive shadows he chased darted away. *You just want to be the hero to everyone.* The thought disgusted him. He couldn't deny the need to be important. His father wasted his life. Murat was spared for a greater purpose. He sucked in a deep breath through his mouth, held it for a second, then slowly released it. *Focus on one problem at a time. One day at a time.* Otherwise, he might collapse under the pressure, like a tiny shell at the bottom of the Black Sea.

"Yes. Barry, can we talk?" Murat stepped into the bright room, the sun streaming in. A soft breeze lifted the curtains in a smooth dance. "I'm concerned about Pinar."

"Oh? Well, let's sit." Barry gestured to the deep orange and red wool pillows that served as seats. He went to the small refrigerator and pulled out two cold bottles of Coca-Cola and popped the caps off each. He handed one to Murat as he returned and then sat across from the younger man. "Please. Tell me what concerns you."

"Barry, I went today to bring Pinar bread. I've done this for a while to check on her after . . . even before the day she left. She smelled of alcohol today and . . . " Murat stared at the bottle of brown bubbly liquid, his face hot as fresh-baked bread. "She asked me to stay and . . . she wasn't dressed all the way."

The ending statement probably didn't make much sense to Barry, but Murat added it anyway. This man was like a father to him—well, not anything like his father, but the kind of father he longed for. He knew telling the truth was safe.

"Hmm . . . I'm sorry to hear that. Barry rubbed a hand over his beard making a scratchy sound. I checked on her myself, with June, and we're concerned as well. I don't see any signs of abuse, only neglect and ignorance. June planned to speak with Ella about maybe modeling how to care for the kids and the home better."

Murat shook his head. He didn't want Ella anywhere near the woman. "She's not to be trusted. What about the alcohol? She's not capable of doing anything, not even learning, if she's drinking. Ella will just end up doing all her work."

"I didn't realize she had any means of getting much for herself, let alone alcohol. I suggest we rotate so she's monitored more closely and the kids are being watched as well. What do you think of that?"

Barry leaned in and placed his hand on Murat's shoulder as he often did when having a heart to heart. He looked into Murat's eyes. "I'm sure you believe she deserves at least a chance to learn and grow. She's never known the goodness God hands to us with His gift of hope. She's never known a mother who loved her and showed her how to manage a home and care for young ones. She

says her mother was a prostitute. I'd guess that's why she stayed with her husband through all the abuse, because she figured she deserved nothing more than that life. This is our chance to turn a legacy of ugliness into victory. What would you say to that?"

Murat never grew tired of Barry's ways. His outlook, unchanged by any problem, gave Murat hope that one day he'd find a vision beyond the immediate job to right all the wrongs he encountered, or to protect these little ones from harm.

Tired of his burden, hope seemed foolish. But what could he say? He knew all too well he had little control over how things were done at the orphanage.

"*Tamam*. Perhaps arrange this with the other women too? I'm sure *Anne* will help. I will talk to her and to Ella, too," Murat said. "Consider it done."

Murat rose and shook Barry's hand before being pulled in for another customary bear hug.

The doubts that never fully retreated paced alongside Murat on the walk home. Like the man lurking behind the myrtle bushes, his apprehension watched and waited to remind him he couldn't fix anything. Couldn't protect anyone. That his weakness spread like black-blue water all the way to the horizon. ❧

13 PRESCHOOL

I held little Çiğdem's hand, rubbing my thumb over the soft top of her skin. Working with the preschool-aged kids at the orphanage infused purpose. It's why I came. Mostly. With all my visions of reconnecting with the past and finding peace at last, teaching the kids filled me with resolve and calm. Nothing else compared.

"I pick you flower?" The girl tugged at me to drop to eye level with the buttercup in her tiny hand.

"Yes, but wait. First, I want to ask you questions." She plopped onto the dirt and waited. "What color is this flower?"

"Yellow."

"Good. Can you count the petals for me?"

Çiğdem looked at me and asked, "Petals?"

I sat cross legged on the ground and pointed to the petals surrounding the fronds in the center.

"Yes. I do it. One . . . two . . . three . . . four . . . "

"And what about the leaves. How many leaves are there?"

She pointed to the stem. I shook my head, 'No.' She pointed to a leaf and I nodded. "Is one, two."

Noticing her comfort level with basic conversation skills, I considered a new challenge when I noticed a man peering over the wall, beckoning one of my students his way saying something I couldn't make out. Umut sprinted toward him.

I shot up and ran after him. "Umut. Come back here." I translated the request into Turkish, alarm filling me, yelling now. "Umut!" *Is this his father, the same man who stole away Pinar?* I gulped in breaths, part panic induced, part out-of-shape induced, and snatched him up. I stared at the person near the wall.

I fixed his features in my mind. He looked familiar. I had no clue why. I knew only the women and kids at the orphanage. He glared at me, then turned and sprinted away.

Murat skidded the van to a stop between me and the wall. He jumped out and rushed after him. The whole scene unfolded

in a strange, slow motion sort of way. I watched Murat leap the wall all too easily and heard his shouts calling out to the man now lost from view.

By the time Murat returned, the kids he drove home from school disappeared to their respective homes. He walked up to me, touched my arm, touched Umut's face. "What happened? Did he try to take Umut?" The heat and comfort from his hand lingered on my skin.

The reality of the moment settled in. The weight of Umut in my arms, of the responsibility I carried left me cold. I covered Umut's trembling head with my hand, needing to use it for some good. "I don't know. Umut ran toward him. I was able to grab him. The man tried to get him to come over to talk. What's going on, Murat? Why did you run after him? Do you know who that was?"

Murat stared at me, his eyes darker than usual, the golden brown almost invisible. "I saw this man before on Sunday, watching someone. Maybe watching Umut. I noticed a scar on his mouth."

"I paid attention so I could tell you what he looked like." In that moment, Murat was my first thought—to share the load, to come to the rescue maybe. "He was about six foot, black hair, brown eyes, not freshly shaven, no wedding ring. I saw the scar too. His clothes looked ratty. Do you think it's Pinar's husband?"

Murat searched my face like an answer would appear. "No. I don't think so. He had no scar in the wedding picture I saw at her home. Her husband is shorter, just a little taller than Pinar."

I rubbed my hand in circles on Umut's back. "Umut, did that man speak to you?" Umut shoved his face into my chest to burrow to safety. "Umut, you aren't in trouble. Murat? Would it help if you spoke to him in Turkish?"

"Yes, *tamam*." Murat questioned him slowly, gently, tweaking the boy's cheeks. Murat's smiling face mesmerized me. He spread his legs, squatted, and leaned back at eye level with the boy.

Murat ran to the van and emerged with a loaf of bread in a brown paper bag. He tore off a huge hunk and handed it to me, then gave Umut a small piece. The child nibbled and soon talked. Murat listened casually like the two were merely shooting the

breeze. I heard him thank Umut then offered to take him home.

"Ella, we'll talk later. Can I come get you tonight after dinner?"

"Sure, I'll be in my room."

He winked. The trembling I'd ignored moved into my chest. I hardly knew him, yet I felt connected in some deep way and for the first time I experienced fear that had nothing to do with my past. And everything to do with the present and my future.

I opened the door and waited, having no idea what time Murat planned to come, then went back in my room and sat, looking out the window, jiggling my foot. A soft knock filled the quiet of my room.

Murat leaned in to kiss both of my cheeks. Did he feel the heat in my face or the thumping pulse in my temples? My comfort zone sat in an indistinguishable blob somewhere near my feet. Never before had I genuinely cared what a man thought of me, of everything about me. The vulnerability ticked me off. *Just keep your distance and then he won't have any power over you.*

Murat sensed my tension. His hands still on my elbows, he looked at me like I needed a lifeline. Which is exactly what I didn't want. I wanted to radiate strength and power. All my mess exposed with Murat around. I shoved an annoying curl behind my ear.

"So what's going on with Umut? What did he tell you?"

Murat scanned the room to appraise the seating options. "Want to walk?"

"Yes." Walking would push past the tremble, account for the waver in my voice, and race away from his intense gaze. "Where?"

He reached for my hand and pulled me out the door. "I have a good place."

14 THE BEACH

Minutes later we strolled the beach. Cool watery tentacles crept in, grabbing our ankles. Tugging. *It's only sand.* The ocean glittered black, a plane broken by sluggish waves catching the moonlight.

I tipped my head back to find a constellation I knew. Find some solid anchor to remember that not everything shifted and changed and moved me. Some things never changed. Constant as pain. The big dipper tipped in the sky. I inhaled a deep, massive breath then whooshed it out, slow and steady like Lamaze.

Murat's profile silhouetted against the full moon that hung pregnant over the glistening Aegean. He angled his face toward mine.

I turned away. I couldn't bear to let him see I needed a life vest right here on the edge of the sea. Frustration pulsed in my throat, pulsated through me until I feared I might pop and shrink like a deflated balloon. My self-centeredness spun its web, holding me in place. I read someplace that trauma could be triggered, over and over again. But I was sick of reliving it. Sick of fixating on me. I wanted a brand new, untainted present.

"You seem upset," Murat said, angling toward me.

"I'm not upset." I said with a little more emphasis than I should have. "Well, yes, I'm upset about Umut. About the man. What did you find out?" *That's why we're here after all.*

The decoy worked.

Murat's breath fizzed out between his teeth. "Nothing. Pinar is no help. She sleeps her days away and leaves those kids to themselves. I don't think she cooks for them any days. The house is a mess."

He tugged my hand to halt my march forward, almost like he figured out he couldn't delve into the heart of this with me moving. Which was my plan.

This conversation has nothing to do with me, so why am I so scared?

"What Murat? I really don't have answers. I have no idea what to do. The whole thing feels beyond our control." He looked at me as if my saying the truth woke a sleeping monster.

Without uttering a word, Murat moved toward the water line, then stood in the ebb and flow, staring out to where the black water met with a black sky.

I stepped in the cool water until our shoulders rubbed. "So what did you find out?"

"Umut said his *Baba* hasn't come around since the last time. The man by the wall wasn't him."

"If it isn't Umut's dad, any ideas who this man might be?"

Murat didn't answer. Didn't respond at all for a long while. "No." He added the word more like a command than from any real conviction. I suspected he lied. But why?

"Murat, what are you worried about?"

He ran all his fingers through his thick hair and tugged near the roots, his arms swung open. I laid a hand on his elbow and forced him to pull back from wherever he balanced so precariously. *Now who's running?* The thought tugged at my throat. What pain has Murat suffered? I missed it completely. Hadn't even considered.

The internal battle exhausted me. I longed to live and react in a normal way to life instead of endless thinking and considering and reminding myself of what I should do.

Murat turned to me, his face whitened by moonlight, the city line now behind him. Even with his skin dulled to a gray-white, he took my breath away. Behind him the lights from businesses and hotels and restaurants formed a zigzagging constellation.

"Let's walk." What an idiot. Walk, stop, walk, stop. *Make up your mind, woman. Are you going to engage in the moment or not?*

I mentally ranted and raved until Murat broke the argument with, "What if I set a trap?"

"A trap?" Our thought processes were like north from south.

"*Evet.* What if you teach the kids outside all week? I'll wait on the street, on the other side of the wall near where he stands to

look, but far enough he won't see me. I watch to see what he wants. What he'll do."

"I can't put the kids in danger."

"Is no danger to the kids. They'll be with you. I won't be far away. When he comes, I'll grab him when his back is turned."

"Then what?"

"Then I make him tell me what he wants."

At this hour, the shoreline extended in a long, unobstructed line, clean and uninhabited. The cool ocean water washed over my feet. "Murat, I think we should talk this over with Barry and June, don't you?"

"No. They have too much to do already. And Barry just thinks I worry too much."

"I'm sure it would concern Barry to know the same man has been lurking around and luring kids over to talk."

"Yes. Maybe is true. But I think we must find out for myself first."

"Hey, what did Umut say the man asked him?"

Murat turned, slowed his pace and squinted at me, as though regret hung like rocks around his feet.

"He asked about his teacher. He asked about you, Ella."

15 UMUT'S HOUSE

Every day I taught the kids outside, near the wall hemmed in by bougainvillea vines, a tumble of billowing fuchsia against gray stone, near where the man stood seven days ago. Like a one-person surveillance unit, Murat sat in the van, scoping out any passers-by. Nothing happened out of the ordinary. Perhaps Murat scared him off when he chased him. Maybe the man wouldn't return.

I studied Umut, his eyes bloodshot, his tiny frame looking even tinier for some reason. I rubbed his shoulder and asked what was wrong. He shook his head and looked away, hunching his shoulders like he needed to protect his heart from exposure. The boy's sluggishness filled me with concern. Boys his age should be running—I should be scolding him for not sitting still in class.

"Çiğdem, will you see if you can find out what's wrong with Umut?" Regardless of my limited Turkish, I recognized the two kids shared a deep connection. Most days Çiğdem stayed close to Umut like she was assigned as his protector. I even watched her lift the boy off the ground to tend to a skinned knee.

"*Tamam.* I do it."

I observed the two conversing, Umut unfolding his body like a morning glory opening to the sun's warmth. Still their words remained hushed and sober.

Çiğdem turned her lanky frame to me and threw the words out, "He say he *Anne* no feed him for two day." I saw her hands squeezed closed and her shoulders lifted, ready to take the woman on herself. Even though my heart pounded with anger, I touched her fist and offered my most genuine smile.

"Thank you, Çiğdem. You've helped so much. Will you run to my room and bring me a few things? I need a box of *vişne suyu* and some *ekmek*. They're both on my desk in a box."

The sharp peaks of her shoulders softened. She returned with the cherry juice and a half loaf of bread and I pulled Umut onto my lap, offering the *ekmek* first. He pecked at the bread like a bird.

Within moments he wolfed down the last quarter of the loaf. He slurped all the tart-sweet nectar and set the juice box on the grass.

"Umut?" I ran my fingers through the back of his dull, black hair. His skull against my palm felt like a baby's. Gray storm clouds crowded in my mind. *How can anyone treat a child this way, especially his mother?* I stood and asked Umut, "Do you want to walk home or should I carry you?"

He said the word in a whisper. "Walk." The boy turned to Çiğdem and spoke in Turkish. I recognized two words: 'no' and 'home.'

A dull ache filled my chest. Of course he didn't want to go home. Nothing at home except more of the same. More neglect. More longing for what he'd not received. Even though he was surrounded.

I spotted Murat watching us from the van. I signaled for him to come. In moments he stationed himself beside us.

"Yes. What is it, Ella?" I admitted even in this tense moment that my name spoken with his accent affected me, though I couldn't put into words how.

"Umut hasn't eaten for two days." The words appeared to inflict physical pain in the man. He stepped back and twirled toward the child, appraising him, then his eyes fixed on mine.

"I wanted to go over to Pinar's and talk to her. How can this happen here, Murat? It's the opposite of what this place is supposed to offer. I don't get it." My voice shot up an octave. I paused to get my emotions in check. "I just need to go talk to her. Can you watch the kids?"

Murat blinked. "Be careful. She's not to be trusted." His eyes looked glossy, "I'm so sorry. I was going to ask the ladies to teach Pinar about being a mom. With the strange man I forgot to tell them." His eyes flicked to the wall, then to his feet.

I squeezed his hand and turned toward the path to Umut's home where he lived with three older kids. Given Pinar's history, most likely June and Barry didn't want to overload her with too much responsibility. I wondered if any kids should be under her care. When I reached the home, the door was open, but I didn't see any signs of Umut's mom. I called out her name.

"Pinar." No response.

The messy space spoke volumes. Dishes stacked on the low brass table, filling the sink. Clothes scattered without a shred of anything sentimental anywhere. No pictures. No vase of flowers, nothing. I turned and left.

Where could she be? The idea she'd have any place to go provided little comfort, since any connections she maintained couldn't be good for her. I returned to my group of kids.

Murat lay on the ground with the whole group tackling him. Umut transformed in the short time to a child rather than a small, sad adult with problems too big to bear. I watched him dive into the chaos and let out a high-pitched squeal.

I sat on the grass a short distance away, my back pressed against an olive tree. The lime-green fruit drooped the branches. I plucked one off and bit into it. The unripe, bitter fruit squeaked against my teeth and cramped my taste buds.

I needed to figure out what to do with Pinar. What to do with this child under my care. For this moment, I closed my eyes and listened to the sound of unaffected glee. ✎

16 PINAR'S HOUSE

Murat insisted the children go to his house until Pinar was located. When the older kids returned home from school, the afternoon sun lay thick and tangerine yellow on the horizon. After a quick explanation, the group shuffled toward Murat's home. I walked with them, splitting off toward Pinar's once again.

In case she was still gone, I came prepared with a pen and paper. I stepped over the trash and clothing on the floor and peeked my head inside her room, expecting it to be empty. Then I spotted her in a space hidden somewhat behind the door not visible from the living room. In the corner of the room sat Umut's mother, eyes dark and glazed.

I hadn't spotted her before. *Was she there all along?* Her face drawn like a character of agony. Like a sad-faced clown from the circus. The spectacle shot tingles up my spine.

Disarray defined the space, life continuing, not stopping to get her help. The woman looked up, staring past me to the light outside.

Tears sat in her cool eyes like tide pools. Nothing I could say right now would break through whatever trance possessed her. I set to work straightening the house. At least I could make the space feel more welcoming than this.

I organized the dishes, piled them on the counter, and filled the small sink with water and soap. I let the water run hot, steam rising in front of my face, imagining the answers I needed materializing before my face. I scrubbed the dishes with a course squash sponge, not even caring my hands burned a little. My anger fueled my work, removing filth from the space. I finished by wiping all the surfaces and sweeping food crumbs out the door.

With nothing left to do I gazed at the ceiling as if God might be sitting there like a giant floating genie with an answer on a silver pillow. Nothing. No shining wisdom scrawled across the off-white surface.

I returned to Pinar's room and plopped beside the woman allowing my side to touch hers. Maybe jar her zombie-like state. She didn't register my presence.

I began to pray, quietly at first, then out loud. She might as well know where I stood. I prayed for peace to fill this home. For breakthrough. For demons to get out. For a miracle.

By the time I finished, my throat felt wooden. She hadn't moved. I looked over, her eyes were closed and two shimmery streams moistened her face.

I grasped her hand in mine, holding on even though the cool limpness repelled me. Maybe the warmth from mine would find its way to hers.

"Umut was hungry today."

She tipped her chin downward ever so slightly. I wouldn't have noticed if I hadn't watched her like a deranged woman needing answers.

"Can I help you?"

The woman turned to look at me, our faces just inches away. Her lips parted like she needed to say something. No words came out. The pinch of skin between her eyes convinced me that my words struck somewhere deep inside.

"*Evet.*" The quiet word screamed resignation. And need. *Yes.* That was all she said.

She might as well have shared her deepest secret. Her most intimate weakness. Whether she knew it or not, the word meant a new beginning. ❧

17 THE BAR

"*Anne.*" Murat called out as he entered his home after helping at *Ekmek Fabrikasi*. Work. The only place he escaped the thick feeling slumped around his ankles. His nagging unresolved questions needed to be dealt with. He'd put off this conversation long enough.

"Yes, son." Meryem stepped out of the bedroom, her head covered in a muted-blue head-scarf, her face red from the exertion of cleaning.

"*Merhaba, Anne.*"

"*Merhaba,* son." Meryem leaned in and kissed both of Murat's cheeks, then huffed as she lugged a pile of dirty laundry to the washer in the corner of the room.

"*Anne.* Let me do that."

"Why? I do this all day when you are gone." She dropped the basket on the floor in front of the ancient machine.

The woman pulled a clean load out of the washing machine, started another load, then carried the wet wad in a basket to the line outside. Murat followed her and together the two pinned the clothing until the laundry stretched like a cut out paper chain of children holding hands. A call to prayer beckoned and wove together with afternoon traffic and the faint drilling of a jackhammer on cement. Meryem shot Murat a sidelong glance, but remained quiet. She snapped a T-shirt in the air, breaking the silence.

Having no idea where to begin, Murat rubbed his forehead. "*Anne?*" He stared at the ground like the words laid there in a heap with the remaining wet clothes.

Meryem moved over to him, "What is it, son? What are you waiting for? You've never stopped yourself from asking me anything."

If only she knew how many times he'd wondered about his father and held back his questions. Waiting hadn't eased the need

to know. And truth hadn't miraculously set him free. *Maybe that's because you don't know the truth.*

"What was so terrible about *Baba*? Why has everyone disowned us because of his disgrace? It's not so unusual for a husband to beat his wife." Murat looked away, realizing his words weren't coming out right. "I mean, it's normal enough for a husband to feel his wife needs to be taught submission. Sadly, we've seen it's rarely the man's fault. So why? What is it he did that's earned us such scorn?"

Meryem searched his eyes to figure out something before speaking. She looked scared too, like a small mouse backed into a cage. She rubbed Murat's arm. Her eyes fixed on the spire of a minaret slicing the horizon peeking, elusive, between the trees.

"Maybe it is time." She turned away. He noticed the rise and fall of her shoulders preparing for battle. She half turned as she spoke. "Your father was a leader. I admired that. He did not wait for others to make things happen for him—he envisioned taking it for his. When we moved to Izmir we were going to finally have our dreams come true. Live by the water. He bought a boat. For a while he fished and sold what he caught."

His mother stepped away from him, putting distance between them. And Murat suspected she couldn't talk about the ugly parts without separating herself from her role as a mother and protector.

"It wasn't long before he was caught up in something different. At first I didn't know he wasn't fishing anymore when he left each day. At first I didn't want to see the obvious. His clothes, his skin, didn't smell like salt water anymore. They smelled like . . ."

"*Anne*. Don't continue. I'm sorry I asked." Murat understood. His father was unfaithful. Perhaps had many mistresses, or worse, prostitution being common enough. He turned to leave. He needed to escape the sad pool of green in his mother's eyes. A whippoorwill quavered, its chant soft, but insistent—*a warning.*

"No. You asked. I'll tell you."

"No. I don't want to hear it. I cannot bear to hear the details." Murat brushed his mother's limp hand off his forearm. "I'll be back to help with dinner." He paused and without looking back at her and asked, "Could *Baba* still be alive?"

He heard the sucking intake of her breath, a step back, and a deep sigh. He couldn't force himself to turn and meet her eyes.

"No. He cannot be, son. He is gone. He cannot hurt us any longer."

Murat didn't fully believe her words. That sounded more like what his mother wished to believe, that life hadn't gotten so complicated. That ghosts of an old, ugly past couldn't still hold their stronghold in the present. He'd never ask again. Murat knew the terrible, twisting pain he caused to even voice the question.

"*Tamam.*" The word "Okay" tasted metallic. It hadn't been okay in such a long time. This pain persevered. Stagnant. Ever present. Get away. *Run away from all the need.*

Murat followed the path, away from his home, then sped up to a full sprint. Down the dirt lane. Past trees that blurred. Past the kids playing in the courtyard. He couldn't stop.

His heritage tossed away for something as trivial as sexual pleasure. Because of his father's bent toward loose women, the family abandoned him and his mother. How could a woman and her child be left because of one man's choices? And even worse, he suspected his father to not be gone after all. Perhaps he planned to harm his mother. To harm Ella. Anyone Murat cared about. He must have observed for a long time. Who else kept watch over the wall?

Murat slipped into a seat in the back corner of a local bar and ordered a Malibu and Coke. Moments later, the coconut liquor warmed his throat.

Murat enjoyed the sense of aloneness. Away from the needy stares of children looking to him as a role model. Away from the sad truth his mother held back, now laid bare. *I can no longer look at her without thinking of the betrayal.*

Time smoothed by. The ache ebbed with each drink, with ice clinking against the glass. A dark horizon engulfed him, but the drinks pushed the pain further away. Soon Murat found the light of day no longer fanned through the doorway, only blackness.

He thumped his heavy head on his arms then jerked up. A man, who looked like the man peering over the wall at Ella, sat at a table

across the room watching him. The vision swam and shifted and he really couldn't tell.

Murat shot up, knocking over his chair. He lunged forward. The man slipped out of the bar. Murat stumbled out the door and scanned the street. Only taxis lined the sidewalk. A black cat slinked beneath a parked car.

Murat twirled around and re-entered the bar. The phantom of fear could not be escaped even with alcohol. It sat, as real as any person, just across from him, dark eyes burning into his barricades.

"Was there a man there?" Murat heard himself yell the words as though he watched some other person, not himself. But right now he didn't care. It felt good to finally release the frustration caged in his ribs. "Tell me."

The bartender looked confused. He nodded his head, backing away from the bar.

"Then who is he?"

"He's nobody. He sat down just before you chased him out."

Murat slammed his fist against the bar, then swiped his hand against a line of glasses, shattering them to the ground.

The man stepped back, arms up, palms out. "Please go. I don't want your problems."

Murat glared at his hand that had never before been raised in violence. Splintered glass glittered in the dim room like the façade of decency he'd tried so hard to create. Now scattered and revealed for everyone to see, he was a phony and his father an abusive adulterer.

Disappointment fluxed in the room. Murat scrambled out of the tavern and staggered across the road toward the sea, the last place his father did something other than shame his family. The blue-black Aegean like a bruise as far as the eye could see. ✖

18 THE BEACH

Like it or not, the man helped me more times than I could count already. I couldn't leave him to deal with whatever drove him away tonight. I saw him jet out of the property not stopping so much as to scruff a child's head or look my way. I wasted a perfectly good wave too. I watched him duck into a bar across the road. And even though I wasn't stupid enough to go in there alone, I watched and waited from my perch on the low wall stretching around the orphanage property. For a minute he came out, as if chasing the guy who'd ducked into an alleyway, and then slipped back into the bar.

He stepped out again, unsteady. His hair stood up, like he'd tugged at it with his hands in frustration.

He's drunk. I couldn't believe the image. This pillar of goodness swayed on the sidewalk like a bum. I followed him down the road leading to the beach. He mumbled angry words in Turkish, slurred and also staccato, like he yelled at someone invisible.

"I didn't take you for a drunk." The beach felt cool on my flip-flopped feet.

Murat spun around, kicking out sand from beneath his heels, stumbling backward. "Ella?"

"Yep. It's me."

"You shouldn't be here."

"Well, I am. And you can't do anything about it." I decided headstrong and sassy worked the best. Besides, push a woman too far with shouldn'ts and can'ts and she'll push back.

"Go home."

"Nope." I crossed my arms, then sauntered toward the shore. A swim suddenly appealed to me. I resisted moving into the coolness of the salt water. "What happened, Murat?"

"I don't want to talk this with you." Murat's voice boomed, but couldn't compete with the persistent whoosh, crash, whoosh of the waves rolling toward us, then pulling back.

"Why not? You have to sober up before going home anyway."

Murat's sandy hand scratched against his stubbly chin. I reached over to brush the golden grit off. Murat placed his palm on the top of mine. Tears slipped from his closed eyes, pooling on the top of my finger. "What is it?" I whispered realizing the tough approach no longer applied.

"I'm a man just like my father. Weak and violent and . . ."

"And what? What other terrible things are you?"

"Well, he was an unfaithful man. Many women. Our family wants nothing of us. They must think his life stained us." Murat's hand flopped down. He collapsed onto the sand, as if he planned on staying all night.

"Hmm . . . so they, your family, who is that?" I sat beside Murat.

"My *Dede*. My grandfather is the only one alive that still lives nearby. My father's family, my aunt and uncle, are kind enough to send us money now and then, but only in the last few months have we heard from them. For fifteen years, we've lived as leopards." He paused, letting that sink in, pressing his hand over mine.

I almost gagged on my spit at his slip up. I imagined him and his mom prancing around the orphanage, spotted and sleek. Pretty sure he meant 'lepers,' I covered my mouth and coughed to stifle laughing out loud. That would definitely break the thin trust Murat extended my way.

He began again, saving me from the moment. "Separated and pushed away. Is why my *Anne* moved to the orphanage in the first place. She had to take care of me." I heard regret in the word 'me.' Like he almost wanted to blot himself out of the picture to make it easier for his mom. The depth of his load dug my fingers into the sand until I touched the wetness of the sea beneath. Murat flopped back, arms splayed above his head. The black hair from his armpits peeked out of his T-shirt. I looked away.

"Am I missing something? Where's your father in all this?"

"He's dead."

"So why hide away anymore? He can't hurt your mom anymore."

"We're not hiding. We're trying to live. To do something good with the kids. At least he can't take that from us." Murat spat out the last sentence like a vow.

"It kind of seems to me like going out and getting drunk and doing whatever you're doing tonight is letting him win just a little, don't you think?"

Murat rolled up like an athlete doing crunches, looked toward the water with his arms strapped around his spread knees. He didn't respond. Only brooded for a bit. The waves washed between our words, in and out through the silence, until finally he looked at me over his shoulder.

"How did you know to find me here?"

"I followed you." I flicked my chin up to make sure he wouldn't even consider scolding me.

A crooked smile flickered on his lips. "You're stubborn, you know this?"

"Yep. I do know this, sad to say."

He turned his face toward the water again. Then added quietly, "Thank you, Ella."

"My pleasure, sir. We all need help now and then."

"I'm not used to this."

I laid back on the sand, the moon so bright above me, and closed my eyes. "I know."

The waves kept hushing.

"Murat?"

"Yes?"

"Are you an alcoholic? Do you do this regularly?"

At this Murat laughed out loud. His belly laugh made my chest feel warm and my cheeks hot.

"No. I'm not. Is the first time for me. Well, since I was teenager."

"Just checking."

He embraced my hand, sand and wetness coating his. Together we waited for him to sober up. I couldn't remember ever feeling so comfortable or staying quiet with any person, man or woman, for this long. Like it was all right not to have answers or smart anecdotes.

I relaxed as the sea air whispered over me next to a man I hardly knew, yet somehow, I'd always known. Ours was a shared cavern full of healing, salted water. ✎

19 MERYEM'S HOME

Murat dropped Ella off at her room. He walked home and pushed open the front door of his house after 2 a.m., certain his mother was worried. Never before had he given her reason to be afraid. She'd dealt with more than enough already.

As he entered, the door squeaked. A lamp cast an orangey glow across the small living room. His mother slumped in a chair, her fingers interlaced under her chin and her shoulders rising and falling in exaggerated huffs. Murat moved to her and kneeled. He noticed the way her lips drooped at the corners. The black of her shoulder-length hair shone in the lamp's light.

He touched her chubby hand. "*Anne*?"

"*Evet.*" She repeated a robotic 'yes.' Her body lurched. Her eyes popped open forgetting where she slept. Recognition and a flash of anger lit in her green-brown eyes. "Murat."

"Shhh . . . the kids."

"You scold me?" She yanked his ear as she stood to her full height, a full foot-and-a-half shorter than him.

Murat scrambled to rise. "*Anne*, I'm sorry. I needed time alone."

She inhaled an exaggerated sniff. "Drinking? This is the man you want to be?" The pitch of her voice lowered, deep and commanding.

"No. It isn't."

"Well then, why?"

"Because, I'm tired. I'm tired of trying so hard to be perfect. To take care of everyone. To take care of you." Before he could snatch his words back, they flew out, like black crows lifting off the sand carrying rotting flesh in their beaks.

Stunned and silent, she pounded her hands against his chest as he attempted to draw her close to hug her. "I won't lose you like I did him. I won't." Murat thought her thick sobs might kill him.

"*Anne*, I'm so sorry. I didn't mean that. I don't know why I did it. I just feel so . . . "

"Outside." His mom ordered him out the door with a flick of her

head, her fingers brushing her tears away. The cool of the evening surrounded him, taking the final hold of the alcohol and shooing it off, a dull headache lingering. His mother pulled his hand and together they walked until they came to the bench where she sat each morning and read her Bible. The place hidden inside a draping of willow branches created the feel of a separate, private room, like only they heard what words swirled within the green walls.

"You are like your father in some ways, Murat. Not everything about him was terrible, son. Failure is measured by different people in different ways. To your father it was measured by losing a sense of power in society and not having enough money. At times he loved us. He tried to make a good life. Other things crept in. Anger. Hate. It didn't happen all at once. Little pieces here, there." She looked at the canopy of black, shadowy leaves.

"What are you telling me, *Anne*?"

"You must forgive him. Must let it go. Give the anger and taking care of everyone to God. Or you will end up like him." The last words clapped like a death sentence. Murat couldn't comprehend ever being like his father. Not deep inside.

Meryem rose and walked to the edge of the hanging wall of green, the tips of her fingers brushing at the sagging, oblong leaves. Even though the evening wasn't cold, she rubbed her arms warding off a chill. Meryem turned to Murat, her face splashed with the blue-gray shadow created by the moon filtering through the tree. "Stop trying to do everything, son. You cannot possibly protect everyone. You will go crazy with this task."

"*Anne*, this is the job I must do. Even if I wish sometimes I could run away from it. I will not let you or the children down."

"Will not let Ella down." His mother said, low with anger.

But why? Didn't she realize how things would be if he stopped? She had no idea all he cared for without her knowing. She only spoke as a mother, considering his good, nobody else's. He didn't have the benefit to live selfishly like his father. No, he'd continue carrying this load for all of them. His future wasn't important. He must stay the course for them. ◆

2O ANKARA, TURKEY, 1981

Ali said only a few words before he left the next morning. "Get our things together. We leave tomorrow." With that he stepped out, closing the door with finality.

Meryem blinked against the sunlight's glare stretched across the room beckoning her to get up before hope faded all together. Her husband's harried words pushed her up. *Tomorrow?* It hardly seemed possible.

Preparing to leave in such haste would be difficult. Getting her parents to agree to leave on the spot would be the harder task. Meryem nudged back the questions. *Why so soon? What is my husband running from?*

But she allowed only one thought to take root—leaving this place. She grasped onto the tiny fragment of hope, like a secret, not daring to broadcast it out into the open, for fear it would catch on a breeze—whisked away from her forever.

Meryem knelt beside her bed and tugged out a large suitcase to hold their belongings. The rest had to fit in the back of the Fiat or be left behind. Without any order she tossed their few possessions in the luggage, though she carefully packed the black sea urchin from her time at the sea with *Anne* and *Baba*—a skeleton of a time when their smiles beamed against a butter-yellow sun, unrestrained.

She owned so little that mattered at all. She kept the essentials, but nothing that spoke of her heart. Meryem protected herself by not decorating or making the space a home. Caring about any of it spread her heart out like a doormat. The gray-white walls could not become more empty or bleak. No, they reflected the truth. She never did well with façades.

She only dared decorate the private room inside her chest. In her heart the walls were painted an aquamarine; on tiny silver nails hung pictures of her and her parents, faces all pressed together, smiling. A glass bowl full of white sand and delicate sand

dollars the size of her pinky nail rested on a side table. A beautiful, little baby boy played on the handwoven blue and green rug. This place she visited often—the place where she cried.

Meryem lifted the cumbersome bag and stepped out of her bedroom. An irrational notion flitted through her mind. Perhaps within the walls of this empty house she could trap and leave behind the sadness. Click the front door behind her and start again.

Either way, leaving meant some dreams stayed alive despite starvation. Almost giddy, she imagined their new life on the seashore. Maybe Ali would do as he dreamed. Maybe they'd be happy. That's all they needed—a fresh start.

Meryem descended the steps to her parent's apartment calling out for her parents. *"Anne. Baba."*

Time had come for a new life. Her crystal clear sea awaited.

21 MERYEM'S HOME, 2007

Pretending to ask Murat to take me some place, rather than coming right out and asking, "Are you better?" seemed easiest. With the nightmare from the past evening pressed back for a bit, we could play all was right with humankind.

As if my thoughts conjured him, I spotted him coming my way. "Ella." He leaned in and kissed me on both cheeks. I didn't detect any lingering effects of his drinking, no stale alcohol tang. Instead he smelled like he just stepped out of the shower and splashed with lemons. "I wanted to check in on you."

Tiny fireworks went off in my stomach and I wondered if I'd implode. I breathed in to calm the feeling. "Me? I was coming to do the same," I said.

"Oh, thank you. The headache is bad, but that's okay." He paused, looking at his feet, then at me, his dark eyes orbs of depth and history. "I'm sorry about it. I shouldn't have done this. I'm sorry you saw me this way too."

"I didn't expect everything here to be perfect and I didn't think you were without issues."

He huffed some air and chuckled. "Well, I should say thank you, but this doesn't sound like a good thing."

"I knew you weren't perfect from the day I met you."

His eyebrows drew together. I spotted the smile behind the glare. "Oh, so quickly?"

"Yah. Like when you cut off someone just minutes after picking me up. I thought I was going to die."

"I cut someone?" Murat shook his head.

"Cut someone off, you know, drove right out in front of another vehicle?"

"Ahh . . . this is how you must drive. You should know this." Now he really sounded like a Turk.

"Hmm . . . I guess you had no choice then. It was necessary."

"Necessary." The warm morning air already heavy with humidity hung with silence, forcing me to fill the gap.

"Murat, I better go. I need to go check on Umut. Can I come by to say "Hello" to your mom later on? I haven't really gotten a chance to get to know her."

"*Tamam*. We'll be there." He shuffled backward for a second before turning and heading toward his home. I watched him disappear around the bend. I didn't even ask him to take me exploring. The man made me lose all coherency.

I walked to Murat's home and spotted Meryem outside beating a rug hanging over the clothesline. Shading her eyes from the sun's blinding, melon-colored glow, Meryem waved a hand at me and began hitting the rug again, dust floating in a ball around her.

"*Merhaba*," she said, not stopping her work.

"*Merhaba*, is Murat here?"

Meryem looked at her feet and stalled to answer. I wondered why. Looking at me like a woman unsure and confused, she plastered a painfully false smile on her face. "Murat inside." She didn't move.

I wondered about fooling her with a, "Hey, what's that?" and running around her into the house while she craned to look. Instead I just said, "Oh, well, can I talk to him? Just for a minute."

"*Tamam*." The word 'okay' sounded dead. I shrugged off self-doubt, coaching myself that her reservation surely had nothing to do with me. How could it?

"We go together." Meryem pulled the rug from the line and together we walked into her home.

Murat's back in all its glory, his T-shirt clinging, greeted me. He scrubbed a plate and didn't turn around when we entered the room. Instead he said something in Turkish, pointing a soapy hand to a package laying on the table nearest him.

Meryem stepped forward, opening the package then pressing the contents to her nose, inhaling deeply. She barked at him, a sound that didn't fit with her sweet face complete with laugh lines. She changed so quickly, I wondered if the woman was bipolar. Or maybe a serial killer.

"Murat." She said his name like an order.

Murat swung around, a feminine apron tied around him, soap dripping onto the floor in front of his bare feet. He looked from his mom to me then at his apron. Red tinged his face. He scrambled to remove the apron, tossing it in the corner.

"Hello, Ella." Murat stammered, clearly flustered. "I didn't know you were here."

I forced down a laugh forming in my chest. "Yes, I see that." I couldn't help it and laughed out loud, covering my mouth to muffle the sound. "I like your apron." An unfeminine blast of laughter escaped, but I thankfully suppressed an accompanying snort.

Murat's eyes widened. "I use it when my mom needs help. I don't want to get my clothes wet. Perhaps you'll need one." Murat turned to the sink, still filled with dirty dish water, then twisted the faucet handle, a clear stream of liquid filled his cupped hands.

"Why? Why would I need . . . ?" Murat spun around and splashed me right in the face.

The liquid dripped from my chin. I paused for a few seconds, then dashed to the sink, dunked a cup in the water, and threw it on Murat's shirt. Meryem stood there, the package she opened still in her hands, looking back and forth between the two of us, the dark cloud she trudged under, now gone.

Clucking her tongue she snapped, "Murat. You know better than to treat a guest like this." Murat looked momentarily repentant, then shocked, as his mother dipped a large plastic pitcher into the dishwater. "It isn't proper to treat a woman in this way either." She ambled over to her son and poured the full pitcher over his head. At that she let out a scream-laugh, dropped the pitcher, and dashed out of the front door.

Murat looked at me with an expression of complete amazement, water dripping from his hair, and sped out the door

after his mother. Within moments he carried the chubby, squealing woman back through the front door, trapped in his firm grip. She screamed hysterically and kicked her fat feet. I noticed one of Murat's hands stayed pinned under her armpit.

"*Hayir! Hayir!* No, Murat." Her face reddened gradually, like mercury in a thermometer. She gasped for air, "*Çok fena. Çok fena. Hayir,* Murat. Very bad boy, Murat."

The scene mesmerized me. Murat's arms tensed against her body's thrashings. He carried her to the chair in the corner and set her down. Leaning over her, he tweaked her cheek and kissed her nose.

"Behave, *Anne.*"

I felt like a tree rooted in the center of their home. He turned to me and offered a stunning, wet smile, his entire shirt soaked. "I'll be back in a moment. Please have this seat." He turned and left the room, like a graceful master, closing the bedroom door with a quiet dignity.

"Well, that was most fun." Meryem giggled as she opened the box Murat gave her and offered me a piece of the honey-soaked dessert. "Come, sit." She guided me to the low copper table in the corner surrounded by blue and rust wool pillows. "Baklava. You like it?"

"Yes, I'd love some." I picked out a sticky piece, a flake of the delicate pastry falling onto my skirt. "Very tasty."

"Is this how Murat behaves at home?"

Meryem tugged at her wet T-shirt and smiled. Suddenly she looked sad. The change was subtle. A slight tip of her head to the side, the far-off look in her eyes. "No. He not laugh so much these days."

No idea what to say, I focused on the baklava like an offering to the gods. "This is delicious. Thank you." The flavors kept my mind from wandering dark roads again, to just savor this moment. The room fell silent aside from my chewing.

"*Çay,* Ella?"

"Yes, please." She stood to grab the pot simmering on the stovetop. Like her home remained perpetually ready for any visitor

that might happen by. For some reason that image struck me as important. How open have I made my small home? How open have I made my heart? Do I ever prepare for a possible guest who might need me? Or am I solely in the business of protecting myself? Doing things on my terms, with all the proper buffers in place? The realization of the answer soured the pistachio-sweet taste in my mouth.

Murat came out, saving me from further introspection. His brushed, jet-black hair curled damp on his neck. An amused look on his face, Murat squatted at the copper table and plucked a square of baklava for himself and wiped some honey from his lip with his thumb. I stared until Murat caught me gawking.

"You see how she treats me? I bring her gifts and she pours water on me."

"Is that how you see it? I don't feel sorry for you." Surely my face glowed maroon-red with the word "pervert" scrawled clearly in black Sharpie on my forehead.

"No, I'm sure you don't. The women always stay together." With feigned pride, Murat stood and walked over to the apron laying in a ball on the floor. He picked it up and hung it carefully on a hook by the small sink, then turned back to us.

Clearing his throat with a deep cough, he announced, "I must go to work on fixing this van." With a manly stride he headed out the door.

I let out the breath I held and laughed like a smitten twelve year old. The only thing I didn't do was ask Meryem to pass a note to Murat in gym class.

I rose and thanked the woman for her hospitality, then stepped outside into the hot sunshine determined to leave with some semblance of self-control still intact. I spotted Murat's muscular legs sticking out from under the van, sprawled apart on the dirt. Careful not to startle him, I knelt and tilted my head under the vehicle. "Murat?"

Pulling himself out, Murat looked up at me, a wry grin on his face, "What can I do for you, *Madame*?"

"I wondered if maybe you could drive me to a few places tomorrow after you get off work." At Murat's stare, I fumbled to explain, "I can take a taxi if you're busy. I just know how you feel." He still lay flat on his back, a smudge of grease marking his cheek.

"No, no problem. I can take you. The van should be fixed soon. We can leave at noon tomorrow, *tamam*?"

"After my class?"

"*Evet*. After your class."

"I'll see you then." I stood and walked away, but couldn't help peeking back his direction. Murat watched me from his position on the ground.

"I like your mom." The dampness of the collar of my shirt made me smile.

Murat blinked his eyes and replied, "Me too."

On the way home I realized for the first time how much I missed my mom. Before taking the job at the orphanage I never considered leaving her. She came up with the idea for me to return to Turkey. In fact, she found out about the position and urged me to go, saying it would be good for me to get away. But from what? A girl can't escape her brain.

I wrestled with whether it was really good for me. Whether I helped anyone except myself in coming. My motivation appeared the epitome of altruism.

Girl returns to find her father's murderer to forgive. Yah right.

Selfishness marked each step. That's what being wrapped up in myself did—blurred the rest of the world—a magnifying glass burning my fixation of that day so long past, until it burned me. And not in the good clean-you-up sort of way. The scarring, leave-you-marked sort of way.

I'd lived long enough making do, treading water. I dreamed of jetting out past the safety zone. To discover what might be found in the deep waters. To where a sea of mystery awaited. To ignore the fact that sharks lived that far out too. Stunning Arabian ones. ✎

22 THE RESTAURANT

Ella and Murat sat in silence in bistro chairs on the sidewalk outside the restaurant watching the bustle. They enjoyed a meal and fell into a comfortable lull. Ella leaned an arm against the metal lattice fence observing all the activity—cars buzzing by, workmen digging up the road on the other side of the street, a vendor yelling out his wares in a monotonous, nasally tone. Murat even admitted the mesmerizing scene begged to be noticed. Ella glanced over and found him watching her, his arms crossed over his chest.

"What?" Ella ripped a nugget of bread from the long loaf in the center of the table to soak up leftover sauce on her plate.

"You remind me that each day is a gift."

"Really? Me? The woman who second guesses every single good moment offered her?" Ella smirked and popped *ekmek* in her mouth.

"Yes, you. You're watching everything with so much interest. I never do this. I forget about all the good things around me. I get tired by life."

Ella looked at Murat, then out at the street. "I know what you mean."

Murat broke the seriousness. He didn't want to weigh down this time with problems. "Like that man yelling about his food. That's funny, don't you think? He sounds like he's chanting. Maybe he's one of the men doing the call to worship and this is his other job."

"Bread seller by day . . . man in the minaret by night. He almost sounds like he says it without any hope anyone even listens. I wonder if he says it in his sleep," Ella chimed in.

"His wife must get tired of him trying to sell her bread in bed," Murat said with a chuckle, enjoying laughing with someone to forget responsibilities and just relax.

"Or yelling in her face to worship Allah," Ella said, her voice like a balm somehow. "Thank you, Murat, for taking me all over the place. I know you have other things you could be doing . . . "

"Yes, I do, though I'd rather wait all day for this woman than do anything else." He smiled, pretending he joked. Pretending he had other things to do without wanting to spend every moment with her.

"Oh, right. You're flattering me." Ella looked at her plate, her cheeks a little more pink than usual. He hoped he affected the woman in some way. He noticed her little glances. Noticed her acting nervous in his presence. He didn't understand what triggered that. He flattered himself thinking maybe he caused the fluttering.

"I never tell a lie, *Madame.*" With that he pulled off a huge chunk of bread and tore a piece away with his teeth. Without waiting to finish he asked, "Where would you like me to take you?"

"Hmm . . . how about Ephesus?"

If the woman only knew how much he wanted to do that. Maybe run away and not return. He'd hide away with her any place she dreamed up. "Yes . . . , or maybe we could go get ice cream. Is better anyway, yes?"

"Fine, I guess if we can't drive all the way to Ephesus today I'll settle for ice cream. Could you maybe take me by the base? I want to look around there too. Oh, and I want to get some roses. You know, the ones they sell in big buckets? For some reason I remember that."

"Yes, I know this. There is one place with many flowers for sale. Kemeralti Bazaar near Konak Square." He pictured the labyrinthine, rambling alleyways and knew the exact spot where vendors set up shop in the photogenic flower market. Bunches of colorful, fresh cut flowers offered at bargain prices soaked in water in buckets stacked in stair-stepped rows.

A tall waiter interrupted the moment with the check, which Murat snatched before Ella had a chance to act like an American woman and demand she pay her part. Murat didn't care if it bothered her—as a Turkish man he couldn't allow her to pay for a meal they shared.

The waiter asked if the food had been good. Ella tried out her Turkish by engaging him in a little conversation about what was in the meal. He grinned and answered in English which Ella handled

with grace, while extending her hands for the *limon* cologne the man squeezed all over her palms. She scrubbed her hands together with the pungent citrus cleanser and then pressed her palms to her nose. "Mmm. That smell is probably the strongest one I have from living here. I love it!" Ella snapped out of the moment and squinted her eyes at Murat. "I hope I'm not being too demanding about all the places I just asked you to take me." She fidgeted and looked to the side.

"This is my pleasure." And it was. Being with her away from the orphanage made him feel less tethered. More free to just live—to be a boy who liked a girl.

Ella stood to leave. Murat sprang to his feet and pulled her chair out.

"Thank you."

"No problem, *Madame*. Yes, first ice cream. Then the base. Then I'll buy you flowers. *Tamam?*" Was he actually flirting with her? He didn't recall ever acting so obvious before.

But he'd never really cared before. Sure, getting the attention of girls at his school as a young man amused him. However, he'd never let anyone get close. Too risky. Look at his mother. She'd loved once. What did she have to show for it? Besides he didn't have time to think of his desires.

"Oh, please, you don't have to buy them. I remember doing that with my mom. She bought a bouquet practically every week. Said they made the apartment cheerful. I think I'll get some for Pinar too."

Murat nodded, thinking of Ella as a little girl, maybe buying flowers while he played soccer on a nearby street. He smiled, liking the picture of them so long ago, close to each other, but on very different paths.

Even now he wondered how his journey could do more than cross hers—he carried a different burden than she did. For the hundredth time he talked himself out of pursuing Ella. How could he stop his heart from chasing after her like a dog with all the longing he pretended didn't exist? ❧

23 THE AIR FORCE BASE

At the front gate of the Air Force base, Murat pulled up to the security guard on duty. I leaned toward the MP and showed my military ID out Murat's driver-side window.

The man gestured to Murat, "Do you have I.D.?"

"No. I'm just driving."

The gate guard pointed to a line of taxis. "You can wait for her over there with your vehicle."

Murat didn't argue. He pulled through and parked where the MP indicated. "Ella, I'll be here when you return."

I hated the idea of Murat sitting for hours like my chauffeur. "I can catch a taxi back so you don't have to wait around. I don't know how long I'll be."

"I brought a book." Murat turned up the radio and leaned back in his seat, no book in sight.

"Oh, I see. Well, if you're sure then. Enjoy the book."

I exited the car feeling small and childish all of a sudden. Could I do this on my own? I didn't know why I'd assumed Murat would be by my side. I looped my purse around my neck and began to walk, resisting the urge to turn back and climb in beside Murat like a wimp. Or worse, like a helpless girl.

I had no idea the location of my dad's old office. And even if I did know, would it still be in the same building?

I asked a man in uniform where the judge advocate general's office was and he gave me quick directions. As I turned the corner and spotted the building, long, low and tan, I recognized it as the same place. How many days did I walk after school to my dad's office to stay and watch him work, to pretend I had business of my own to do, spinning in his squeaky, gray office chair and stamping envelopes with his big, rubbery stamp?

The place hadn't changed at all: a simple rectangular structure with four identical square windows lining the front. A sign hung outside: "Staff Judge Advocate General, Larry Burns."

With an ache, I admitted some things changed. The earth didn't stop spinning when Matthew Gardner died. The base didn't close or demand a time of mourning. No, the sign was changed. The job he held, filled. My mom and I left with nothing but our household belongings and a great sense of loss. How could life possibly continue?

But it had. I remembered my pride as a seven year old seeing my dad's name etched into the metal placard. Now it was as though he'd never been here at all. Would anyone still be there who knew him so long ago? Extremely unlikely, given the short terms military men and women served before moving to a new place. However, I needed to ask.

I walked into a room with multiple gray desks lining the wall and several private, glassed-in offices to the right of the main area. I stepped forward into a din of activity and concentrated minds. I ventured a meek clearing of my throat and waited, hoping someone noticed me. A petite African American woman looked up and squinted in my direction. She wore the typical pressed light-blue, short-sleeved top and starchy navy-blue pants. She held a Holey Joe in her hand, the standard manila envelope covered in holes used for inter-base communications. Around her neck her tie formed an "x" giving her the look of a bull's eye. The picture I held of the military stood in front of me. The familiarity squeezed my throat and I closed my eyes. I drew in a deep breath, hoping I could do this.

"What can I do for you, young lady?" The woman said, friendly, and clearly all business.

"Yes, I was wondering if someone might be able to help me with something. My dad, Matthew Gardner, was the Staff Judge Advocate General here about fifteen years ago. I wondered if anyone might have some information for me on his death."

I paused and cleared my throat. "He was killed in a car bombing." She didn't respond right away, forcing me to explain. "They said it was a terrorist act . . . nobody was ever found. Or maybe they never told us who it was. All I know is one minute he was starting the car . . . the next minute . . . "

I wondered if it might be better if a giant hole appeared in the floor and gulped me down. The woman looked at me like I escaped from a mental facility. And she wouldn't be far off. "I want to know what happened, so I can put this to rest."

Chewing on the inside of her cheek, she stared at me trying to figure out this creature standing in front of her. "Well, I don't know if anyone here can help since it was so long ago. And that kind of info would be kept someplace else, I'd expect. We don't keep records that far back or that easily accessible anyway. Research would have to be done. Nobody I know worked here then. Have you written to the base commander? He might be able to help."

"No, I haven't. What is the commander's name and where can I find him?" I dug in my purse and retrieved a pencil and paper.

"Colonel Robert Taylor. He's just down the road on the right. You have to make an appointment. Can't just waltz in there and see the base commander."

I tucked the paper back in my bag. "Yes, I know. I'll set that up when I get there." My hackles started rising. I had issues, but I didn't lack the basics of problem-solving.

"Good luck then." The woman shrugged and began working again.

"Thank you, you've been very helpful," I lied. I figured it best not to create enemies so quickly. She lifted a hand without looking up.

Remind me not to help you if you ever need it. She'd never want my help, so the internal vow provided little comfort.

I stepped out the front door, adjusting to the transition from fluorescent bulbs to blinding sunlight. I strode toward the Base Commander's office.

What a dummy. Why did I think anyone would have answers for me? They don't know me from Adam.

I heard fast-approaching footsteps and turned, ready to use my limited Tae Kwon Do moves if need be. A gentleman ran toward me and stopped a few feet away. He stood about a full foot taller than me and sported a military haircut. He looked very Turkish with his

dark skin, salt and pepper mustache, and eagle-like, Arabian nose. "Hello. Did you say your father worked here?"

"I'm sorry. Who are you?"

"Tell me his name. Please." He ignored my question and I decided to indulge him. *What harm can it do?*

"Matthew Gardner."

The man pressed his hand to his mouth and stepped back appraising me, like I slapped him across the face. He whispered, "Why did you return?"

I forced myself to ignore the twisting in my stomach. I asked again, "Who are you?"

Taking in a deep breath, the man sighed. "Yes, of course. My name is Koray Yurdagüven. You see, the Turkish workers do not change postings. I've been here a long time working in this office. Twenty years, actually." He pressed his lips together for a moment then added, "I knew your father." ❧

24 THE COCOON

Koray said we'd meet when the time was right, whatever that meant. He didn't commit to a date or a time, claiming to be in the middle of some difficult projects at work. I suspected the man stalled. Getting straight answers equated to trudging through sinking sand carrying a refrigerator.

I leaned against the tree near Murat's house in my private outdoor room. The leaves hung so low they almost touched the ground. Cocooned. I struggled with the realization I was just that, surrounded by euphemisms for the pain to protect me.

I knew my mom understood more than she was willing to share and that made me love her—and hate her. Why all the secrecy now? What harm would it do anyone for me to finally have answers? My father was dead, so what more could I lose? I wanted to feel things again, allow myself to get lost in my life rather than bobbing like driftwood.

I watched Murat approach, looking muscular in his jeans and fitted black T-shirt. I looked at my hands until he stepped into the shade, otherwise I'd look like a creep under a tree. Besides, in my state of mind I might do something I'd regret.

"What are you doing?"

"I like sitting in here. I do my Bible time and think."

"Hmm. *Anne* too." He squatted in front of me and looked around the space.

"What are you doing today?" At this moment, I wished for better conversation skills.

"Escaping." He plopped beside me and loosely wrapped his spread knees with his arms. A lopsided grin graced his face.

"From what?" I asked.

"From *who*," he said.

"What do you mean?"

Murat chuckled and looked at me. I held his gaze, though I didn't know how long I could keep it up. Girls with issues don't

consider things like boyfriends, or dates, or even fine tune the skill of flirting. Maybe this place bewitched me because someone set fire to the rule book. Or my pants. Then scattered the ashes. I dog paddled in uncharted waters.

"My *Anne*."

"You're escaping from your mom?" I couldn't help laughing.

"She has much for me to do. Do this. Do that. I think she does not want me to get fat."

"Or spend time with a certain American girl." The words waltzed out of my mouth without knowing they were coming.

Murat shifted and turned beside me. "You? Of course this is not true. My *Anne* does not tell me who to see."

"She might keep you busy so you won't see me."

He considered this, surveyed my features, and leaned in an inch. It might as well have been a mile. "I would not let any person stop me from seeing you."

Help me, Lord.

As if realizing the intimacy of his words, of his closeness, of the space and the privacy, he pulled back, then leapt up. "Have a good Bible reading."

As he jogged toward his house, I heard his mother's voice beckoning and his muffled, low response. Perhaps my insecurity found a new fear to latch onto. I couldn't imagine why she found me unfit for her son. I reminded myself it shouldn't matter anyway.

This was a limited thing, my time here. I'd spend the year doing my job, find the answers I wanted, and then return home. Best not to grow attached to anything I couldn't fit into my carry-on. ❧

25 ANKARA, TURKEY, 1981

Always the detractor, Meryem thought as she watched her father's mouth move. "Why so soon, daughter?"

All she wanted to do was escape—forget the rationalizations.

"What is he running from?" *Baba* clothed her doubts with words, echoing her worries in the open, giving them life and truth.

The urge to choke her fear and pretend forced her to say the lie to her *Baba,* as if speaking it might make it so. "He cannot wait another day or he'll lose his courage is all." She paused then added, "It is hard to leave what he knows and start new. You know his family is here."

Her father always saw past her walls. At this moment she hated him. Hated the sad compassionate way he looked past the pretense her eyes failed to mask.

"He is not running," she finished without conviction. Her father wasn't buying it. Fear strolled in, like a ragged dog once slumped in a corner, awakened, and pacing at her feet.

Meryem slung her next words out, not to wound her father, but to move him. Still, regret filled her throat. "Father, you have not worked for over six months. We both must follow Ali. He is the one providing."

Hurt showed only in the soft crease that deepened between his gentle brown eyes. She dishonored him. A pain twisted in her throat.

Ankara didn't provide the same market as the ocean-side towns for *Baba's* beautiful hand-painted pottery. She sensed her father hated his powerlessness. No excuse pardoned being so impotent, so dependent on a man for whom her *Baba* held no respect.

Meryem reasoned Izmir offered a new beginning for her father. One day he'd thank her for saving them all. Still, shame lay with the dog heavy around her ankles; the pile of regret accrued so quickly. She felt herself sinking with the weight.

Father, forgive me.

Meryem touched his hunched shoulder.

Only love caused her father to stand and begin gathering the few belongings in the room. Meryem ran her hand over the empty shelf.

Her mother who remained silent through the exchange joined his efforts, shoving an old clock, blankets, and other items into a plastic woven bag.

Meryem noticed she wouldn't look her in the eye. "*Anne. . .*" She needed her mother to engage. Needed to know she understood. Her mother's head remained bowed, hands busy.

Heavy guilt circled and panted at her feet. ✑

26 PINAR'S HOUSE, 2007

All my broken fragments filled the shadowy black night, leaves casting strange shapes across the path as my feet crunched on the pebbles. My concerns tumbled around like rocks under a strong wave.

When will I ever find out about my father? When will I talk to the one responsible and close and seal that door with cement? If I had so much unresolved in myself, how could I help Pinar and Umut and the other kids? I was no mentor. Weak and unsure, I was mostly scared to death.

The ache in my lower back fluxed and I worked out the knots with my fingertips. Hearing my deep sigh in the quiet fed my irritation. I hated the atmosphere in Pinar's home, hated the thickness of the place, like a dark cloud hanging full and fat with sorrow.

The children who chattered before entering Pinar's home spoke only a few words once stepping into the house. Throughout the whole meal they acted tense. Were they scared I'd find out what life was like for them, like they'd all be asked to leave if anyone knew? Pinar never looked at the children. She did her duties. Nothing more.

I cleaned and then tucked Umut in bed before leaving. It all felt so short-lived and painful. Powerless to do anything, leaving them there to deal with more of the same was like handing a foster child back over to an abusive parent.

A warm breeze stirred the leaves, breaking the quiet of the evening, hushing me, calming me to remember that the God I loved could work all things out for good. Only—did I really believe that? How could that be true given all the suffering in this place? The recovery from life's blows.

The snap of a twig jarred and tossed the thought off to the side. The entire space around me shuttered with an unseen enemy. I parted the center space unable to do anything. I paused. Listened.

Maybe an animal? Or the wind? The tickle rippled down my spine. The almost too-still night transmitted a creepy feeling.

I'm not alone.

I experienced a fear so intense I stood in a room of darkness without even the tiniest light to guide me. I twirled in a circle like a plastic ballerina in a little girl's jewelry box scanning the area around the path, hoping with all my heart I wouldn't discover someone hiding. Only darkness blurred around me.

It's so terribly dark.

I bolted toward my home. All I could think? *Run. Don't stop.*

Run until hidden safely in my room under the covers with my door locked. I heard breathing. Was it mine or someone else's? I turned to look back, praying like a freak a face wasn't behind me when I rammed into someone. I started punching and screaming.

"Ella," Murat's voice broke into my hysterics.

"Murat? What. . .?" None of this made sense. *What happened?*

"Ella. Is me. What's wrong?" He grasped my shoulders and peered past me. "Who's following you?"

"I don't know. I heard a twig and then you. . ." *I feel like a fool.* A girl afraid of monsters. "I'm sorry. I don't know why I was so freaked out. I guess I'm scared by the strange guy we saw peeping over the fence. I heard a sound . . . it was so dark." I sucked air in and out of my lungs to calm down and looked behind me again. "It must have been nothing. I feel stupid." The quiet, cozy glow from Murat's home spreading across the area only added to my embarrassment.

Murat wasn't laughing or giving me a wizened look of 'how ridiculous are you.' He scoured the darkness. His brow pinched tight. His arms flexed, in a fighting position at his sides.

"Why were you out this evening?"

"I was at Pinar's house."

Murat visibly stiffened. "Why? Why were you there so late? Others can do the dinner times. I don't want you out so late alone."

"I brought Umut home and just stayed. Pinar wasn't feeling well, so I made dinner and cleaned a little. It got late before I realized what time it was."

"Ella, do you know why anyone would follow you?"

"No, no . . . " My strength depleted, I didn't want to have this conversation. Didn't want to even consider I might have anything to fear beyond old ghosts from the past. "Please, I'm sorry I bothered you. I'm exhausted. I need to go to sleep."

"I'll walk with you to your house then." Murat gave no room for argument and I had none to give. Just thinking about being alone again, even for the rest of the short walk home, made my hands dangle, like wilted rags at my sides, with no fight left.

Murat led me toward his home and didn't release my hand while leaning his head into his house and saying something in Turkish about being back later. He slipped his hand around my back and under my arm like he was afraid I might collapse. The heat of his hand soaked into my skin. I had the ungodly vision that if he touched me more I could ward off the chill, escape the fear.

"I don't know what's wrong with me."

"No problem," Murat said. "I've learned from *Anne* a woman's sense is often right . . . somehow you notice more than the boys."

"So you think someone was there? That someone was following me?" A cold chill burrowed even deeper.

Murat stopped and turned me toward him, his hands holding mine, grasping my fingertips. "If there was, I will find him. And I will stop him. I promise you this." ⇲

27 MERYEM'S HOME

Murat's heart felt thick and swollen. Ella's arrival triggered a deep fear snaking through every thought, every word, every action. Something about her made him feel out of control—like she'd be harmed and he'd have no way to stop it. He cared too much already. *Lord. What does it mean? I'm trying to let go of the shadow of my father's sins, but I can't seem to. Why does it feel he's still here, lurking, watching, and waiting?*

A dark inner voice whispered. *Because he is.*

Murat stood quiet and still, on the path back to his home, dampness forming on his neck and back. His father's death was a story he'd heard from *Anne* after a time of squid-ink-black, blurring the outlines of everything. A car accident, she said. One that Murat nearly lost his life to as well, she said. But looking back, Murat couldn't blow back the blotchy fog. He only knew one moment his *Baba* lived and breathed and shadowed everything and the next moment he disappeared, like some terrible magic trick.

Gone, but still hurting them. Murat's uncle arrived at the door some weeks later, eyes cast downward, "You must find a way now. You have no family here who will call you theirs. Leave. There's no other way." He pressed a bundle of money into *Anne*'s hands then turned away, but still Murat saw the regret in his eyes. His mom moved like a Roman statue at Ephesus, marble beneath flesh, and walked into her room, and closed the door. An otherworldly wail broke through the walls. Broke through Murat too.

After that, Murat and his mother left their apartment—found the orphanage. They never saw his aunt and uncle again, nor his grandparents. That was all Murat had of his father: an unsatisfied longing to be accepted and banked coals of dread.

No funeral to say good-bye. Nobody to speak of. Just a missing place at the head of the table and a horrible guilt at having loved him at all.

The moment Murat walked in the door of their small cement home, he called to his mother.

"Yes," Meryem stepped quietly out of the room. "I'm here. I finished getting the little ones settled for the night. So full of imagination, those two."

"What's that?" Murat rubbed the back of his neck as he slumped to the floor pillows trying to relax.

"They say a man asked them questions over the fence today. They said he looked like a madman. Probably someone wanting a coin or two."

"A man?" Murat rose and walked over to his mother. "They say a man asked what?"

"Son, you seem frightened. What is it?"

"*Anne*, what did they say he wanted?"

"Some nonsense about our home. They said he asked about a woman who lives here."

"You mean, he asked about Ella?" Murat paced the small room, eyes searching for some answer, illusive and stalking.

"Son, why are you so upset? Why assume Ella has anything to do with it? I'm sure it was nothing. You know how old men harass little children for a few *lire* hoping to find a sympathetic heart. It's nothing. I'm sure. Rest yourself. Can I make you some *çay*?"

"No, *Anne*, thank you. I saw a man watching at the wall a few times. Then tonight Ella thought someone followed her. I don't know what's happening. Could it be?"

The words swirling through his mind wouldn't come out. His mother's face appeared so calm. He forced the words back into his throat. He swallowed the ache, the unspoken possibility. Besides, he'd made himself a promise never to voice his theory again.

"Son, we mustn't live in fear. We did that for far too long. We must not turn back that way." His mom grabbed both sides of his face. Her eyes took on a fierceness. A warning. "Besides, you are getting too crazy with this idea of protecting, protecting, protecting. Enough of it. Ella is not your family. Not your responsibility." Her words slapped him across the face.

Murat stepped back. The pain of his mother's rebuke felt almost physical—the feel of her hands on his face still lingered.

Lord, it's too much. Too much for me. Please take the burdens off.

Meryem approached Murat again, embraced his hand in hers, the warmth seeped in, slowing the pace of his heart to a dull thump. "I'm sorry, Murat." She closed her eyes tight then looked at him, tears glossing over her greenish-brown eyes. "I just don't know how to help you see. You are just a man. Not the Lord himself. Why not let Him do the work? Please." The last word begged with concern. She flicked her gaze away like she couldn't bear to look him in the eyes anymore.

Could he really release control back to God so the ownership stayed there? He'd lost count of how many times he'd prayed and committed his future to the Lord, then minutes later snatched back the job of solving everything. How could he really, once-and-for-all, release it? No matter how hard he tried, there seemed no way to escape the role he must play. If he didn't, what would happen to everyone? What would happen to Ella, to his mom?

"*Anne*, I will do it. I will do as you say."

She nodded. Murat could tell she didn't believe him. "Good-night then." His mother untied her head-scarf and pulled her glossy, black hair smoothed free from a low ponytail. Wiry gray lines like pathways spread from her part here and there. Shuffling into the bedroom, Meryem glanced back once more. "I know your *Baba* is sometimes like a ghost you cannot run from. He is gone, son. He is gone. This new life we have been given is a gift." A pained look crossed her face, pressing her brows together. "But even gifts can be lost if we keep pushing them away. I love you, son."

"I love you too, *Anne*." Murat stood, then walked out into the darkness again. He kneeled on the gravel to collect the tools he spread out to work on the van earlier, placing each carefully in the toolbox.

He tried to find peace in his mother's words, "He's gone . . . " But no rest could be found. He didn't believe her words. ✒

2 8 IZMIR, 1982

Meryem's mother stepped into the kitchen with a stack of clean rags in her hands. "Where is Ali?"

"Out. Looking for work." Meryem stopped. The salty scent of the warm sea air glided over her face. She could stand almost anything by the ocean. Something about the endless, soothing lap of the waves made each day feel new, washed before beginning. No heaping of one burden on another like a tomb.

Meryem's mother laid the stack on the counter. "Daughter, don't forget to pray for him, your husband. He is looking . . . " The word "looking" dangled. Like more needed to be said. Like Ali didn't look for work, but something else entirely.

"I will." Meryem corrected herself before *Anne* discovered she failed in that regard to this point. "I have been." Anger and hurt drove any such plans off the landscape.

The older woman shut her eyes for a fraction of a second longer than a blink, making Meryem realize her lies didn't comfort her mother, rather, pained her. She laid her hand on her mother's. "*Anne*. Can . . . " *What can I say?*

Their closeness long ago scooted away like crabs hiding in the shadows of a sea cave. And it was her fault. The relentless "why's" left Meryem secluded, speechless. No, now Meryem and her mother worked side-by-side, except in two different places.

Anne covered Meryem's hand with her scratchy palm. "It is never too late, Meryem. Never."

Fear clamped a hand over the words laying mute on her tongue. *Never too late for what?* She turned away from her mother's gold-brown eyes. Instead Meryem asked, "Have you walked down by the sea?"

"Not yet. But soon. *Baba* wants to look for a place to put a storefront. Right near the ocean."

Thin hope filled Meryem's throat with a lump. Thankful all over again Ali brought them here. At long last.

The door to the second story apartment squeaked. Meryem turned to find Ali entering, arms full of *ekmek*. *Anne* escaped without a word. Meryem was not foolish enough to think her mother suddenly needed to be someplace else, doing something else. *Anne, you hope too much.*

Her husband dropped the pile of bread on the counter and said, "I have found a job." The yeasty smell filled the small space and her stomach growled. Unpacking all morning, she forgot to eat.

"On a boat?" Meryem asked, reaching for a loaf, pinching off a small portion from the crusty heel.

"No. Working on cars. But still, it is work and I thank Allah for that. You should as well."

He chewed his bread with his mouth closed, nostrils flaring as he breathed in. Most women would call his face handsome. She never cared much for such things. He was a provider to them. All she ever needed him to be.

At that moment, the salt air lifting the sweat from her forehead and the waves hushing her questions, she let herself look at her husband. This man in front of her, so tall and noble and rugged with his black hair curling at his temples. His wide shoulders enough for her to lean on. He took away her breath. Pulled her in. She stepped forward and pressed her palm to the side of his face. He flinched, then relaxed. His pupils opened just a fraction. She felt the thump of his pulse on her pinky.

"Why do you look at me?"

"Can a woman not look at her husband?" She ventured the next words. "Especially one who looks like you?"

Ali didn't move, just stared at her, into her. Like he'd never seen her before now either. Like he suddenly realized she was a woman.

"So tell me about this job." She stepped closer so their faces were only inches apart.

"It's. . ." He glanced at her mouth, then at her eyes. "It's just something to earn money while I save for a boat."

"Hmm. . ." She didn't dare push any further, not wanting to break the enchantment. Maybe the ocean possessed magical qualities, as she dreamed. All the ugliness would sink away.

"Meryem. . ." He didn't finish the sentence. Somehow she knew what he wanted to say.

She imagined her mother was right. She imagined he said he adored her, that he was sorry for not loving her well before, for all the angry words. She imagined he said her beauty rivaled a princess.

Instead he kissed her soft and sweet and now she knew. The salty waves took away the pain and gave them a new beginning. ✒

29 IZMIR, 2007

For several weeks I'd come. Though things were slow going, maybe I'd have some effect on Pinar. I wondered if my efforts would ever pay off. Not just for Pinar, but for the kids who seemed convinced they needed to remain sober and unfeeling, showing no reaction to my attempts to draw them out.

I cleared the breakfast dishes. All the kids, except Umut, left for school. A cool breeze lifted the gauzy white curtains I hung a month ago.

The undulating call to prayer echoed and staggered from all the minarets across Izmir. "*Allahu ekber*." I breathed a prayer to God thinking, even though I didn't worship Allah, I appreciated the reminder as I waited for a breakthrough with this almost catatonic woman.

Pinar shuffled out in her pj's and dusty flip-flops. As was her way, she yawned and glared at me out of the corner of her eye. She snatched a stray hunk of *ekmek*, slathered honey on it, then chewed and walked away. No "thank you." No "Wow, you're helping me out here making my kids breakfast every day and doing all my chores."

I forced down the comment I wanted to make about her being a lazy, good-for-nothing, before the words flew out audible and irretrievable. Besides, Pinar would surely agree with that assessment. My goal all along was for her to realize her purpose and destiny. I forced my feet her way and tugged the back of her ill-fitted shirt with my fingertips until she stopped and turned. In her eyes something stewed, churning around.

"Good morning. Are you okay?"

She pitched her chin up. "Sure. *Tamam*. Pinar *tamam*."

I reached out to give her a morning hug. I'd attempted this many times before only to be received by a wooden statue. Still, I couldn't give up. She most likely never was given the kind of love I hoped she'd learn to give these kids.

Instead of standing rigid and unmoving, she shoved me back, her eyes dark coals of anger. "What you want?" She practically spit out the words.

How to answer that? Where to begin? "I want to be your friend, Pinar."

"Why?" She moved a small step forward. I wondered if the shift forward caused her physical pain the way she worked so hard to push me away. Either that, or she planned to deck me.

"I . . ."

She squinted with enough fury to pin me, like a bug against a board. Pinar's balled fists forced me to pause before replying, "I just do."

"I not your friend." Her words said without feeling. No, not true. They leaked regret.

"I want to be your friend." The lifeline Pinar begged for got harder and harder to extend. The buoy bobbed and dipped on choppy water.

"No. Pinar no want to be." She whirled around. Her shoulders, puffed seconds ago, sagged like a person dragged down by sandbags. She couldn't help and look back to see if I walked out. Her self-defeating behavior still surprised me.

"I'm sorry to hear that." My eyes willed her to see my heart, praying she'd stop pretending and start living for once.

Pinar closed her eyes for a half a second, then walked like a thin stray dog out the front door.

I sighed in the small, boxy home. As I leaned over and wiped the low copper table, it gave off a hollow sound, as empty as Pinar's hope.

In only a matter of minutes I finished. Table cleared. Floor swept. Small vase of flowers sagging on the counter—my daily offering of cheerfulness into the dreary home.

I grabbed my bag to leave, then turned and prayed quietly for this sad person I tried to connect with. Maybe Pinar would never change. Maybe she'd never realize what she pushed away. Maybe Pinar would never stop being fearful and just grab at the gift of life extended.

Stepping out into the brightness of the morning, I spotted Umut sitting in the dust near the path, scratching aimlessly with a stick in the dirt yard. Pinar sat at the edge of the drive. When I looked toward her, she turned her face away, pretending she couldn't care less about anything. I didn't buy it.

When I approached, Umut tipped his brown face toward mine. "What are you drawing?"

He shook his head and continued his doodles. The dirt contained a fish, a dog, and two stick figures holding hands. "Do you like to draw?" I spoke to him in Turkish to make things easier. This wasn't about English acquisition right now.

He nodded.

"Do you have any paper or pencils or crayons?"

Again he shook his moppy, brown head. Interest caused him to tilt his head at me, not committing to a full-on stare. Not so unlike his mother in that way.

"Would it be all right if I got you some?"

At this his mouth pulled up on one side, a sort of half-smile. "Yes," he whispered though he didn't need to.

"*Tamam*. I'll do it." I knelt, the pebbly ground biting into my knees. I forced him to look my way by hooking his chin with my finger. "Remember who loves you?"

He nodded.

"Who?"

"Jesus." He said the word without hesitation.

"And?" I smiled, hoping he believed me.

"Teacher."

"Yep, that's right. Teacher loves you too."

He grinned without reservation. I pulled him onto my lap and hugged him tight against me. "Don't forget, *tamam*?"

His smile faded as quickly as it came. The shadow of Pinar clouded the sun over us. She glared at me and yelled, "Why you lie to Umut? God no love him. God no love me."

I rubbed Umut's back, his spine tight and straight under my fingertips. "Pinar, let's talk inside please."

She lifted her chin enough that I knew she agreed, then I lowered

Umut to the ground and scruffled his hair. "I'm going to talk to your mom for a minute. Then we'll walk over to meet the other kids in a little bit." He stared at his drawings, now destroyed by his mother's feet. I couldn't help see the irony. "Could you draw me a picture of your favorite animal?"

Back to the nodding. He turned his body away and I heard the scratch of his stick in the gritty earth. My hands tightened into fists. How could she wound her child's spirit like that? I resisted the thought of strangling Pinar.

I marched into the house and stood there taking in deep breaths through my nose and blowing them out slowly through my mouth. "Why do you do that? Why do you hurt your son like that?"

"I no hurt him. You hurt. You tell lie."

"No, I don't."

"Yes. God no love. God hate. He leave me die like dog. Let my husband hit, hit, and not care." She yelled out the words half in English, half in Turkish.

"Pinar, God didn't leave you. God used Murat to bring you home. God did not hit you. Your husband did. We hurt each other all the time. Your husband, you, me. Now you have a chance for a good life. With love. And children. And no terrible husband." I simplified a truth that should be simple, but wasn't for someone who ran from true love all her life. Or maybe more accurate, ran toward destruction. "God wants to give you another chance. Make your heart clean and start over."

She grabbed the vase of flowers and hurled them across the room. The glass broke. The stems scattered and lay in the shards. I ran over to Pinar and embraced her. "Stop doing this. Stop doing this, Pinar." I pressed her hard shoulders into me, smoothed her hair like a little child, whispered words of truth into her ear so maybe she'd believe them. "Please. I love you. You aren't alone. Don't push me away."

The transformation was so subtle, like the melting of ice in warm water. Her body softened, stopped the pressing away. I heard the tears before I realized they were there. She must have been so used

to hiding, even the truth came out painstakingly slow. "I not know how."

I held her at arm's-length, searched her black eyes. "It's not hard. Let me help you."

And this time the nod wasn't subtle. It was clear and full of longing.

We spent the next hour leaning against a tree in the yard, watching Umut tentatively playing, peeking up, then snatching his gaze downward again.

We talked about Pinar's questions. I shared my story, without all the details. Pinar eyed me now and then like she only just now realized she hadn't been the only person to suffer. Like maybe if I found some sort of peace, maybe she could too.

She made no life-altering decision to follow Christ, but the door cracked open just a bit. A thin stream of light found its way in, sweeping back the darkness that I feared took up permanent residence in Pinar's heart. ❧

3 O THE WINDOW

Each evening, Murat made it a habit to walk the circumference of the grounds. He wasn't sure if there was anything to be worried about. He figured better to be safe. On this night his mind stayed caught on Ella. After her trip to the base, she acted restless. She hadn't shared what transpired. Ella hid something out of sight, out of his reach. Murat decided to pray for her. As much as he wished to know what troubled her, he knew it wasn't his place to force anything. His lack of control left him feeling on edge.

He stopped below Ella's bedroom window. A warm glow of light illuminated the space inside. He saw her walking across the room unaware of the visibility from the outside. The sheer curtains suddenly seemed a terrible idea. Any person could watch from the darkness. Like hot coals banked and stoked back to life, anger filled his chest. Murat moved his flashlight back and forth, revealing the area below the ledge. Something caught his eye.

Scratches scraped the paint on the wood. No, gouged out, like someone attempted to pry under the crack and open Ella's window. He swept the flowers below with light to investigate clues as to the purpose for the damage. Maybe Ella did it somehow.

The stems of a peony bush brushing against the house were crushed. Footprints graced the dark soil, only they weren't small footprints. They were man-size—the same size as his shoes. Murat ran his hand along the trim like the wood would speak to him, tell him what happened, and why.

Then the curtain pulled back. He watched Ella squinting out at the darkness. Murat stepped into the shadows not wanting to frighten her. He tapped lightly on the glass and Ella jumped, jerking her hand away. The curtains fluttered across the window. Why had he done that? Of course it would scare her.

"Is me. Murat." He said the words loud enough for her to hear.

She opened the window, the frame groaning. "Murat? What are you doing out there?"

"I was . . . I thought someone . . ." How could he explain his intentions?

"What? What did you think?" She rested her elbows on the sill and leaned her head out, the ends of her hair brushing the scratched wood.

"Ella, did you get locked out of your room?"

"No. Why?"

"I just noticed . . ." He couldn't stand the vulnerable look on her face. How could he voice his concern that someone tried to break into her room? "Nothing. I was walking around to make sure everything is safe and saw your light on. I wanted to say 'Hi.'" The lie sounded ridiculous.

Ella eyed him like his heart was see-through. And with her, he felt sure it must be. He couldn't hide the intense need to be near her, protect her, solve the problems she hid poorly.

Then with a soft lift of the side of her mouth she said, "Hi."

Murat couldn't help himself. He needed to touch her. To feel the warmth of her skin. To feel her heart beat. To hear her steady breath. He reached up and brushed his fingers on her elbow. "Will you do me this favor?" Her eyes opened wider. She shifted her arm so his hand fully cupped her elbow. "Get darker curtains. *Tamam*?"

At his words she sunk back just a bit then grinned. "Tomorrow I'll go shopping."

"I'll take you then."

"Great, you can help me bargain."

"*Tamam.* In the afternoon I will get you."

"I'll be waiting."

Murat forced himself to step back. Even though his hands tingled from holding them above his heart, he could stand here all night. If he could be near Ella, it didn't matter. If he could only stay this close, then he could protect her. ✑

3 1 THE SHOPS

For a man totally driven to take care of the entire world, Murat drove like a freak. I grabbed the bar above my shoulder, pretending I only wanted my arm there. Trying to act like I wasn't terrified of the van rolling off the road in a ball of dust, plunging us to our deaths into the sea.

Murat's low chuckle made me wonder if he drove this way on purpose. "What are you laughing at?"

"Nothing." He squinted into the sun. I liked the way his smile rested on his lips.

I released my hold on the Jesus Bar, as Mom always called it, pressed my sweaty palms into my lap, then wrapped them together in a gesture of prayer. Might as well be authentic.

"Almost there?"

That sounded casual, right?

"*Evet.* This way." He whipped the vehicle around someone on a blind turn. I squeezed my eyes shut, bracing myself for my final moment on earth. When it didn't come, I opened them again after I felt the slowing and the crunching of the wheels on rocks on the cobblestoned street.

"Oh good." I popped open my door, leapt out, and resisted the urge to kiss the ground. That would be too blatant. Besides, someone might mistake me for a Muslim.

The din of movement at Kemeralti Bazaar gave the area a bee-like feel, portions covered in ancient, stone-arched ceilings, others open to the sky, then shaded with colorful flapping rectangle fabric swatches. Chattering voices, men and women stacking and scooping, a maze of tiny makeshift storefronts. Warm and nutty orangey spices piled in heaps in burlap bags. Silvery fish nestled in ice beds. Dried fruits and nuts displayed in buckets, alongside stacked, olive-green grape leaves.

A boy who looked to be only twelve, but clearly a capable business man, waved his hand showing off his jewel-colored

spices. Since I had no way to cook in my room, I shook my head 'no' and moved on.

Shining copper glowed from another storefront. I stepped toward the shop and watched my face distort in the nearest platter. The owner gave me an over-friendly look and Murat stepped forward and grabbed my hand, holding it snug in his. He leaned over and whispered, "So no one bothers you." His breath skittered down my neck. "And hold on to your purse."

Not allowing my mind to travel that scary road I nodded, but stayed mute, hugging my bag against my stomach with a vice grip. Murat's large hand wrapped around mine and I savored the sensation. I admitted the feeling of being taken care of was foreign to me, though I was perfectly capable on my own. I allowed myself to sink into the moment, wriggled my toes into it, lowering my guard.

"So which way to the fabric?"

"Follow me this way."

Somehow the man knew his way around the bazaar's maze. He led me to a place piled with bright, colorful cloth. I loved the idea of my room decorated completely Turkish. I leaned in and touched every fabric I liked.

I decided on a blue-green, paisley-patterned piece and waited for Murat to drive down the price. A few *lire* later, I owned the bolt of fabric the color of the shallow pools in the coves of Izmir, enough to sew curtains and even cover my bed. I imagined myself wrapped in the water, hair floating on the surface, face tipped to the sun.

"Lunch?" As we left the store Murat reached for my hand again. *He's getting used to this. So am I. And I'm not scared to admit it. Mostly.*

"Actually, I want to buy a few more things."

"Like?"

"Some lemon cologne and a *çay* set. Two of them. I want to send one to my mom."

"*Tamam.* I know this. I will take you."

At the tea shop I leaned over to check out the tiny cups of one set, clear hourglasses circled in a painted silver band. Each one sat on top of a tiny tin saucer.

I straightened to begin bargaining when Murat jerked beside me and said, "Wait here. I'll be back." *Weird.*

With that he sprinted away. I craned my neck, but couldn't see past a few feet in the congested space. The storeowner pushed the tea set closer.

I shrugged off the fear, claws piercing soft soil, and began my wagering. Feigning disinterest when his price edged above my goal, I relented once it dropped, then informed him I'd take two. He wrapped the tea sets in newsprint smelling of cigarettes, then deposited both in a thin plastic bag.

"*Teşekkür ederim.*" I thanked the man who turned away to deposit my dollars into his apron.

He waved at me over his shoulder looking somewhat dejected. I assumed he took me for a sucker and was disappointed. I breathed in through my nose, feeling a tad smug. Scanning the congested walk leading through the shopping area, I searched for Murat. He wasn't there.

What now?

Next door a vendor sold *vişne suyu* and *tost*, or smooshed-cheese sandwiches, the name I called them as a child. I ordered, sat at the plastic blue table, and took my time eating. When I sipped the last of my cherry juice, Murat arrived, out of breath.

I wondered where he'd been. How on earth could any person sprint in the marketplace? The place tangled with tripping hazards, alive and not alive.

"What happened? Where did you go?"

Murat looked away, then at me, like he didn't want to tell me. His shirt, wet with perspiration, clung a little too well. I ignored his muscles and his glistening lip. And his dark eyes.

"The man. He was here."

"The man?" It took a moment to register to whom he referred. "Oh. Well, did you catch him?" Stupid question given the fact Murat stood in front of me empty-handed.

"No. He got in a taxi on the road. He got away." Defeat was written all over his face. Sagged across his shoulders. Drew in his chin.

"We'll catch him, Murat." Though I didn't believe my words, I said them so the man in front of me didn't collapse.

A terrible twisting dug low in my stomach. That feeling I experienced for years whenever I thought of my dad's death. The feeling that someone lurked out there. And he killed my father. And that he wanted me dead too.

But what would anyone gain from me being gone? *I'm nothing.* A threat to no one. Just a girl, really, whose only goal was finding peace.

3 2 MERYEM'S KITCHEN

The leaves tinkled in the breeze making the evening feel more like a dream than reality. I gazed up through the trees lining the path to Meryem's house. Breathing in deeply, calm settled in my chest. I expected something to happen to spoil it.

I tapped lightly on Meryem's front door. A moment later Murat opened the door, handsome in a black T-shirt and blue jeans. His shaggy hair looked boyish and appealing. I resisted the urge to brush back a stray curl falling over one eye. Hands soapy from washing dishes, Murat leaned his head forward to kiss me on both cheeks. I took a moment to recover from his familiarity, so intimate and comfortable.

"Please, come in, Ella." Murat signaled with his head for me to enter and sit. The man seemed unfazed.

"I can help," I managed.

"No. No. You just sit and talk to me. I'm almost done. *Anne* is just finishing putting the little ones in bed."

"Oh." This meant we'd be alone for a few more moments, which felt intimidating at this point.

"What's wrong, Ella?" Murat turned his brown eyes on me, thick lashes and all, one hand in the dish water, the other placing a plate in the strainer.

"Nothing . . . I'm fine. I just . . . " I fumbled. *What is my problem, exactly?* The man made me feel like a teenager swooning at the star quarterback. "I guess I'm feeling nervous for some reason."

"Nervous? Why? To cook with *Anne?*"

"Oh, no. She doesn't make me nervous." *Liar.* "I don't know. I'm . . . " I paused again, "I don't know what my problem is. I'll be fine."

Murat finished the last dish, drained the water, and wiped his hands on his jeans. He sat beside me and leaned in lifting my hand gently in his.

"I don't know what's wrong, sweet Ella. Please don't be nervous in our home. You're a welcome guest. I'm very happy you're here. I always love any time I get to spend with you." He smiled genuinely, then released my hand.

Swooning, definitely swooning.

"Now, may I offer you some *çay* and a taste of baklava?"

I sighed, relaxing a millimeter. "You know the way to my heart."

Murat removed the *çaydanlik* and poured the boiling water from the larger bottom kettle over the tea in the top pot. He set the smaller kettle on the table. Then he placed three clear, hour-glass tea cups on a small tray along with a bowl with sugar cubes and brought them to the table.

Sitting across from me, Murat poured the tea through a small strainer that he placed over my cup.

"Sugar, *Madame*?" Murat pinned me with his eyes again.

"Yes, please." My voice cracked like a pubescent boy. I cleared it for an embarrassingly long time before saying, "Yes, one please." I fumbled with the small spoon and stared into the transparent gold tea as the sugar slumped with the heat. I related to that blob at the bottom of my cup. Steam swirled up as I stirred like an OCD patient. I kept my eyes lowered and my hands busy, then lifted the glass by its delicate rim and successfully singed off the top layer of my lip.

"This is good, Murat. *Teşekkür ederim.* Thank you."

"My pleasure." He leaned in and touched my hand again.

What's going on? How come all of a sudden I'm hormonal and crazed?

Ten minutes with Murat felt like an hour. Meryem entered, closed the bedroom door softly, and turned toward me. Relief flooded my face like cool water licking out the dark corners of a cove. I stood and moved her direction. Murat followed behind me.

Meryem glanced at Murat, then at me and frowned, but recovered quickly. Murat made arrangements with her to teach me a few Turkish dishes after I commented on wishing I knew how.

"Ella. I am sorry I was not out to greet you. The little boys were a little too much like being boys tonight." Meryem sighed. "How I wish I had same energy as them. So, ready to cook?"

"Yes," I said a little too loud. "Are you sure this is okay?" The woman's moods shifted almost as much as mine.

"Yes. So we begin make *İskender*."

I stood in the kitchen feeling awkward and clunky. "I hope you aren't too hungry. Is it all right that we waited to cook until now?"

"Yes, yes." Meryem waved a hand. "Is Friday night. Is nice to just sit us adults and enjoy quiet meal, yes?" She didn't look me in the eye, just made her hands busy.

"Yes. That will be wonderful."

"Murat brings me more baklava. I eat it all evening." The woman smiled at her son, all caution gone. "He wants to keep his *Anne* nice and round, yes?"

Murat pinched her cheeks. "Yes, just how I like my *Anne*. Plump and smiling."

Clearly, the woman adored her boy and would do anything for him. Meryem grabbed the flat bread wrapped in a thin white plastic bag. "Here, Ella. Take this and cut it into small square. Then put it on each plate."

I nodded my head and watched every move Meryem made. I'd waited years for the *İskender* recipe and wasn't about to miss a thing, despite Meryem's awkward greeting and the hot Turk in the room.

Meryem reduced the tomatoes to sauce in a large pot. "I do this early today. *Domates* 'tomatoes,' *sarımsak* 'garlic,' *su* 'water,' *tuz* 'salt,' *soğan* 'onion,' and *limon* 'lemon.'" The mixture thickened and simmered to a thick paste.

"Taste." She held the wooden spoon out to me.

I dipped my finger into it and tasted. "Perfect." I grinned at the older woman. "I can hardly wait to eat."

Murat stepped toward his mother. "May I?"

"Of course, son, taste." Meryem held the spoon up and Murat leaned in to taste it off the spoon.

"Mmmm . . .*Çok güzel.* Very good." Murat licked some of the sauce from his lower lip and smiled at me.

I ignored him and stepped toward the pot with the tomato. "Now what?"

"Is simple." Meryem placed a little of the paste into a small pot and added olive oil. "Just make thin this a little by water. Then we get lamb. Murat got for me at restaurant."

I reached for the package of meat and dumped it into a pan to heat through. "Oh, it smells so good."

"Now melt the butter. Murat, will you do this?"

"*Tamam.* Sure, *Anne.*" Murat moved to the space beside me and reached above my head for another small pot.

I eyed his muscular arm stretching across my line of vision.

"Excuse me, sorry, Ella."

"No problem," I mumbled.

Then Murat reached across me to the large block of butter on the counter. He cut off a hunk, dropped it into the pot, and lit the gas stove, the blue flame dancing like my nerves.

"Thank you, *Madame.* Is fun cooking with you. Maybe if you come over every day, I'll cook every time."

Meryem slapped a clean rag over Murat's head. "You are a teaser, son. Melt butter." The order was given with little humor and soon all the parts of the dish were ready to be assembled.

With an air of authority, Meryem directed us. "So, Ella, lay the lamb over *pide.* Now I pour this tomato sauce over. Murat, you pour butter. I'll get yogurt. Is fresh."

She reached into the refrigerator and pulled out a white bucket with a lid. Meryem spooned three large, creamy-white scoops of yogurt onto each plate. Snapping off some parsley from a window planter, Meryem garnished the meal with a small sprig. "*Tamam.* Is finished."

"Let's eat." My mouth watered and my stomach growled like a bear trapped in a box.

"Let's eat," Murat echoed.

We brought our plates to the small round table. Meryem offered up a brief prayer, then said, "*Afiyet olsun. Bon appétit.*"

I took a bite, heaven and earth meeting in a perfect balance of buttery symphony, and getting married. I considered writing an ode, but decided against it. Meryem was too sensible for odes.

I closed my eyes to enjoy the moment, to pretend Murat wasn't sitting across from me like one giant smolder. When I opened my eyes, I caught Murat staring at me.

He glanced away and coughed, then eyed his mom who frowned. Murat didn't move or respond to her, only lowered his eyebrows like he didn't get what she tried to say.

I knew the look. A warning. A huge "No Trespassing—Stay Away from the American" sign.

Only, Murat was already fused, like a brand in my side. *And I might just follow him right out to slaughter.* ✍

3 3 THE LANE

Murat wished the evening wouldn't end, though his *Anne* made it awkward. He anticipated walking Ella home alone without strange glances and cryptic messages from his mom.

At ten o'clock, Ella stood to leave.

Meryem stood too. "I teach you more cooking if you want." Knowing her usual warm personality, the offer sounded begrudging to Murat.

"I'd love that." Ella smiled then turned and grabbed her shawl.

As the summer gave way to the crisp breezes of autumn, the evenings cooled off. Still, being positioned off the coast of the Aegean, it was never cold.

Murat grabbed his jacket and stepped into the darkness ahead of Ella. Though she lived a short walk down the lane, he wouldn't think of allowing her to return home alone.

They hadn't gone far when Murat reached for Ella's hand. Without a word they walked hand in hand. The quiet hung like a room around them. Murat wondered what ran through this woman's mind. Did she care for him as merely a friend? A co-worker?

"Ella, may we talk before you go in?"

"Sure." She turned to face Murat. "What is it?"

Murat released her hand, then stuffed both of his hands into his pockets. "Would you like to sit?"

"Maybe here?" Ella waved her hand to the place under her favorite tree.

"*Tamam.*"

Both walked to the spot and sat on the crunchy leaves. Murat allowed the breeze to calm him, to absorb the quiet, the hush of leaves clattering around them.

I want to see dry bones, living again. The words floated in, then left, and he swallowed the ache that never fully left him. *Not now.* This moment wouldn't be stolen too.

"Ella. I wish I could see inside your head."

"Me too. Inside your head." She laughed softly.

"Even I cannot do this."

"What do you mean?" she asked.

"I feel mixed up. One minute afraid, the next wanting. . ."

"What," she whispered.

"Wanting a life. Wanting a kiss." He turned to her hoping she wouldn't run. *What's so wrong with wanting to live? Wanting to forget how he came to be here?*

She stared at him, her eyes glittering in the dark and light of the black night broken with lights from the homes.

"Will you think of spending time with me?" He paused again, searching for words, and mumbling something in Turkish.

Ella's laugh comforted. "Do you know you speak Turkish whenever you're nervous or upset?"

Murat's head shot up and he grinned. "Really? Sometimes I don't find the words I need."

"Well, I'm still impressed. Your English is flawless to me. I couldn't have this conversation in Turkish, that's for sure. So, you were saying?"

"Yes, I wanted to ask you something." Murat's voice dropped low. He cleared his throat. "I wanted to ask if I could grab a kiss. Or just, can we have a date?" His eyes searched Ella's face, wishing he could see her more clearly.

Ella smiled. "Let's wait on the first. Could be dangerous." She raised one eyebrow. "But, definitely, yes, on the second."

Murat clarified, "Yes, to the date?"

"Yes, to the date."

"Why dangerous to the kiss?" Murat reached out and pulled Ella to himself. She rested her forehead against his chest. A moment later Ella pressed her hands against him and gently put some space between them. Murat wanted to pull her back and take a kiss, but resisted. He'd never force her to stay close, no matter how much he needed her near.

Murat couldn't remember when he ever felt so much longing except for with his dad. The feeling terrified him. Still, her decision

to keep their relationship on 'safe' ground raised Ella a notch higher in his mind, though that seemed impossible.

"Dangerous because. . . ?" Murat teased knowing her meaning, but enjoying watching her awkward stumbling. She let a breath rush out. The wind kicked the leaves into full chorus.

Her quiet laugh blended with the trees. "I think I won't finish that sentence."

"*Tamam*. When can we have this date? Tomorrow night?"

"Sure. Where?"

"Let me think. Somewhere special. It will be a surprise."

"When?"

"I will come at seven."

"*Tamam*." As she stood to leave, he gently tugged at her hand.

"Why did you look sad when you came to the house tonight?"

Her hand tightened in his. "I wasn't sad. Only nervous. Because of you."

"Why?"

"Because of wanting to grab a kiss." Her nervous, quiet words made him want to take the lead—to remove any anxiety with action.

"Really?" Murat couldn't hide his grin.

Ella slapped his arm playfully. "Don't get any ideas and take advantage."

Murat traced his finger over her hand. "*Tamam*. I will not get any ideas." He paused, then reworded. "Actually, I will get ideas, but I won't do them."

"I guess that's the same as me then."

"Yes, the same is good. I don't want to have ideas all alone." Murat couldn't help but laugh. Ella joined in too.

For that space of time—nothing—not even old ghosts, suppressed the hope that filled the moment like liquid. ❧

3 4 THE AEGEAN

I grabbed Murat's outreached hand and pulled myself up to the rocky outcropping that jutted to a point overlooking the breaking water of the Aegean Sea. From this vantage point I surveyed the coastline, zigzagged in spots and stretched in others. The sun hid below the horizon. A burnt-orange hue radiated across the surface of the water. That blaze fanned out, then melted into a deep blue-black.

Murat spoke first, breaking the rhythmic thunder of the ebb and flow of the waves against the sand and rocks below. The pounding that hushed in turns, never stopped. "Is my favorite place. I once came here as a boy and remember it made me feel so sure of God. His voice does not stop here."

I considered Murat's words. God's voice might sound like the waves, curling and tossing in the white foam or booming over the crest of a huge wave or hushed as froth and bubbles floating across the sand.

"It's beautiful. I love this. Thank you for bringing me."

Murat leaned close, wrapping an arm around my waist, pulling me to his side. His distinct scent, a hint of olive oil and bread mixed together with his musky cologne gave me the chills, or had the wind done that? *Yes, definitely the wind.*

I stepped away to stay on safe ground. "Dinner was good, thanks for treating me."

Murat tilted his head to the side and smiled. "Is my pleasure, *Madame.*"

I couldn't help but laugh. "You know you sound just like a taxi driver when you say '*Madame*'?"

Murat's dark eyebrows rose in surprise. "Really? I didn't know this. The taxi drivers say to you '*Madame*'?"

"Yes. All the time."

"What else should I say? Is not the right word?"

"No, it's fine. It makes you seem like a man trying to please his customer, that's all."

"Should I say, 'Is my pleasure, 'woman?'"

An unladylike guffaw burst out too loud. "No, definitely not. If you said that in America, you'd get your face slapped."

Murat cocked his head as he crinkled his eyes. His confusion made me laugh more. Murat asked, "Why would I get my face slapped? Don't American women like to be women?"

"Hmm . . . good question. Some women would rather be treated like a man, whatever that means."

"Well, you're my teacher in this. I didn't know this was a problem to be called a woman. I will be careful."

"Good idea." I grinned at Murat as he rubbed his thumb over my hand.

He leaned in and pressed his nose into my hair. A tickle fluttered down my spine. "I love your hair."

Slow down there, gorgeous.

"Murat."

"Sorry," he said then dropped my hand and walked forward a little.

To move things away from awkward, I said, "I used to collect mini crabs as a little girl. Near here, I think." Though I had no clue where exactly the memory occurred. "They were so small their pinchers didn't hurt." I hunkered over, looking into small holes in the rocks.

"Yes. Me too." He chuckled low and distracting.

I snatched a look at his face as I squatted like a woman baking bread over an outdoor fire. Then I turned my attention to the small tide pools shimmering in the dusky light.

A tiny crab skittered from one side of the rocky bowl, darting around the edge to hide. I reached in, but missed the spidery crustacean.

Murat called to me and lifted his hand to show me he caught one. He lowered the small creature into my palm, his skin dark against mine. The crab squiggled sideways from his hands into my cupped fingers.

Murat laughed, "I used to pull off their pinchers. For fun."

"What?" I stared at him, my mouth hanging open wide enough to catch flies. "That's terrible."

"Hmm."

"Such a boy thing to do." Despite the image of an evil child pulling off millions of tiny pinchers for no reason, I shook my head and couldn't help but snicker.

Murat sat on the rock, beside where I still crouched, and leaned back, giving me his full attention. I turned away not liking the way he made my heart feel like a fish arcing out of the water. I turned back to him and only said, "Murat?"

Still watching me, he said, "Yes, *Madame?*" Then tipped his mouth a bit.

"I like your hair too." ✎

35 THE DIRTY SIDE STREET

Getting away always proved difficult. All the responsibilities sometimes made Meryem wonder what her life would have been had she just taken Murat and tried to make a way on her own fifteen years ago. But she couldn't imagine it.

Though worry twisted inside her, Meryem knew God's provision brought them to the orphanage. God managed every detail. Even her longing for more children. Now she had four in her care including Murat, though as a man he required little from her.

Except this.

An inner drive pushed her legs on, along the dirty side street to his house. It wasn't like Meryem to keep secrets, but some things couldn't be avoided. Some things she knew God allowed to play out. Though she normally trusted Him in all areas, this must be steered the right way.

She couldn't risk Murat being hurt further. She didn't think his heart could take it. He'd been through so much already. Meryem had to protect him from finding out.

"Hello?" Her weak voice echoed in the empty shell of a home.

The man played his part well, filthy and less than welcoming.

"Meryem. I hope you have money. I don't plan on continuing for free."

"Yes. Here." She pulled a wad of *lire* out and plunked the pastel bills on the metal table where he lounged, nursing a beer. The scene dug into her gut, making her second-guess the approach she chose.

He sniffed, his nose twitched. His left eye blinked. "Good. What now? Your son is on to me you know." His bloodshot eyes held hers for a moment then lowered, too inebriated to maintain her gaze.

Causing Murat greater fear wasn't Meryem's goal, but what else could she do? She had to put a stop to things before everything unraveled like the day her husband died, leaving them with nothing. *I was passive then, but no longer.*

"Perhaps just scare her a bit." She leaned in to make eye contact. "Don't hurt her."

Meryem wondered if she could even trust he'd remember this conversation. His breath so foul, she wondered how long he slouched here drinking, like a dog waiting for orders, with no hope of any life beyond odd jobs to feed his addiction.

This reminded her of her husband. Not the drinking or slovenliness, but the sense of sinking.

I need to get away, before I change my mind.

At the door she turned and scrutinized the man's dejected frame. "Don't hurt her, I said."

He lifted his hand, then let it drop with a thud on his thigh. "As you wish, my lady."

She pulled the door closed with a click and shuffled away, her gray-blue head-scarf pulled tight around her hair and under her chin. If this worked, all would be well. ✺

36 ELLA'S ROOM

June knocked on my door, even though it stood open.

"Busy?" She stepped into my gray room and offered a weak smile.

"No, what is it?" I closed my journal and slid it under the other books on my small desk.

"I received a phone call for you, earlier, while you were teaching."

"A phone call?" *Who would call me but my Mom?* We agreed to talk the first Saturday of the month in the evenings to account for the eight-hour time difference.

June withdrew a crumpled piece of paper from her pocket and opened it. "Koray Yürdagüven?" Her thin voice sounded far away.

I stood, knocking my pencil onto the floor. "Oh . . . what did he say?"

"He said to tell you he'd like to meet you tomorrow afternoon at a restaurant near here."

"Oh."

"He said to come on your own." June cleared her throat. "Ella, are you sure he's someone you should meet alone?" She paused, then asked, "What's this all about?"

My face prickled. *Why should I have to explain myself to her?* I opted for honesty, because what could it hurt?

"He knew my father. He said he had some information about his death."

"So is that what brought you here?"

The question weighed heavy. At first, I didn't have words. *Of course, it's why I came.* But not only that, I came to see if I could create a different outcome than the first time, like a bookmark in a choose-your-own-ending novel.

I came to make a difference to somebody—unlike that day when I just stood there like a tree rooted in the cement sidewalk and watched my dad blown to nothing.

June moved closer and took a seat on my bed that ran the length of one wall. Her legs appeared shorter since her feet couldn't touch the ground with her legs bent over the side.

I opened my mouth to answer her, then closed it. June sat there like she had all day and didn't plan on leaving until I spilled it.

"Yes." I waited, wondering if she'd lecture me on doing things for the right reasons. Or, if she'd call me selfish.

Instead, she only offered, "Can I suggest something?"

I shifted from my right foot to my left, awkward since I was pretty sure being right-handed made me right-legged too. I shifted back and crossed my hands over my chest.

"Maybe coming for one thing will lead you to another place. One you hadn't anticipated."

I decided it couldn't hurt to join her, so I plopped on the bed too, bouncing her a little.

"I've never been a rule follower." June scooted all the way back, pressing her spine to the wall. "I've always sort of craved making my own way. Carving a brand new path. When I came here with Barry, I knew doing the whole orphanage thing ranked me right up there with saints like Mother Teresa." I looked at June over my shoulder. She grinned and said, "Seriously. I waited for the praise and guess what I got?"

I shrugged my shoulders.

"My family told me I wasn't only naïve, but wrong to come to another country and impose my beliefs on others."

"But you don't make anyone believe anything, right?"

"No, we don't. All of the women are accepted as they are and never expected to convert. The children too, though we don't hide our faith either. We try to mentor these women and children in life skills so they can eventually move out and choose a new path. Anyway, my family, they didn't know that. They saw it as me acting like the giver of all good things."

"What if someone comes to live here and never chooses to believe in and follow Christ?"

"Well, that's always their choice."

"Do they face any problems among the Turks if they do become a Christian living in a Muslim society?"

"Some of the women and children have made the decision to become Christians. For them, there is a hard road ahead in many ways, living in a Muslim country, even though being here at the orphanage helps with a support network. We share our faith in Christ, but never push conversion."

"Hmm." I liked the idea—no conditions to being invited to stay.

"A decision that important needs to be a choice made without compulsion—they need to be sure if they want to choose Jesus. I've always believed in love being the most convincing voice anyway. We'll always help anyone who arrives at our doors, if we're able, with no strings attached. Either way, we'll have done our job to show love to those with few choices." June paused then added. "You might have come because of what happened to you. To your dad. But maybe, just maybe, you'll be like me. You'll be completely changed and rerouted."

"I hope you're right," I said. Nothing about my fixation on the past made me feel alive, only like someone trying to steal something back. Once there is nothing left to chase, what does a person do?

June squeezed my hand and said, "I know I've been the opposite of the wise mentor to you, Ella. I have problems of my own. I'm afraid they've done a number on my so-called, godly perspective."

She wobbled from side to side on her butt, scooting to the edge of the bed, and stood up. "But I know something to be true. You were brought here for a reason. No matter why you think you came, I know God will do something with you and through you and in you. You'll be different. Your little students will be different. Just watch."

I studied my fingers, swallowing an unexpected ache in my throat.

"But just one favor." She turned at the door, looking over her shoulder. "Be careful." ❧

37 THE MEETING

"Want some fun, American?" The voice yanked me out of the labyrinth I wove through in my mind, trying to convince myself to be confident. The man walking near me threw me off my groove.

"No. Thank you." Even though he wasn't that far from me, I hollered the reply, and kept moving. I didn't want to tell Murat I came out tonight. He had enough on his mind. Besides, the powerless thing grated. Koray said to come alone, so I basically followed directions.

The stalker kept time with my strides. He angled in closer, smelling like CK One and looking like a Middle Eastern Shaun Cassidy with black feathered hair and a plunging V-neck, complete with a swatch of chest hair peeking out.

"Why not, pretty lady? I will buy you a drink."

"Leave me alone, creep." The thick thump of my heart gained speed. *Was it really so much to ask to not be harassed the minute no male accompanied me? Do I really look so easy?* The man had the good sense not to follow.

I marked one tally on my mental list of accomplishments. Evaded a creep. Check. I chuckled to myself thinking that needed to find its way into my journal, or a letter to Mom, or my memoirs everyone would clamor to read one day.

The street wound toward the sea. Storefronts ushered me toward the water. I closed my eyes, breathing in the smell of diesel fuel, salt air, and *ekmek*.

I tripped on the uneven sidewalk and decided I needed to focus, to walk with my eyes open. June's words, "He said to come alone," made my stomach turn like I had the Turkish trots. What could he possibly need to say that required me to meet him alone?

The restaurant sagged on the second story of a crusty building with the name *Soğan* painted over a hanging shop shingle. Wondering whether food poisoning might be in my near future, I climbed the steps to a room reminding me not to judge a

book by its cover. The space looked like a sultan's palace. Teal and purple fabrics draped from a central point on the ceiling, flowering out to each wall. Since the room was full and contained no empty tables, locals clearly knew about the unlikely place.

"*Madame?*"

I turned to the host. "Oh, yes, I'm meeting someone here."

"This way." The man led me to a table tucked into a recessed wall with a curtain to offer privacy.

Koray stood and shook my hand before sitting. "Ella, thank you for meeting here."

The host pulled the curtain closed behind me. I took my seat. For a painfully long time we made small talk about my job, about what I'd done for the last fifteen years. Koray ordered dinner and we tore into the disk of bread on the table, though my stomach started screaming for me to go easy.

"I want to make sure I understand. What are you looking for?"

I nearly gagged on the plug of bread lodged in one cheek. *Doesn't he know?* "Well, who was responsible? Why target my father? Why nobody was ever convicted."

The older man leaned back, long lines stacked his forehead, like files of paper. *Is that what he does at the office, file papers?* Maybe this man knew nothing, but saw an opportunity in me.

I gulped the water to force the bread down. Gray hair filled in Koray's sideburns and streaked his combed back, cropped black hair. *Would Dad look this old if he'd lived?*

"Ella. I'll tell you what I know, but it would be best not to dig further. I fear if you do, you will suffer more. Do you understand?"

"Yes," I said, though I lied.

Koray's eyes looked kind. *But something tells me he doesn't like to be questioned.* I decided to listen. Keep any disagreements to myself.

He leaned forward. The golden candle light flickered olive on his face. "Your father was a Colonel. That's why he was targeted. Not because of who he was. But because of what he was."

I folded my hands in my lap trying to wait, to remain composed.

If I can't handle the news, Koray won't fully explain. Even though I didn't move or speak, the blood drained away from my fingertips, away from my lips, away from my heart.

This man sighed, clearly unnerved by my silence. "You look like him."

I ran my fingertips over my eyebrows. *I've been told I have his eyes. Is that what Koray noticed? Or is it something more? Do I have his courage, too?*

"Please, tell me more."

He lowered his head, leaned closer and whispered. "A terrorist group, *Dev Sol*, claimed responsibility. They wanted to send a message to the American military. They didn't want Turkey involved in the western war against Iraq. They didn't want to be pulled into the so-called sin and corruption. With the housing off base, your father, your father's vehicle, made an easy target. Others died that same day. Turkish civilians." Koray stared at his fingers interlaced, moving his thumbs in a slow, spinning motion.

"What about a name?"

Even before I finished the sentence, he shook his head. "No. No name."

I pounded a fist on the table causing the crumbs on my plate to shift to the side. Frustration was more a friend to me than most people. Faithful and constant.

"I'm sick of no name. I'm sick of my mom pretending the whole thing was an accident. Why did you have me meet you here, like a spy, if you didn't want to tell me anything?" My pulse pumped in my neck. I inhaled deep breaths to slow the thumping in my ears. "What is the name of the man responsible?"

"I cannot."

"You cannot, or you will not?" *How long have I waited to get answers, so I could confront the person and be done with the mess?*

Again he shook his head, "No."

"Well, thank you for nothing then." I shot up to leave, scraping my chair against the wooden floor. *How stupid to get my hopes*

up. Why did I think anyone would help me? Of course they considered the whole thing too hairy.

What have I got to lose? So what if it's dangerous? I'd gambled, hoping for an answer. A life full of waiting and wondering and spinning clockwise like a dreidel, forward. And now spiraling counterclockwise, toppling. Halting with no answers?

"Ella." The warmth of his fingertips pinched mine. "Please wait."

"Why should I? I thought you were going to help me. I guess I was wrong." Still I didn't pull my hand away, I couldn't resist this lifeline to the past. My only hope for answers.

"No. You weren't wrong. I hoped you'd not be so persistent. I see you're just like your mom."

"My mom? She didn't do anything to find out. To get justice. We just left like two dejected dogs. And now she works at a library doing nothing with her life. Kind of like me until I decided to come here." I ignored the thought she'd set it all up.

"Ella, your mom didn't give up. She fought hard and refused to stop until she got what she wanted."

"How did she fight? She'd never do something so risky as finding out who killed her husband." The disdain in my voice triggered instant regret.

Love for my mom didn't forgive her lack of action. Especially when it ate away at me over the years like cancer. Never would she say so much as a negative word about the killer.

"Yes. She would. And she did."

His words flung ice-cold water in my face. *Mom knew? All this time she knew and never said anything? When I asked and asked and she insisted it was an accident?*

I shoved my chin up, pretending his news didn't hurt. "So tell me then. What was his name?"

"Ali."

"Ali who?"

A thick sigh escaped his mouth. He closed his eyes as he said the name, as if the utterance would conjure the man. "Ali Yenibay."

"And how do I contact him? How do I find out where he lives?"

"You cannot."

"Why? Why can't I?"

Koray's eyes harbored regret and defeat. "He's dead."

Nausea rose, burning in my throat. I swallowed repeatedly, but couldn't move the tightness. All this, the wondering and waiting and aching.

I'll never have the opportunity to look into the eyes of the man who killed my father. Tell him what he did to my life. What he did to my mother. I'll never be able to tell him he killed me that day too. ❧

38 PINAR'S HOUSE

I forced myself to focus on Pinar. She sat attentive as I showed her how to plan meals. My shoulders sagged with guilt, because my heart was drained by what I'd discovered.

My father's killer escaped justice through death. How could it be? The closure I'd come to find eluded me. There would be no reckoning of any sort. And Mom knew about it all along. Even the man's name. How could she keep that from me? I knew it had something to do with protecting me. Why not tell the full story before I hauled my butt all the way over here to get kicked in the gut with the truth? Wouldn't it have been better to hear it from her?

Pinar stared at me like the Virgin Mary herself sat in her living room, that's how high of a pedestal she put me on. *Too bad I'm a total wreck.*

A few weeks ago Pinar yearned for peace. Said she was tired of not knowing whether all of her best intentions would ever tip the balance in her favor. Said she was tired of wrath and anger. Said she'd done too much bad in her life to ever be good enough. Said she didn't know how to make a new beginning.

When I explained that with Jesus, love, forgiveness, and paradise was a sure thing; that she didn't have to earn His love or acceptance; that He could make her a new person; she nearly collapsed. Her small body held up as long as it could. She cried like a baby that day when she believed Jesus could bring about change in her heart through love. Even so, she still seemed as delicate as a flower shoved out to sea.

She's as fragile as I am, only for very different reasons. Better ones.

"Pinar? Can we continue tomorrow?" I asked in my steadily accumulating Turkish.

"Yes. Sure." A slight downturn of her lips registered her disappointment, like my words were a personal rejection to her.

"I just don't feel very well." It wasn't a lie. Besides, I couldn't have this conversation in Turkish. I could barely articulate it in English.

Without a backup plan to the great atonement story I'd planned in my mind, the rest of my time seemed without aim or purpose. *What am I here for? Aside from the kids?*

I thought I was meant to be here. Like God put me here to get healed, or some such nonsense. And now pain drowned my heart, like water soaking into sand. I didn't see any way of getting to the bottom of my agony, of clearing the way to sea-glass-blue water.

"Is everything okay?" Pinar leaned close and brushed my hand. A monumental gesture given her state a few months ago.

I nodded my head back and forth like a bobble-head doll, all ridiculous, lacking feeling. Then I looked at my palms and tried to swallow the ache filling my throat.

I'm so tired of putting on a happy face. So sick of being a fake.

"No."

She clasped my hands in hers, leaned over, and touched her warm forehead my palms. It took a few moments before I realized she was praying.

For me.

This woman having no history with God, totally new in her faith, surpassed me by miles. She perceived my problem enjoyed no earthly answers and decided to talk to the only One who could do anything about it.

She lifted her head then patted my hand, filling the quiet with a soft smacking. "Better soon. Better soon," she said in English. She smiled then stood and gathered food to prepare dinner for the kids.

So what if she only knew how to make three different meals? She took action. Unlike me. A girl stuck in stone hard cement. ✦

39 THE ORPHANAGE

Murat leaned over to jerk the cord on the lawnmower, eager to clean up the property. Though he didn't mind, keeping up the property took second place to helping Ella—taking her where she needed to go.

The afternoon began with pulling weeds, picking up trash that blew onto the grounds, and trimming the edges of the grass. The steady routine shifted all the mixed-up parts of him, putting them in order, giving them a place. For now.

In the distance the midday call to worship echoed from the different minarets throughout Izmir. The *Zuhr* prayer created a hypnotic ripple effect. As always, the meter and rhythm blaring through the speaker of the nearby minaret reminded Murat to pray for his extended family.

"Lord, if it's your will, allow me to share my faith with them someday." *Who am I to pray like I have anything figured out?*

The past few weeks was like a storm cracking between moments of light—but no, Murat could not claim he possessed peace just now. He knew God's promise to provide rest, should he ever release his tight grip on his past and on those he loved most. But how could he when danger lurked everywhere?

Murat spotted Ella coming out the front door of June and Barry's home, heading toward the front gate of the property. She snatched a glance Murat's way, but didn't stop, only lifted her hand in a brief wave, then moved on.

Murat felt sure she evaded him intentionally. He strode toward her anyway. He could see his concern sometimes frustrated her. Like it or not, a woman walking alone in Turkey drew attention and with Ella's beauty, it drew the wrong kind of attention. He clenched his teeth so hard they hurt.

"Where are you going, Ella?" Just a question from one friend to another.

She slowed, but didn't stop. "I'm headed to the coffee shop.

I want to do a little catching up on my letter writing." Obviously not wanting to be deterred, Ella continued along the path, acting as if she didn't have a care in the world.

He discerned she did though—by the way she pushed her shoulders up, almost too rigid, like she needed to prove she could hold herself up straight.

"May I take you there?" Murat pressed.

"No. Thank you, Murat. It's only two blocks away. I'm fine. I'd enjoy some time to myself. I'm sure you understand." Her blue eyes looked rimmed with red and she wore no make-up.

Murat laid a hand gently on her upper arm. "Please let me take you. You shouldn't go alone."

"No, thank you. As I said, it's not far and I'm fine. Besides, you're busy."

"Ella. We've talked about this. I know how men will treat you."

Ella stopped with a sigh and turned to face Murat. "I do appreciate your concern. But you cannot babysit me all the time. And anyway, it's important to me to have some sort of independence. What would I do if you weren't around, Murat? Just not go anywhere or do anything? Live in fear? I won't do that. Now, please, try to understand. Besides," she shot her chin up and finished, "I left yesterday without you and did just fine." She flicked her eyes to the side, then studied her feet.

Murat stared at her, shook his head, turned his back, and trudged away. *Stubborn woman.*

A moment later Murat jerked the mower to a roar. With one last glance at Ella, he shoved the mower across the grass.

He wouldn't condone her decision by offering a smile and a nod. His concern must feel to her like an unwanted gift, perhaps—but he knew his culture better than Ella. And American women were viewed and treated differently. Murat didn't make up the rules.

He mowed right over the tulips he planted on the side of the Lovell's home below the front porch and cursed. He chanced a glance back, hoping she chose not to leave after all.

But no.

If she wanted to be stupid, he had no choice but to let her. ✒

4 0 THE TAXI

"I'm not a child." My small-sounding voice couldn't compete with the noise around me. I ignored all the glances cast my way by men heading home from work. At four p.m., the blue worker's buses pulled up one after another transporting piles of weary bodies home from work.

What am I supposed to do? Be carted around like a child every time I feel the need to do anything? I can't live that way. Not even for a year.

Besides, I needed to write this letter to Mom and didn't need someone looking over my shoulder. I glanced in the direction of the coffee shop, dreading the harsh words for Mom tumbling through my mind like throwing stars. Some things should not be dealt with from a distance. What choice did I have? Mom put that on herself by keeping the truth from me.

Taxis honked like the most obnoxious driver won a free loaf of *ekmek*. A line of bumblebee-bright yellow *taksi*'s slowed to the side of the road looking to get my business.

Like I'm the only person here.

The traffic sounds pounded on my skull: engines revving, air brakes hissing on bus after bus, voices of food vendors yelling above the din. In short, a normal afternoon in Izmir, Turkey. Even though I still held a grudge, I couldn't help admit, I loved the cacophony. However, the same old struggle—alive and dead all at once—intensified in this place.

"Well, I'm still alone. Sort of. That's what I needed."

On cue a man walked close beside me and started keeping pace.

Not again.

He huffed and puffed like he'd been jogging. His breath smelled like sour milk.

I veered off to the side picking up my pace. At least yesterday's interested suitor looked good. This man could have crawled out of a box of trash. His hand clamped under my elbow, steering me

back, pinching at the skin. I tried to jerk loose, but he wouldn't let go. Then he shoved me into a waiting taxi, climbing in beside me.

What's happening? I tugged at the door handle, but it was child locked. The man beside me pressed something sharp into my ribs. Someone I knew if I moved or spoke, it would cut.

In a matter of seconds the city whizzed by. The clueless taxi driver asked what street we needed to go to. The man growled, "*Tunali Sokak.*"

I turned to face my attacker. His lowered head stayed tipped away. The depth and the bass of adrenaline hammered in my heart, and swelled my hands.

What do I do? What do I do?

I reached inside my bag hoping to find something to use as a weapon. Without thinking about whether it would work, I grabbed a pencil and stabbed the man's leg.

He bellowed out. A thud landed against my face, a black, glittering pain. The taxi lurched to a stop.

Like a bear, the driver exited and ripped open the back door. He yanked the man out by one arm and shoved him onto the sidewalk, yelling loud enough that several people stopped to watch the commotion. The driver kicked the man in the side and waited while the coward scrambled to his feet, then staggered away.

The older man turned and stared at me, meaty arms hanging to his sides, hands clenched in two round balls, his eyes squinted and probing. My hand, still gripping the pencil, shook. I dropped my 'weapon' to the dirty floor mat.

The cab driver slumped into his seat, rocking the vehicle. I swallowed acid. Then I forced myself to look in the direction of my attacker, watched the man standing down the street, looking right at me, eyes like tiny black rocks. And that's when I noticed. The scar across his chin. The man following me. Who watched me from over the wall.

The taxi driver turned to face me, anger pinching the skin between his eyes. "*İyi misin, Madame?*"

I tasted the blood on my lip. Hot pain pulsated on my cheekbone.

"Yes." I nodded and my head swam like being underwater. "Please, will you take me to *Güvenli Bölge?*" Like calling it Safe Haven made it so.

I offered the address then allowed my back to sink against the stiff seat. Hot tears trickling down my cheeks caught on the bloody spot on one side, and dripped from my chin. I didn't even bother wiping them. The short drive reminded me of my weakness. I made it a few blocks away from home before being rerouted.

Story of my life.

The taxi driver pulled up to the front gate. I reached in my purse to get out the *lire* amount flashing hot red on the dash. But the man shook his head at the bills I held out, concern clear in his expression.

I didn't have the strength to argue. I felt like a loser and, worse than that—scared.

This must have to do with Dad.

With Koray's warning.

With my father's killer dead and gone, what would this man have against me? What use am I to him? I couldn't analyze it.

I just wanted to crawl into my bed, pretend I was home and safe. Far, far away from terrorists and creeps, and a man named Murat without whom I could no longer even walk two blocks by myself. ❧

4 1 ELLA'S ROOM

The knock came later. Much later. Jarring, sharp raps reverberated in my room. I instinctively curled up under the blankets, pulled the turquoise-blue fabric from the market over my head, and prayed the noise would stop.

It didn't. I crawled out of bed and shuffled to the door.

"Who's there?" I made my voice sound deeper, more intimidating, just in case.

"Is me. Murat. Can I come in?"

I allowed the door to ease open a crack. "What do you want?" I knew I sounded like a jerk, but I didn't care. Knowing I needed to leave Turkey, I might as well sever ties, even fragile, stringy ones.

"Were you sleeping, Ella?" My name spoken by his deep, accented voice stirred me, helped me ease away from the cliff I loomed near.

"Yes. I was."

"I'm sorry. Can I to talk to you?"

"Not now Murat. I'm tired."

"Please, let me come in."

"No. That wouldn't look right, Murat, you know that."

He pushed the door back. The light from the hallway crossed my face causing the man to nearly yell, cursing in Turkish. "Ella, what happened?"

He shoved open my door and flicked on the room light, blinding me. Murat nudged me toward the chair where I read my Bible in the mornings, where I ate my breakfast alone. Like I had no ability to do anything on my own, he eased me onto the soft seat, then knelt in front of me, hands on my knees. His stare nearly burned a hole through me, and he repeated, "What happened?"

I recoiled at the fight, the searing light in his eyes. I couldn't handle his intense scrutiny, the embrace of his hands on my knees. My heart was one big bruise. And violence pulsated from this man. His hands cupped my knees, as if to keep me still.

Tears filled my eyes. I kept swallowing the warm lump in my throat. If I started crying again, I wouldn't stop. Then how would Murat survive that? I needed to keep it together, if only to protect Murat. Protect me from him.

Murat gently skimmed my cheek with his knuckle, sending a shooting pain to my eye. I flinched. Sadness drooped from the corners of his mouth. His hand lurched back, like my skin burnt his.

He moved his fingers forward again, brushing back a curl hanging in front of the bruise on my cheekbone. A shallow rim of tears rested on his lower lids, like the rest of him filled up, revealing he was drowning. That he had been for a long time.

Deep inside I felt the urge to cover this up, come up with an explanation that wouldn't send him reeling. But how could I do that? I remembered I wasn't lying anymore. Not to myself. Not to anyone. I'd been deceived enough and refused to be a part of the well-meaning, "protecting" game.

"Murat." I reached for his hand still extended toward my face, hanging in midair. He turned and pulled the other chair in front of me. We sat so close our knees touched. His stare unnerved me. I lowered my eyes to gain my bearings. "He grabbed me. The man with the scar. On the way to the café. I was walking one minute and the next minute I was being shoved into a taxi."

Murat scanned the room, like a predator sure the prey hid in a hole nearby. *He's ready to pounce and kill.*

He snatched his gaze back to me. "How did you get away?"

"I stabbed his leg with a pencil. Then he hit me. The driver realized I needed help, because he pulled over and threw him out the door, and drove me home."

"I just don't understand. What's happening? Why would anyone want to hurt you, Ella?"

I shook my head, but stopped. The room was still a little slow to catch up with my movements. Pressing my eyelids together to stop the tilting of the chair, the space around me, I reached for Murat. He wrapped his arms around me, pulled me in so tight I shook from the strength of his embrace, from the fear sinking in.

"Murat, I don't know. My father . . . "

How can I explain? I never talked to anyone about that terrible moment, except for my mother. *Could I trust him to hear it?*

"I wanted to know what happened. Why he died. Who killed someone so full of love?" My voice grew louder. I didn't care. I choked on a sob, allowing it to tumble out.

Ages of anger, loneliness, and pain billowed into the quiet, giving my agony voice and life. I pretended I'd forgiven the man. Now I knew that to be a lie. I realized if I saw him right now, I'd have trouble holding back the hatred.

He took everything from me. Even my childhood. The little girl in me hid in a dark corner, cowering, waiting for that moment when things would stop hurting so badly.

Murat pulled back, our faces just inches apart. I felt his breath as he spoke. "Ella, did you go looking for someone?"

"No, I wanted to go to the coffee shop and think. And write a letter to my mom."

"Then, why is this man after you?"

"I don't know. Maybe he was part of it. Maybe he helped."

"Ella, I don't understand. Helped with what?"

Of course he's confused. He doesn't know. He's completely in the dark about my father's murder. "Murat, my father was killed. By a terrorist. That's why I came back. I needed to find him, tell him what he did to me. To my mom."

Hot tears pulsed down my face, on autopilot. *Why did I think I could handle this?* I felt like a fool for the millionth time.

"Ella, this is too dangerous. Maybe he's afraid you'll find out he was part of the . . . " He didn't say the word out loud.

"But how, Murat? I haven't talked to anyone. Except for the man my father worked with. He wouldn't say anything to anyone who was involved. He didn't even want to tell me the man's name in the first place. He thought it wasn't a good idea either. I guess I'm too stubborn to listen to reason from anyone."

"Ella, you know the name of who did this? You're not going to go to him. Please, tell me no." Murat vice-gripped my hand. "Is it the man from today?"

"No, he's dead. Isn't that just my luck? I've come all this way and he's dead. Now I can't do anything about it. I have to live with the anger. Why did God let this happen, Murat? Why would He have me come all this way for nothing? And now some crazy person wants me gone too."

I buried my face into my palms and sobbed. Mainly because the ache wouldn't recede. Letting out some of the pressure felt good. Maybe now I wouldn't implode with all my introversion and contemplation.

Murat lifted my face so his hands barely touched both sides of my chin. He moved in quietly, brushing tears back, tucking a curl behind my ear. Then he kissed me, warm, sweet and soft.

I couldn't pull away. I needed to leave and forget I even came here. For this one moment, I dared to enjoy the moment. I sank into him. He tasted like garlic and olive oil. I swirled in midair, except his hands grounded me from flying away. When his kisses deepened and his hands gripped me tighter, I pulled back.

I can't go that deep.

Not now, after what happened today.

"I'm sorry, Murat." Not for the kiss, though I knew I should be. Sorry for allowing myself to believe I could have a normal life, for allowing my heart to sink in this far. "I have to leave. I shouldn't have come here. I know that now. I need to go home."

The idea sounded like a punishment. I knew how trapped I'd feel back home. I pictured myself an old woman, inside my mom's tiny house doing nothing with my life.

He shook his head, but no fight was in it. "Ella."

What more could he say when he saw the truth? I was in danger. The one thing I could count on with Murat was—if it boiled down to his wants or my safety—he'd always opt for the latter.

His chivalry made my decision hurt even more. I loved being cared about that way. I never allowed myself to lean into someone so fully. I had no idea how I'd survive without him. ❧

42 JUNE'S LIVING ROOM

I tapped softly on June's bedroom door. Like a pillar holding up a building, Murat stood behind me. I knew if he stepped away for even a second everything could tumble on top of me. He kept his hand on my back, like he suspected I might collapse.

Wise man.

I needed to tell June why I came for three months and now had to leave so quickly. *Deserter.* Why leaving was the best thing for everyone.

She opened the door and nearly threw herself at me, pulled me into a hug so tight I felt instant concern. This woman kept me at arm's length since I arrived, and now this?

"Ella, Murat, I've been meaning to talk to you, I just didn't know how. I hoped I'd be able to skip this conversation all together and throw a party instead." Her bloodshot eyes drooped at the corners. She jerked her head toward me. "Goodness, what happened to your eye?"

Instinctively I covered the dark spot, then blurted out a lie as easily as ordering a cup of tea. "I fell. I'm fine." Something told me right now wasn't the time for the truth.

"Oh." The word sounded flat as *pide*. June pulled me into the living room and Murat followed without saying a word.

Together we sat on the cushions, only this time no tea warmed on the stove. No fragile glasses graced the table. Only quiet filled the space. I watched her face, hoping for some clues of what she planned to say. Is she asking me to leave? That would be just as well. Then I wouldn't feel so guilty.

"Ella, I . . ." She smiled, a painful smile, like holding back a whole wall of floodwater, then she looked at Murat. "Barry has cancer. He isn't doing well. We thought if he received treatments here we'd see improvement, be able to say that was that, but, no. It's growing. The tumor." Her words came out in staccato notes, maybe to make them less personal, less terrifying.

"June." *It will turn out fine? I know how you feel? By the way, I'm leaving.* I reached for her hand and offered, "I'm sorry. What can I do to help?"

Murat sat like a pole, back straight, eyes riveted to the older woman. He didn't move or say anything. *He's barely holding himself together. How will he handle this, too?*

Finally, he spoke. "What kind of cancer?" His voice remained low, like he dared God to do something to the man who'd been like a father to him.

As June looked at Murat her face held something different now. *Is it compassion? For him?*

"Brain."

That single word crashed like a death sentence. The dropping of a guillotine. How many people with aggressive brain cancer survived? The odds were stacked against Barry. I pictured him lying in a bed, waiting to die, instead of running a ball down the field with kids at his heels. The two images couldn't possibly be for the same man.

I reached my hand beneath the table to grab Murat's, rubbing my thumb over his rough knuckles. He turned slightly to acknowledge my touch, tears streaking his face. "What do you need us to do?" His voice cracked. He swiped at the tears with the back of his free hand.

June's face assumed a look of all business, like a To-Do list could solve problems like this. She spouted off things she needed taken care of. "I'll continue with the paperwork and financial side of things from the States. The rest runs itself with how we've set things up, so you don't need us really."

June folded then unfolded her hands, maybe realizing what she just said—that things could go on without them. Perhaps that gave Barry permission not to fight so much. "We'll be leaving in a week for Colorado. We have family there. Two kids. They said we can stay with them during his treatment."

"How long?" My plans to leave slipped away like fine sand through fingers. Disappointment and relief wrestled inside me. *Selfish.*

"The surgery to remove the tumor will be in two weeks. Then whatever follow-up. Chemo might be unavoidable. The tumor is fighting back." She smiled like someone who knew her adversary and had a healthy respect for him.

"We'll take care of everything, June. Please don't worry about the orphanage."

I needed to make that promise. The rest of it, the surgery the battle for Barry's life . . . I had no idea about.

Lord, how can you allow such suffering?

Sadness covered me like a black prayer shawl, dark and all-encompassing, driving me to cry out to God.

Barry stepped into the conversation and stood behind his wife, spreading his hands over her shoulders. Even though he'd just entered the room, he sensed the conversation centered around him. About the balance between planning a future or a funeral.

"Let's pray right now. Is that all right?"

Murat blinked and nodded, then lowered his head. Barry's voice broke the quiet, like a wave on jagged rocks. Barry petitioned God for Murat and me, not himself.

A prayer so full of anguish I squeezed Murat's hand tighter to keep him from breaking down all together. From keeping myself from falling to pieces too. Barry finished, then looked up abruptly. Tears sparkled in his eyes.

"I'll talk to *Anne* about me staying here in your home." Murat turned to me. "That way I can keep my eyes on things." He pegged me in my place with his dark gaze, then a slight tip of his head, like making some agreement with me, though I wasn't sure what.

Sometimes one struggle trumped another.

I conceded, knowing I couldn't possibly run away now. What kind of a girl chose self-preservation over helping someone in need?

Certainly not one who came across the Atlantic to help orphans. Besides, it was the kind of thing my dad would have done. And, I admitted, Mom, too. ❧

43 ELLA'S ROOM

I nibbled at my thumbnail, a habit that worsened with stress. For years I'd tried and failed to kick it. *What am I supposed to do?* How can I keep this place from falling apart with all my strength yanked out like a rug snatched away?

Murat barely held himself together. Then add in the psycho stalking me. We had a perfect recipe for the whole place crumbling like a sand castle swallowed by a wave.

A rap at my door forced me to snatch my finger from my mouth and stop wallowing in worry. I opened the door to June who stepped in and scanned my room. Without saying a word, she walked over to my desk and picked up the framed picture.

"This is your dad." She didn't ask. In the photo Dad and I lay on a Turkish rug grinning with Charlie Chaplin mustaches on.

"Yes. He was funny."

"He died when you lived here, right? A terrorist attack?"

I sifted through my memories and couldn't recall bringing that up. "Yes. How did you know?"

"When you applied you mentioned it. In the letter." June turned back toward the photo, so I couldn't read her expression.

"Oh."

She walked over to the window, then her hand stroked the blue-green curtain. She gripped the blue fabric tightly. Her knuckles turned white. She let it go, leaving a faint wrinkle in the fabric.

"Ella, I'm sorry I haven't been much of a mentor to you. I imagined your start here so different than how it's turned out. When you arrived, I'd just found out about the tumor. Then Barry had tests done and that's all I could think about. It's like the cancer grasped hold of me too. Eating away the good things I meant to do and be." She turned her attention on me. "I hope you can forgive me." Minuscule wrinkles lined her face. The good kind: crinkles around her eyes and mouth showing a life of laughter.

Now what? Would more furrows be added for very different reasons? Signs of worry and suffering?

"June, I understand, I do."

She took a seat at the table then said, "I'm worried about Murat."

"Me too."

"I don't know if he can take this on. Murat has already got so much . . ." Her sentence dangled, allowing the unspoken to scream into the space.

"I know."

She toyed with her ring finger, twisting the wedding band around and around, then fixed it in the right position. Pulling her gaze back to me she added, "Can you promise you'll keep me posted. On how he's doing?"

Ironic that in a place full of orphans, she worried about a grown man. But I got it. "I promise. But you already have so much to deal with."

"Both Barry and I will be leaving our hearts here. This is our home. Our family. It would help, I think, to not be so disconnected. Not to have all our focus on ourselves. That's never a good thing." She chuckled, then abruptly stopped, like it was wrong given the situation.

"I'll write. Email. So you can be right here with us," I promised.

"I don't want Murat to quit his job at the bakery. He needs that. To escape a little."

"I'll see what I can do."

"You have quite an effect on him, you know?" June looked straight at me, a faint smile lifting the corners of her mouth.

My face warmed. "I know." I assumed our affection for one another was a secret.

"Take care of his heart. He's been through a lot." She said the words quietly then stood to go. "Thank you, Ella. What would we do without you?" With a squeeze to my shoulder she left, tugging the door shut behind her. ❧

44 THE ORPHANAGE

Preparations for June and Barry's departure to the United States stirred throughout the entire orphanage. Cards made by the children wallpapered every space available in their home. The women delivered meals each day so June could focus on her husband and organize the administrative details.

I leaned in to polish the squatty table in their living room, considering what might be the end result of this trip home. *Will Barry return? If he doesn't, will the orphanage close? What will happen to all these women and children?*

I stared into the soft golden glow of the brass table, searching for answers that failed to come. I realized in my daze I'd scrubbed the round vintage table to a bright gleam—so different than the dull ache in my chest.

Desiring to be strong for Barry and June, I determined to keep working until the place glowed. I knew June didn't need one more thing to worry about.

Without knocking, Meryem entered, bucket and sponge in hand. "I have no rest since I hear of Barry. I want to help please. Working helps me." Her bloodshot eyes avoided my gaze. She knelt on the kitchen floor and began scrubbing.

With the table polished I moved over to the sink to wash and dry the few dishes. Meryem worked backward from the furthest corner. I watched how intently she moved, strings of silky black hair coming loose from beneath her head-scarf. Like she battled with something other than the smooth, cold tile floor. Meryem's lips moved as she stared into the spot she buffed. She leaned back on her heels, tipped her head back and closed her eyes, a glisten of tears streaked her face.

Battle wounds.

She looked over her shoulder at me and said, "I sorry. So sorry."

I walked over to her to offer comfort. *She's obviously mourning over Barry's health.* I took a spot beside her on the tile floor and

grabbed her hand, sponge and all. She pulled it back when she saw my face for the first time. Clearly noticing my shiner, the back of her free hand covered her eyes.

"It doesn't hurt anymore." I offered a smile to convince her.

"I so sorry. So, so sorry." She repeated, a low moaning chant.

What's going on? Maybe this is where Murat gets his Savior complex.

"Remember, God works everything for good." Maybe the ancient truth would bring comfort to this woman. Though I'd lost count of all the times I doubted that promise.

She sucked in a huge, jagged breath and said, "Not this time." Then she set back to work, almost violent in her scratching motions, scrubbing the tile, scrambling back, then scrubbing more. I rose and left her to her work. ✒

45   IZMIR, 1982

"Hand me the paint." Meryem's mother tossed the request over her shoulder. Her round hips bulged below her dusty T-shirt. Her dark hair peeked out beneath her head-scarf.

Meryem grabbed the jar and handed it to her mother. Her hand lingered for just a second, forcing her *Anne* to turn. "What is it?"

"Nothing. I'm just happy. For you and *Baba*." Did she dare risk being happy for herself?

Anne turned and faced Meryem, pinching her daughter's cheek like when she was small. She moved her eyes back and forth, searching for something. "Meryem . . ." Her hand dropped like a fallen olive tree.

"What is it, *Anne*?" Her arm created a bridge across a thick body of water. "Please . . . "

Meryem's mother brushed her hands on her dusty shirt, then placed the paint on the shelf with the others, the store almost ready to open.

Baba stayed busy in the back room firing the pottery he created late into the night. His purpose for life returned. For breathing. For wanting to get up in the morning.

"You must find joy now. You mustn't worry over us. Be with your husband and see if you can fall in love."

Of course, she knew Meryem never loved Ali; but saying it out loud, how could she dare?

She noticed her daughter recoil because she said, "Shhh . . . you don't have to pretend. I know marriage is not always easy. It is a gift, if you find ways to love. Even when love is not around." She tugged Meryem's hand and pulled her to the small table at the front of the store, an essential place to sit and drink *çay*, even in a pottery maker's shop. "Do you remember the girl with the pencils?"

How could Meryem forget? The night the child stepped out of the shadows seared in her mind. So small, maybe only five, the girl

said in quiet voice, holding the spiny bouquet up high, "Do you want to buy any?"

Where were her parents at ten o'clock at night when their daughter walked alone? Who took care of her?

Anne dropped on one knee and took just one pencil, then tucked a thick fold of *lire* into her tiny plastic purse. She grabbed the girl's hand, rose up, and guided her to where the street lamp illuminated the child's round face.

I followed her wanting to see what she'd do. *Baba* stood back, allowing his girls space to talk. "Where is your *Anne*?"

The girl only shook her head.

"Can I take you home?"

Another small shake and she said, "She says I must sell these first." She held up the cluster like a burden she wished to be rid of.

"Well, easy enough. I will buy the whole bunch then. How much?"

Meryem inched closer to her *Anne*, just wanting to be near her warmth, her security. Rubbing the softness of her coat between her fingers and only then noticing the small girl wore nothing but a thin, too-small sweater on such a cold night. *Anne* removed her scarf, wrapped loosely around her head, and tied it around the small girl's shoulders.

In minutes the girl had more money than she probably ever earned for her small wares and a little extra warmth too. She dashed into the shadows where her mother must have waited.

The memory stayed with Meryem, vibrant like the lights of the stores and houses glittering on the harbor.

Anne's voice pulled her back, "Ali is like that girl. Desperate for a breakthrough. For some way out of the darkness he is in. He feels trapped by his powerlessness."

She squeezed Meryem's fingertips and then let them go. "Try to find a way to take his burden just a little. Find his joy that has been hidden so long."

Tears stung the back of Meryem's throat. She swallowed them down, down. *My husband, small and alone?* She never thought of him that way.

And here, with their fragile new beginning, could it be that Meryem might help him heal from whatever demons surrounded him? Maybe she could do it.

With Allah's help.

She placed a protective hand over her stomach, knowing the secret hidden there. Perhaps new life would replace all the death.

Perhaps. ✖

46 IZMIR, 2005

I cleared my throat. "I want to talk to you about Murat."

Barry sat beside his wife at their table and leaned forward. "What about Murat?"

"You asked me to help him, June. He won't let me. I don't know how to explain, it's like he's on some sort of mission. Like he's trying to prove something to himself . . . or to God or maybe both. I'm not sure."

Barry turned to June, her eyes webbed with blood vessels, a fragile soap bubble trying to dodge the wind. Wrapping her arms around herself, June said, "Ella, Murat has been through a lot. He came here years ago with his mother. Even then, he tried to act like a big man, to take care of her. I think the trauma of what he went through caused him to pretend nothing happened. He's always tried to be and do everything."

"What can I do to help him?"

June pinched her lips together, then replied, "You can love him. Offer your help, pray, remind him Who's in charge. But really, one person can't exorcise demons without the power of the Lord."

The word 'demons' skittered up my back. "What happened?"

Barry stared at me with his dark blue eyes. "It wouldn't be fair to share his story. That will be up to him. Though he remembers very little from his time before the orphanage. I can say, after a few years, he found some peace."

June folded, then unfolded her hands. "I wouldn't say this unless I felt it might provide some insight. Since we're leaving, you need information to help you decide how to act around Murat."

My heart thumped in my throat. With each word she spoke guilt edged in.

"Ella, I believe Murat has grown to care a great deal for you. Even though I've been somewhat separated from things . . . it's obvious. I think caring for you has only intensified his drive." June

pressed a hand to her chest. "He's in love with you, Ella. I believe that. That's why he's worse than ever."

The words dropped like a smothering blanket over my face. Angst squeezed my heart. I sucked in a slow deep breath, but the anxiety gripping my chest didn't release. *How is it I've managed to cause more harm than good? I planned to be so life-giving to these children, to everyone here.* I imagined myself like Florence Nightingale, loving and ministering to lost souls. But instead pronounced death somehow. I stood up to leave, but June snatched at my hand and pulled me back down.

"Don't do the same thing, taking this all on yourself."

"I'm not helping here. I'm only hurting people. Without even realizing it, I'm doing it."

"You're forcing things forward, that's all. It had to happen sometime. A person who hides out isn't living. He's going through the motions, trying to keep all the balls in the air. Something happens, they collapse, and he's forced to deal with it. It's a good thing."

"So what do I do? I don't know what to do."

Barry placed his large hand over mine, somehow steadying my rickety scaffold of trust for the moment. "You trust the Lord. You pray. And you keep on loving and being truthful. Remember, Murat's the only one who can do this, the letting go part. You can be there when he finally falls apart. And he will, trust me."

"But . . ." *How can that be a good thing? How can I allow that to happen to him? What if he doesn't come back together again? What about me?* The selfish thought caught me by surprise. I was fine with Murat taking care of me. When he took on everyone's problems, that's when I got concerned. That's when I felt the loss of not being his main focus. How sad and sickening. Humbled, I rose slowly, pulled my skirt away from my hot, sticky legs, and turned to leave. "I'll try."

Barry spoke to my back. I couldn't make myself turn around because he'd see all the ugliness in me. "Remember Who our strength comes from." I managed a nod and pulled the door closed behind me. ❧

47 THE COTTAGE PORCH

Sitting on the front stairs of June and Barry's home I spotted her. Meryem stood off to the side, just outside the arc of the porch light, like a pillar holding nothing up. She barely held herself up. She appeared so separate—alone.

The wind whispered against my face, set the leaves in motion, like a hush before the confession. Goosebumps rose on my body, like armor.

I stood and stepped toward her, but wanted to move back. I sensed this wouldn't be a nice visit. "What are you doing here, Meryem?"

"I came for explaining. I never meant for you to hurt." She walked out of the shadows, into the light, illuminating her anguish. Silver-white tears streamed down, dribbling off her chin. I imagined her standing in a pool of water, tears enough to drown.

My heart hammered like a stone banging against the wall of my chest. My throat hurt as I asked, "What? What have you done?"

She extended a hand to my face, butterfly touches to the side of my face. The place that still throbbed and made my stomach hurt thinking about how I'd gotten the purplish-black mark.

Did that only just happen a week ago?

I focused on her head-scarf, creamy white with indigo beads stitched along the edges. Her round face, young, but marked with age inflicted by pain, not time.

"I did not send this man to hurt you."

A vice clamped tight against either side of my ribs. What did the woman mean? She sent the man who attacked me? I shook my head, taking a step back. "I don't understand," I whispered.

Meryem knelt on one knee in front of me, then the other and pressed her forehead to my feet. "Meryem asks your forgiveness." Her moans followed the request. Low and full of

agony. Tears causing her whole body to throb against the gravel. Like she couldn't get low enough.

I don't know what to do. Nothing makes sense.

"Why would you want to hurt me?" I thought I might be sick. My enemy stood, close and fragile. She taught me how to cook. She poured me tea.

"I did not want this. I did not." She sobbed, pressing in lower, hands covering my bare feet. "I cannot say why. I cannot."

"Why can't you? I don't understand."

She stood slow with the tightness of sorrow, then reached up and swiped my tears with her rough thumbs, taking extra care on my bruised eye.

"Only can I say to please forgive."

I studied her face, round and dark and full of grief. I believed her, despite not understanding. I nodded, not trusting my voice.

A sliver of movement pulled my gaze. That's when I spotted him, darker than the night in his dark jeans and T-shirt, with his dark hair. He looked almost menacing, standing just out of the light, trees shrouding him like arms crouching over the top of his body. Murat stared at his mother like he hated her. Like he took in her words, calculating revenge.

A sob escaped my throat, unexpected. I covered my mouth to stop any more sound from coming out. Only the hiss of my breath sucking in and out could be heard above Meryem's sniffling.

Noticing me staring past her, she turned around. Seeing her son, she released a loud wail, then ran.

Her retreat left me feeling more alone than ever and afraid of the man I shaped into my savior. Only now he resembled a man deranged. ⚬

4 8 THE BREAD SHOP

Murat shoved open the front door to the bread shop, the acrid smell of Mustafa's cigarette habit the first greeting of the morning. Fatigue weighed on Murat. The truth, too.

He hadn't slept at all. Hadn't even gone home. Still, he had to do this. Responsibility didn't wait for a heart to start beating again. It was early and he needed to get it over with. Otherwise, he might lose his nerve.

June and Barry left at four a.m. and he was unable to lie back down after that. Fatigue made his neck ache, his eyes burn.

"Where are you, old man?" Stepping into the front room to the store, he saw the ashtray with two crushed cigarette butts. Must have been a rough weekend for the man to burn through two before starting his baking.

"Mustafa?" No sounds came from the oven room. "Sleeping on the job?"

Silence.

"I need to speak with you." Murat walked through the entry to the oven. Bread didn't line the long wooden shelves of the warm room as usual. The strangest sensation filled his chest.

His friend never slacked on the job, not completing the regular bread orders from local restaurants. This place was Mustafa's life.

That and Murat.

Yet, here he stood, like a traitor, planning to tell the man he needed time off to focus on the orphanage and pick up the work Barry put in his hands. No matter what June said, the couple did more than anyone knew at the orphanage. He'd cover what they left behind.

Murat moved toward the storage room. The oven burned orange and hot, but not white yet. Not the heat needed to blister bread in minutes. The space felt relatively cold compared to the usual thick warmth that hit him when entering the baking area.

He pulled open the storage room door and there lay Mustafa, prostrate with his face down against the gray-tiled floor, hands pinned beneath his chest.

Murat yelled out, "Mustafa!"

His friend made no movement. He squatted down and rolled the man back, pressing an ear to his mouth to listen for breathing. Slow and extremely shallow. For Murat it might as well have been a victory bell ringing across an empty courtyard.

He sprinted out to where the phone hung on the wall near the register and called an ambulance, then went back to where the baker lay. Murat sat on the floor near Mustafa's head, placing a hand on his chest to monitor his breathing. And he prayed harder than he had in years.

Murat waited in the too-quiet, oven room until the ambulance cried out its arrival.

Lord, will you take everyone from me? ❧

49 THE PASTURE

Murat didn't return as he promised. Hours later I sat, looking out my bedroom window like a leech unable to move without the life source.

What am I supposed to do? How could I lead an entire orphanage, a tiny dot bobbing in a sea of duties and worries, without sharing the load with Murat?

On top of it all I longed to go to him for my strength—*like he's God himself.* I had absolutely nothing beneath my feet but shifting, pulling sand. No, I was one more responsibility for him.

I growled into the quiet space. *I need a distraction. Think. What can I do right now? What would dad say?*

I stared up at the white plaster ceiling, then bolted to my feet and paced over to the window. Outside a group of kids milled around like aimless ants looking for the trail home.

I wondered for the millionth time where Murat could be, shrugging off the worry. No use trying to figure out more of the impossible. The fact that he didn't show up at my door this morning, the very morning of June and Barry's departure, was more than odd.

And last night still haunted me. Even in the light.

I pulled my hair into a ponytail, tied my tennis shoes, and jogged out the front door. A sorry crowd of faces greeted me, vulnerable to the point that one little boy reached his hands out to me to be held. Being just four, he must have wondered why all the adults stopped noticing him, and couldn't do anything but clean and cry. And now with the main house standing half empty, his world looked scary.

"Adem. I'm so happy to see you. I was coming out to see if you'd like to play soccer with me."

His scruffy head shot up. "Teacher play?"

"Yes. That's what I said."

A slow grin eased back his round cheeks. *"Tamam.* We do it. Boys and girls?" Again his face revealed uncertainty wondering if such a thing was even allowed.

"Boys and girls."

It didn't take long for word to spread. In just minutes both the old and young gathered in the pasture and teams formed. The littlest ones teamed up with older kids.

The game began fast. Laughter floated through the air. My last experience playing soccer was when I was five and joined the base peewee league.

Today, somehow, I managed to score a goal. Ahmed, a gangly 14 year old, quickly snatched the ball away, driving it toward the other goalie and scoring.

The tension hanging like a fat, gray-black cloud melted away, just as the sun sank. The second to last call to prayer, the *Maghrib,* sounded. A few kids turned toward Mecca, distracted from the moment. Torn by loyalties.

The game ended with a tie. All the kids filtered toward their homes. As I sat on the front steps of June and Barry's home, their happy voices travelled back to me.

This is what happened when waiting and fear and 'what ifs' are shoved away by simply living and enjoying the moment. Joy managed to find its way, just a little, in the crack I opened. ✑

50 THE HOSPITAL

Murat waited in the endless, white corridor with its closed doors, hiding the truth about life extinguished or revived. They arrived hours ago and no word yet. The trip took years, a slow swirl of colors and lights filtering into the ambulance's curtained windows, like life passed in slow motion. All the while his friend laid still as a corpse, except for the bounce from the drive on cracked pavement.

Murat wondered at points if his friend still breathed. The paramedics worked on him, his chest compressed like rubber under the rhythmic thrusts of one man's stacked hands— trying to restart Mustafa's body. His cheeks bulged as the other EMT forced air into his lungs.

All the while Murat couldn't do anything. Not even pray. The sickening color of Mustafa's skin a foreshadowing of grayish-blue bleakness.

After waiting for a few hours, Murat called home to let everyone know what happened. He left the van at *Ekmek Fabrikasi* completely forgetting everyone else might wonder what became of him. How selfish given June and Barry's departure this very morning.

A slow shuffling brought his short mother, her face drawn, eyes bloodshot.

"*Anne.*"

"Son."

He couldn't think about her confession. Mustafa needed his focus. His prayers. Nothing should get in the way of that. "He is still in surgery. No word from the doctors."

"These things take time."

"It's been so long. I hate the waiting."

His mother sat on the black, vinyl chair beside him, then placed her warm hand over his. Murat noted the shade of her skin, lighter than his, her palms stained red with henna.

He knew she experienced her fair share of heartache. Having her here almost deepened the pain, because he couldn't shield her from his concern. Normally he pretended, or covered up, or sorted things out.

Not now. Perhaps never again.

The world fell around him in massive chunks, the crumbling of a seawall overtaken by a tsunami. The bleeding happened long before this moment. Now patching and covering wouldn't work.

"Have you eaten?"

Murat sighed into the echoey, sterile space. *Just like my Anne to always worry about feeding me.*

"Yes." Lying came easy. He hadn't eaten since the night before.

At least the falsehood kept her from having something else to consider. What if Barry died? What if Mustafa died?

Nothing made sense. *God, where are you?*

Meryem swept her stubby thumb over the top of his hand. "You and I have forgotten so much. We have been trying so hard to keep everything together. Protect."

"Why, *Anne*?" He couldn't help but ask.

Tears shimmered so thin across her eyes, magnifying the green. She ignored the question and said, "We have both forgotten who our provider is. He is the only one who can make things right. For me. For you."

"I remember. But I don't see Him taking care of things. How long will He stand far off and watch, *Anne*? How long?" He hated the sound of his thick voice booming through the corridor. Hated his faithlessness.

Her face crumpled like a paper ball. She covered her eyes with her hands and wept. Quiet, throbbing tears.

He pulled her shoulders under his arm and pressed his face into her hair. "It will work out, *Anne*. I'm so sorry. I'm just tired. I just feel. . ."

What is it?

"Alone."

She snatched her hands from her face and glared at him. "And what about me? What about the children? You are not alone and

never have been. You've trapped yourself into a corner trying to control everything."

Her eyes flashed anger, then just that quickly relaxed, sadness pulling the lids to half-mast. "And the worst part is . . . I am no better." Her soft cries filled the empty hallway, filled Murat's chest, and flew out the doors. "Father, forgive me."

Her lament twisted a knife in his chest. *What happened to all the peace I felt just months ago? No, to be fair, years ago?* A mirage on the horizon, the promise of an oasis he once knew, but had no idea how to return to again. "Please stop. Please."

Meryem eyed him, her eyebrows rumpled, eyelids swollen. "I cannot pretend with you. I need you to forgive me too."

"I don't understand what you did. Why did you send that man?"

"I cannot explain. You must trust me though." She squeezed her eyes shut maybe realizing confidence had come and gone. "Please, just tell me you will."

Fatigue settled over Murat. Any fight he possessed straggled off like weak, aimless crabs retreating to the sea. He swallowed against the swelling anger.

"Always," he lied.

Her eyes searched back and forth for something in his. Looking at her hands, she said, "Thank you."

The squeaking of shoes preceded the doctor who entered the hallway with the protective face covering drooping around his neck. He blew out air through his mouth causing his cheeks to inflate and deflate like balloons. Then he began without preamble.

"It wasn't easy, but your friend is stable. He isn't well though. I cannot promise he'll be able to return to normal soon. Or ever. His heart is weak. One artery was completely blocked causing stress and today a heart attack. Does he have family?"

Mustafa's sons would most likely swoop in, close their father's bread business, liquidating the profit for themselves. All in the name of helping the man.

"No. There is nobody."

The doctor looked around like he wanted to confirm the fact, or possibly locate someone in the hallway who might contradict

Murat's claim. Then he sighed. "Then I don't see what help there is. He'll need care for several weeks and won't be able to work for some time after that. Even then, he'll need to live a less strenuous life or we'll have a repeat of today's story. Only I'm not sure how much more trauma his heart can take."

Determination rose in Murat like a resurrected battleship, encrusted with barnacles, but still strong and hulking. "I will take care of him. His business. No need to worry."

The doctor eyed him, looking suspicious. Certainly in Turkey family took care of their own. But Murat was no one to Mustafa, not really. Not even a distant cousin.

The man nodded curtly, then added, "Please come back tomorrow to see your friend. We'll discuss the details of his care then." He turned to leave, his rubbery shoes squeaking back out, leaving only the quiet. ☙

5 1 THE PATH

The darkness surrounded Murat like a cloak. He leaned against the Russian elm, his back pressed against the bark so hard it clawed his skin. He settled into the feeling—pushing even harder, letting the sting spread. The sensation almost felt good. Made him feel awake, alert—in control.

I can do this.

The arrangements were made for Mustafa to be brought home to the orphanage. The two would stay in June and Barry's home. If Murat had any chance to pull this off, he needed his friend close by. He'd ask Ella to check in on Mustafa in the morning and after her class with the little ones. Running the bread shop would be difficult. His *Anne* agreed to take the kids to and from school.

Now what about Ella? How could he keep an eye on her being gone from the property so much? He had to find someone to help him. But who? He had no friends, aside from those who lived here. No family who'd help them out. They were abandoned by anyone who once claimed to care.

Murat tipped his head back watching the harvest moon's glow like a halo around the tree top. The moment reminded him he should be praying. He couldn't make himself do it. Anger rumbled like thunder in his temples. He wondered if he'd been chosen, like Lot, to suffer. Only Murat knew he couldn't claim to be blameless. Somehow, this had to be his fault.

He paid penance for whatever evil he'd committed. So why try so very hard to do what was good and right? If a person displeased God so much, he lived to pay the price in suffering, for something he didn't even realize he'd done.

A crunching on the path broke into his thoughts. Murat leapt up, his chest widened ready to fight.

Instead, Ella's voice smoothed his tension. "Murat? It's me."

"Ella. What are you doing out?" If she insisted on doing stupid things, how could the woman possibly expect for him to take care of her? He forced himself to be calm. "You shouldn't be here."

She stood near enough for him to catch the smell of her perfume on the breeze gently rattling the leaves of the Russian elm towering above them. "I was looking for you. Wanted to make sure you're surviving."

"Of course. I'm perfect."

Her soft laugh sounded resigned, lacking in humor. "I heard about your friend, Murat."

"Oh, Mustafa? He'll be good soon. I'll take care of him."

"I'm sure you will." The words came out like an insult. Murat didn't understand what she meant.

She stepped closer and extended her hand to him, touched his cheek so lightly he wondered if he felt the heat only because it radiated. He wanted to take hold of her and sneak away somewhere. Pretend everything remained under control. But that would leave him open, distract him, less aware of what needed to be done.

"Murat . . ." He observed the yellow glow from the moon on her cheeks and lips, shadowing the space under her eyebrows. "I'm worried about you."

He shrugged away from her hand. As soon as he did, Murat moved forward again. His weakness spread hot through his chest, throbbing in his throat. He could barely get the words out. "Please, I'm *iyiyim*." A faker. That's what he'd become. Because he was anything but 'fine' right now.

"I don't believe you." She stepped closer, her face so near, her warm hands grasping the tips of his fingers. "Please, don't do this."

"What? I do nothing."

"You know what I'm talking about."

Murat shook his head, confused. "I don't know."

"You're supposed to talk to me about what needs to be done. We're supposed work together. But you're figuring it all out,

leaving me out of it. You're not able to do everything, Murat. You'll drive yourself crazy."

"You can help check for Mustafa."

"That's not what I'm saying. You're carrying it all. Do you even see you do that? You're trying to be everything. Do everything."

"I must do this. Or it won't . . ."

"Won't what?" Her exasperated words hushed him so he couldn't think or talk. "What, Murat? What is it? Don't you trust me?"

"Yes. Of course."

"Then why won't you give some of these concerns to me to figure out? I can do it, Murat." She sounded so small and unsure. Murat knew what she didn't. That she needed to be cared for, treasured. She didn't have enough power to fight evil, to carry his burdens.

He decided not to remind Ella of the event that happened only a few weeks before. Decided to keep his reservations to himself. She'd just get angry. "I know you can."

Ella grabbed the sides of his face, forcing him to look her in the eyes. Instead he lowered his mouth to hers, because he couldn't deal with looking so deep or letting her see into himself. And besides, he needed her warmth and closeness. Needed her kisses to force back the coldness burrowing into his heart. Like a fish hook.

"Murat." She pushed away and dropped her hands like fallen tree limbs. Shaking her head she stepped back slowly. "When you're ready to quit being God, let me know." Then she turned and strode away.

The criticism—a sucker punch. One minute he was safe. The next he felt more alone than ever.

"Ella?" She stopped, but didn't turn around. "Please don't come out at night again without me."

Without saying a word she walked away again. He followed her at a distance until the house swallowed up her frame, the door shutting behind her, protecting her from a cruel world. ❧

52 GRANDFATHER'S HOUSE

This visit had been years in the making. Murat couldn't bide his time any longer. All his churning unrest needed a place to settle—needed some closure.

Perhaps reaching out to the past could calm the incessant clawing in his chest. Besides, he had to admit, he needed help. Needed another man on his side. With Barry gone . . . he needed allies. Maybe re-tying old connections was the easiest way. Maybe make him stronger, too.

Finding his grandfather wasn't difficult—merely a few keystrokes on the computer. And reading the street address, Murat realized his *Dede* lived in the same home as always, on the outskirts of Çeşme. At the *otogar*, the main bus station, Murat caught the *Çeşme Seyahat* bus toward the nearby seaside town, the last stop on the bus route.

Murat knocked, then buried his hands in his pockets, eyes cast toward his feet. Behind the slow-opening door stood Erol, his grandfather on his father's side. Murat couldn't help but gasp. Sorrow lined the man's wizened face, a near clone of his late father's, though very different in coloring.

Recognition lit the man's gray-blue eyes with surprising speed. He began to close the weathered, wooden entry.

Wedging his foot in the door Murat pleaded, "*Dede*. Please. I need to say some things. Will you let me come in for a moment?"

Murat's grandfather stood still, his shoulders hunched, as if relenting some time ago to the thick arm of worry. Without saying a word, he shuffled backward and opened the door enough for Murat to sidle in sideways.

The old man didn't even look up as he shuffled across the room and sat on the metal chair standing against one wall. The only other items in the room were another chair and an ornate handmade rug. On the floor beside his chair lay a folded newspaper and a pack of Camel cigarettes.

"Grandfather. I have come to beg you to talk to me. Mother and I want to be part of your life again. Will you tell me about my father and help me to understand? Why have you abandoned us?"

The man's head shot up at the mention of Murat's dad. With a shaking hand he rubbed the stubble of his beard covering his jaw. He shuttered as he inhaled.

"Grandfather, what happened to him?" Murat asked again.

"How is it you have come to torture this old man? Have I not suffered enough? My son was a fool, his ways always bent toward violence. The choices he made . . . a disgrace to our good name. I feel his death and the death of so many others. This is my lot. Your grandmother is gone. I am alone. Just leave me with my sorrow."

Murat knelt before his grandfather. "You have mother and me. Why have you turned your back on us?"

"Don't you know?" The man's eyes watered. Something in those old windows masked a shadow. He searched Murat's eyes, then resigned himself to finding nothing.

"Murat, you were always your father's son. You followed him around like a dog begging for scraps. He is so much a part of you." The old man's head slumped against his chest. He began to weep. "I couldn't bear to look at you. I couldn't bear to lose another child to such a life. Such a disgrace."

Murat stroked the man's wrinkled hand, thankful for this small contact with something good from his past. Slowly, he started again. "*Dede*. I don't remember very much. I remember he hurt mother, then he died so unexpectedly. Then you turned your back on us and we suffered more bitterly. We have changed, mother and I. In so many ways. I'd never embrace my father's life of anger. I was just a boy. Now, as a man, I know he didn't honor any of us with his choices. I am my father's son, but I am not my father. I'm new in many ways, *Dede*. Will you allow us the gift of a relationship with you once again?"

Ignoring this last request, the old man began again, "Your grandmother always wanted to find you two. She called me many terrible names for choosing to be cut off from you. I was so angry

and stubborn. And now she's gone. What a life of regret. We can never get back the time."

Murat laid his head on his grandfather's hands, then looked up again, hot tears burning the soft skin around his eyes. "No, *Dede*, we never can. But God can. The Bible says He will restore the years the swarming locusts have eaten. The Bible, *Dede*."

Murat used the word 'grandfather' again to let this man know he still held a place in their small family. "That's a promise from God. And we can choose what we do with our remaining days."

Even with all his anger, Murat knew the only way to peace was through Christ. He'd tried everything else. Tried even still—his path a workaround to his lacking faith. Forcing the outcome he knew needed to happen. Even if he was a hypocrite, something instinctively rose up in him, the truth, real as wood and nails.

The old man stayed silent for so long Murat wondered if he'd turn away again and ask Murat to leave.

"You look just like him." His grandfather's words fell like a sentence. Like Murat couldn't be anything but a disgrace.

The old man searched Murat's face for any sign of the son who disappointed him and couldn't find any remnant of hatred in his grandson's eyes.

"I'm a new creation," Murat whispered, more for himself than his grandfather.

The man's voice scratched out when he spoke again. "Your father had faith too. Faith I taught him. I took him as a young boy to the mosque. Taught him our ways. Taught him about pleasing Allah. Me." He punched his chest. The sound thunked against the quiet room.

"You're not to blame, *Dede*. Not all Muslims live the way he did, or believe as he did. There's so much good he turned his back on. He made his way. You're not to blame. Despite what he chose in the end. He made his choices. Out of his pain. Not because of you."

"He asked me many times about his questions. Asked how he could ensure heaven. But I didn't have answers. I told him he must keep trying to be good. He chose a path he thought pleased Allah. I didn't tell him to do those things." His grandfather brushed

trembling hands over his face, down his chest, tears falling from his chin. "I would never tell him to do those things."

"Of course, *Dede*. Nobody blames you. Nobody." Murat leaned in, pressing his face to the old man's palms. "Your hands were never used as my father's were. Never. I remember that. I remember your kindness. Your willingness to reach out to those in need. Your hospitality, even to strangers. Your love for *Anne* and I. How much you valued family. I remember, *Dede*." Murat yearned for his grandfather to truly see him. "I love you. And I need you. *Anne* and I both need you so desperately."

"I need you too." He squeezed Murat's arms.

"*Dede*, if you will listen, I can tell you about a life of peace and purpose, free and guaranteed forgiveness. Will you hear me? I'd like to tell you about the choice mother and I made years ago."

With a sigh, a quivering smile, and his eyes on Murat, he spoke, "Yes, son. I will listen, though I see no way to save my soul now. I need to see your mother. I have many things to say to her."

"We will do it. This day."

Over the next hour, Murat shared his story of pain, struggle, and redemption. His grandfather, broken for so long, saw no way to change his path.

They talked all the way home, bumping over the streets on the bus, watching a busy world blur by. Murat tried to ignore the pain waiting to be brought to mind as soon as he stepped through the orphanage gates. He had his grandfather back.

One victory—at least for today. ❧

53 MERYEM'S HOME

"*Anne*, grandfather is here."

Murat pushed back the door to find his mother facing him, the blue and white painted pottery bowl made by her father so long ago held in soapy fingertips. Murat took the dish to avoid the impending loss.

"Grandfather. He's here." He repeated quiet and slow.

The hunched man wearing the typical washed out beanie, button up shirt, and baggy trousers stepped forward, his leather shoes scraping against the cement entryway.

"Meryem." The name sounded more like begging. More like disappointment. But not at her. At himself.

Murat's mother, didn't move, didn't speak. The soft tan skin of her forehead pinched in pain. She shook her head so small and uneventful. The denial that this could possibly be happening. Murat placed the bowl on the copper table, then moved to her side, afraid she might collapse at any moment. "He has come. Finally."

Again the shake of her head.

Grandfather inched forward, like a scared animal trying to get close enough to snatch away food, but not close enough to be eaten. He reached out a shaky hand, then dropped it like a log, heavy and dead.

Again he shuffled toward Meryem. He kneeled, slow and painful, removing his hat. His forehead touched the cold floor at her feet, so much like his mother's confession.

"Please forgive me. My son was your undoing. I abandoned you when you needed me most. I pray you will not hold this against me forever. I am but a fool and an old man now." The words spilled out gravelly and tedious, an urn full of tears.

All the while Meryem stood, her hand raised to cover her mouth, tears shining on her chapped cheeks, looking at the man who looked far too much like her late husband.

"Erol, how is it you are here?" She said the words like a robot, monotone and callous.

"Your son. He came."

"My son?" Meryem gaped at Murat, disbelief registering, like he betrayed her.

"Yes, *Anne*." Murat shot his chin out daring her to argue. Murat didn't retreat. They all needed this. The time passed long ago for reconciliation.

Meryem stared at her father-in-law, a battle waging across her face. "I forgive. I already forgave. So long ago. I didn't understand why you punished us for his sin. Why?" She half-wailed the word.

Murat struggled to keep himself composed. Seeing his mother re-living the past this way tortured him. He steadied her with his hand on the back of her arm, pressing her forward, nudging her toward his grandfather. She shook Murat off and planted her feet apart, glaring at the man, almost combative.

"I thought you had been a part of it." He eyed Murat, then Meryem. "I was ashamed. I couldn't stand the sight . . ." He stopped short. "Now I know I was wrong. You were victims too."

"Yes, especially Murat." Meryem growled out. A warning.

The exchange gave Murat the distinct feeling that he was on the outside of the space observing the scene from another room. Like a little boy. Decisions made by others. Talked about as if he was incapable.

"What? I don't understand." Murat leaned in to his mother.

She ignored his question and asked her father-in-law. "What now?"

The man gave her a blank, lost look. He began to stand to his feet. "This was wrong. I see it is too late." Murat pressed a hand under the man's elbow to help him up.

"No." Murat didn't mean to yell the word, but the cycle ended today. "It's never too late. *Anne*, we know this better than most."

Meryem looked at him communicating some things are too little, too late.

"Daughter . . ." Murat's grandfather waited, tears brimming.

"*Baba.*" A sob cut off Meryem's words as she extended her hands and said, "*Baba,* my heart was broken."

Silent, he shuffled forward, pulling her into an embrace, and tenderly rubbing her back. "Time will heal. It will," the old man said.

Meryem only cried until exhaustion put an end to her tears.

After a sober farewell, Murat walked his grandfather to the street and hailed a *taksi.* "Please, visit us Grandfather. Don't let her think this was only a dream."

Murat wasn't sure whether or not he wished this into being. Erol only offered a faint smile, then ducked inside the cab, tugged the door closed, and the vehicle sped away.

His grandfather gazed back through the rear taxi window looking at Murat, until he blurred into the night. ✒

54 JUNE AND BARRY'S PLACE

Murat claimed the couch at June and Barry's place, feeling like an intruder, the house a tomb without them. Tomorrow Mustafa would come to stay, sleeping in their bed. Keeping things the same simplified the situation.

He mentally listed his tasks for the week, including working full time at the bread shop. Murat wondered how to keep an eye on Ella over the next few weeks. Thinking of her so close distracted him. When he realized he hadn't made sure if she slept safely in her room, he jumped up.

A moment later he knocked on her door. There she stood, her hair pulled into a sloppy bun wearing a long night shirt, glasses, and no make-up. He forced his hands deep into his pockets.

She eyed him and said, "Murat."

"I just wanted to check on you."

"I'm fine. Just getting into bed."

"I'm sorry if I upset you." He wanted to bridge the gap between them. The divide stretching, thrusting him back like a forceful hand to his chest.

"I'm worried about you, Murat. You seem so focused. It's almost like you're obsessed. You don't seem happy." She reached for his hand as she said the last words, her eyebrows lowered in pity.

Her words twisted in his stomach. "I only want to keep you safe. You were hurt, Ella." He touched her face, the bruise faded almost completely. *Did she not remember the danger she faced only two weeks before?*

She didn't pull away, just watched him, like she attempted to figure him out.

"It's not just that, Murat. How are you going to make it, if you won't share some of the burden? I can do something too. I didn't come all the way across the ocean to be babied."

The tension he sensed the day of her arrival reared its head. She narrowed her eyes, lifting her chin just a little.

He wondered if she could really be of help. What could she possibly do that didn't involve her being exposed? No, better to give her something simple that kept her close to home.

"I will need help with Mustafa. He must rest and will need food. And you have the children each day."

She smiled a little, "That's far too much, Murat."

He smiled back, feeling some of the strain from the day melting. "Do you want to come and have a cup of *çay* with me?"

She looked back toward her room, dim with only lamp light. "I suppose that would be fine."

He retreated as she closed her door. Being near the woman made him hurt and calmed him at the same time—like observing a life impossible and sweet, within arm's reach—unable to grab hold of. So delicate, a single breath extinguished hope.

Murat brewed the tea and set everything on the brass table. Ella knocked softly before entering the small living room space. She wore sweats and a T-shirt and held an awkwardly wrapped package.

"What's this?" He reached over, touched her hand and she pressed the item into his hand.

"Something for you."

"For me?"

"Yes."

"But why?"

She picked up her teacup with her small fingertips. *So fragile. Breakable.*

He shook his head, looking at the gift in his lap. Neither of them mentioned his mother. Neither were able, clamped down like leeches to their world spinning out of control.

Peeling back the paper he saw a kettle, glittering copper with intricately hammered scroll work all over it. "I don't understand."

Ella leaned back on the colorful, wool pillows lining the wall. "I just wanted to remind you that we do have a job, a responsibility. And when we live that out, it brings comfort to others. Like this

kettle. But," she studied his face, "there's only so much it can hold. And really, overdoing it will just cause us to spend too much of ourselves, so we can't be effective anymore."

Murat nodded. He tried to listen, distracted by her mouth, the way it moved so carefully. By her eyes so full of concern.

"*Tamam.* I will try to keep this in mind." He reached over the table and pulled her hand toward him, though she planted herself far away. Maybe on purpose. "Thank you for this."

She frowned. "Will you really try, Murat?"

He set the kettle on the brass table with a bang, his anxiety failing to keep his frustration at bay. "Pardon." He cleared his throat, embarrassed. "Yes, but, I don't know how to stop." The pressure on his chest increased any time he let himself think too much. "It's my problem, I know this. My *Anne*, she's always reminding and reminding me. But is hard for me."

Murat paused, hesitant to share, but wanting to let some of his story out into the room. "My father was not good to us. He struck anyone who dared question him. I remember one day after spending the day with him working on our car, *Anne* spoke with him. I knew because they got louder as they talked in the other room. Soon I heard a problem. Things breaking. I remember feeling mad at my mother for making *Baba* angry. I had so few special moments with him, I wanted it to last. Instead, he screamed at her. I didn't know she was being hurt."

He pressed his eyes closed, fighting the tears burning his throat. He began again, quieter, trying to steady his voice. "All was quiet when I finally dared go into the other room. My father left moments before. The silence scared me. When I entered the room I saw her right away, lying on the ground, her face so red and bleeding."

Murat touched his forehead, wishing he'd been stronger. "That day I decided I'd protect her whatever it might mean. Even if he killed me, I'd not let her be on the other end of his hand. But it was not to be. Shortly after that he was gone."

Murat reached toward Ella's face and brushed a thumb under her eye stopping a tear. "I don't want to be like him, ruling over others. But fear is always there. I'm so afraid . . ." His voice broke.

Ella scooted around the table to wrap her arms around his neck. "You can't pay for his choices, Murat." She cried into his shoulder, rubbing her hand over his back. "You'll never be able to do that, to rest and be happy, to have any peace if you need to make up for his mistakes."

"I know."

But there is no escaping my life. I am trapped. Though I am supposed to be free, this is my burden to carry.

And loving another person—even just one more—shoved him closer and closer to a cliff overlooking a graveyard of dry, brittle bones, baked ivory by the scorching sun. Littering the beach as far as the eye could see. ❧

55 IZMIR, 1982

Pregnancy wrapped Meryem in light and helped with the unknowns. *Where is my husband? What does he do all day with no apparent job? And still he brings home lire, enough, at least to keep us going. That's why I married him, after all.*

But every time she asked where he went, he growled and told her about his odd jobs. "You know I am good with cars. I fix them. All around the city people need my help."

Pressing only forced out darkness. Quiet and meek worked best with Ali. When he arrived home each day, she doted. Rubbed her fingers up and down the back of his hair, calming the beast.

When she told him about their baby, something clicked. However, not in the expected way. He became more driven, secretive, if that were possible.

He controlled her more than ever, telling her to be careful with this and that and not to go out, not even to the market. So Meryem began putting orders in with *Anne*. Her mother understood, folded her daughter's list, and looked away as she left the house.

Anne didn't mind helping. Meryem always knew that. She only minded the ever-tightening grip of Ali's pressure on her only child.

At home, alone, Meryem allowed herself to dream of the little one inside her. She imagined he occupied the secret room, the one she reserved for dreaming, for hope. The one where she pretended to live a different life. One where she was loved and nurtured and treasured, not boxed away.

And there she told her baby stories about the big man he'd be one day, or the beautiful maiden she'd become. She wove a fantasy where they'd play by the sea, digging to the other side of the earth with just their hands. Where they'd look at the prickly, black sea urchins through the glassy water.

The door slammed. Meryem froze. Waited.

What kind of mood is Ali in tonight?

She walked to the place where he removed his shoes and offered, "Welcome home, can I get you a cup of *çay?*"

He offered only a sidelong glance and shook his head. "No, just dinner. I'm tired."

"How was your day?" She ventured the question, hoping for some revelation.

"Fine." He pulled open the newspaper she always placed at the table where he sat. "You?"

She nearly dropped the spoon she used to dish out the stew. "I stayed home. Cooked and cleaned. Watched the news."

At this he snapped, "Yes, and no good news."

"No," she said. She knew all about his politics. He resented the American military presence so close to them in Izmir. Saw them as encroaching on Turkish control. On the old ways. But the news of fighting in the east between the Kurds and Turks plagued him most. Christians and non-Turks, many of them, two very dark marks on the Kurdish cause.

He cut his eyes away from the paper to her belly. "You are growing. How is the baby?"

As she brought his bowl of food over, she protected her stomach with one hand. "Good. He kicked today." She grinned, unable to contain the joy, even with Ali's dark cloud hovering, wondering when it would strike with lightening anger.

"Really?" He stood and met her half way, taking the bowl and placing it on the table, then covering her swollen belly with his palms. He waited, impatience edging his rough hands outward. "Hmm," he grunted. "Must be sleeping."

Or maybe just scared of you. She shivered thinking how close the words came to being spoken into the room.

As time ticked by, days bleeding into weeks, her husband grew more aggressive, raising his hand to her more than once. But now at times with this baby, he became almost gentle.

His manic swings kept her on edge, like walking right along the edge of the steep rocky cliffs near the ocean. Never knowing whether the winds would caress her face or knock her toward death. ✐

56 IZMIR, 2007

I leaned over my knees, pressing my chest against them, the dark sky cloaking the yard just outside my bedroom. The cool patch of grass spread out around my feet. I ran my hand along the tops, freshly cut by Murat earlier today. *How's he managing it all?*

I sat in the shadows, liking that I could see the space around me and I couldn't be seen. For just a little while, not being seen felt right. Being seen and trying to see all at once blurred the lines for me.

I let myself pray. For Barry. For Murat. For me.

I wondered about Murat, where he was when I lived here fifteen years ago. I wondered about how he was so near. How I didn't even know he existed.

Now the entire city was woven with him, threads of blue and black. The ocean was where he held my hand, drunk and sad. The streets we travelled together, finding my childhood haunts. Even the bread, I imagined, had all been formed by his hands, thrust into the fire to be blistered, and snatched out in the nick of time.

June and Barry's front door cracked open, beaming an arc of light onto me. Murat stepped out, allowing the screen door to snap shut behind him. He walked out to where I sat and plopped beside me. "Are you okay?"

"Yes. You?"

He shrugged. "Yes?"

"Is that a question?"

"Maybe. *Am* I okay?"

He was a little boy who maybe never heard "well done" even once from his dad. What could I say? He was mottled with fissures. *What will it take to make him completely crumble?* "You know the answer to that better than I do."

"Safe answer." He huffed, then turned his head over his shoulder to face me, his arms hooked around his legs. So strong, yet as delicate as depression glass.

Murat watched me in silence then began tearing grass up in clumps, tossing green blades to the side. "Can I ask you something?"

"Sure."

"What will you do now that you know the man who killed your father is dead?"

"I . . ." I swallowed against the gravelly feeling in my throat. "I guess I'll just move on." I knew my answer was lame. What else could I say? "And try to have peace with not confronting him."

"What about finding his family? Tell them your story. Is maybe good to tell them. As a . . ." Murat paused, then said, "substitute."

I let the idea tumble around for a second, then I shook my head. "I don't know. I'm guessing they've been through enough already."

"But it might help, right?"

"I guess so. Maybe."

The locusts that surrounded us, hummed and fluxed and hushed together with the leaves rubbing against each other in the breeze.

"What about you?" I ventured.

"What about me?"

"What would you say to your dad if you could?"

Murat blew air through his mouth, then answered, "I don't think I'd use words." His voice rumbled like an ocean storm.

I shivered, rubbing my hands over my arms pocked with goosebumps. He stayed quiet so long I thought I lost him. Then he said, "How could I have wanted him so much, when he hurt *Anne* . . . and me?"

"Murat, you were a little boy who loved his daddy. He didn't earn your love. As his son, you gave it anyway. You have nothing to be ashamed of."

Murat said nothing, just tipped his head back to stare at the night sky, poking light through the green-black tree canopy. Minuscule specks against the quivering dark.

We sat in silence for a while before turning in for the night, each to our own island. How could we put to rest unresolved hurts and unspoken words—tethered with rocks and submerged to the place where they could no longer send out barbs and anchor in soft flesh? ❧

57 THE NOOK

Murat spun his conversation with Ella over and over in his mind like sea glass tumbling and smoothing out against shells and sand. He sat in June and Barry's small nook and powered up their ancient desktop, the light casting shadows in the darkened room.

Mustafa's bear-like snores reverberated through the wall like it was made of paper instead of drywall. Somehow the sound calmed him. For even just a minute, things were as they should be. Or at least tamed, like a sleeping dragon.

What if Ella's father's murderer still had family in the area? Could anything be done to arrange a meeting? So Ella could snap that piece of the puzzle into place? Close the door on the yawning, open, grave-like cavern he knew tortured a person.

He couldn't let her live without answers the way he had. It would honor her father to know his daughter could move through. Maybe it would take some of the pain away too. He could only hope. Besides, he was like an impotent dog with his mother. Maybe this could be his chance to fight back—evening the score.

Murat pulled up a browser window and began typing in key words. Perhaps after he searched for details about Ella's father, he'd try to find out more about this car accident his *Anne* spoke of. Nobody was forthcoming with the details. Only that he dishonored the family—whatever that meant. What did his death have to do with dishonor? What did *Baba*'s adultery have to do with him and his mother? His memories of *Baba* were spotty and vague, but the feeling of fear and disappointment remained a constant. Selfishly, he wondered if bringing resolution to Ella's questions might heal his heart a measure.

Murat keyed in Ella's father's name then selected "search." Results appeared in a long blue list on the screen. Murat clicked on the first one, a man who owned a dairy farm in Scotland. Not discouraged, Murat browsed more, clicking on each link before beginning a new search.

Perhaps obituaries? Murat scanned archived headlines from the local newspapers for an obituary for the man, but found none. Was it possible the papers reported on the murder of an American military figure; perhaps only as an explanation of the event rather than giving any details on the man himself? Murat rubbed a hand across his jaw feeling the roughness on his palm. Where might he find the information he sought?

About an hour later, Murat still sat staring at the screen. He yawned into the quiet room, Mustafa still hard at work, snoring louder than any human Murat ever encountered. He couldn't help but smile and chuckle.

In a last ditch effort, Murat typed in a search for American casualties in Izmir during the Gulf War. Three listings appeared. After scanning two young, unmarried men killed in Istanbul, he dismissed them. Murat clicked on the last listing. The heading popped up.

His heart picked up speed upon reading the words, "Staff Judge Advocate Matthew Gardner died yesterday morning, October 3, 1990, victim of a car bombing. Gardener is survived by a wife and a seven-year-old daughter. A local terrorist group claimed responsibility. An investigation is underway to determine . . . "

Murat couldn't bear to read any further.

The screen flared up in front of Murat's eyes, like a slow, blinding explosion, blurring the words in front of him.

That date. October 3, 1990.

How could it be? Was it some terrible coincidence—or was there a connection?

Murat's eyes darted to the cause of death "victim to a car bomb." Was this the "dishonorable" way his father died in a so-called car accident? What were the odds this woman who came to their orphanage, with whom he found his heart tangled, that her father and his *Baba* were connected in this terrible, ghostly way?

October 3, 1990.

Fifteen painful years ago.

The same day his father died. ❧

58 THE BREAD SHOP

Murat shoved the dark wooden paddle into the oven to retrieve a long flat piece of *pide* bread. The back and forth movement calmed him. Methodical, predictable. So different than his life.

His frustration made him push the loaves in too hard, too far into the heat with the banked coals, white-hot. Getting too close always ruined the loaf, cooked it too quickly around the edges. Uneven and useless. He allowed his upper body to linger too long in front of the heat, savoring the pain a little.

The screeching of J.R., hanging in his flimsy cage near the front door, drew his attention. *Must be a customer.* He stepped away from the oven and placed the paddle on the hooks that cradled it, and moved to the front room.

Ella stood there with a package in her hands.

"What are you doing here?" *Can't the woman learn to do as she's told?* Besides, he couldn't stand to look at her.

My father is a murderer.

Her smile collapsed and she only said, "You look hot."

He knew the American slang meaning wasn't what she intended. He turned his back to her and only said, "Thank you." He pretended to work, to do anything except make eye contact. She stayed quiet so long he finally peered over his shoulder. "Why are you here?"

"I finished with the little ones, checked on Mustafa, and thought maybe you could use some lunch. I figured you'd forget, since you're on your own today." She sounded small and frail.

He mumbled a "thank you" and took the food wrapped in paper feeling only a little bad he upset her. "How am I supposed to take care of you if you keep leaving the orphanage?"

Pushing her away felt natural. Once she knew their connection, she'd hate him, if it was as he suspected.

Ella narrowed her eyes. "I'm a grown woman, Murat. I didn't come here to be taken care of. If anyone needs help, it's you." Her voice lower than usual was tinged with a little growl.

He clenched his teeth. "Please go home."

She clamped her arms across her chest. "No."

"No?"

"That's right." She looked like a little girl trying to be brave.

"Go home." His voice rising in volume sounded foreign to him. No, sounded like *Baba's*.

"Make. Me." She said, each word, its own sentence, all fire and so angry she trembled.

Before he stopped himself, he took the lunch and hurled it against the wall. The contents burst open and dropped to the floor. Murat stared at his hands, saw blood dripping off his palms, the blood of Ella's father.

He looked at Ella, wondering if she saw it too. She stood so still, unmoving except the tears filling her eyes, betraying her pain. Swallowing her whole. And fear? Murat stepped toward her, reached a hand out to comfort. Only, she recoiled like his touch might burn her. *Maybe she sees the blood.* "I'm sorry."

He couldn't stand looking at her. Her beauty, brokenness, contradictions. Like his constant running around, trying to save, in light of the death brought by his father.

It's in my blood. He's in me.

She shook her head and shoved the door open, allowing it to slam behind her. The bird squawked. Murat resisted the urge to fling the canary's cage to the floor.

A burning filled his throat. He wondered if he might be sick.

You're just like your father. When things get hard, you hurt others like he did. You hurt the ones you love. Murat stumbled to the door pressing his forehead against the glass. *You are just like him. You can't run from it.* He turned the lock and switched the sign to *Kapali.* Closed. Then returned to the back room and found a place below the oven's burning mouth, to slump to the floor.

Like a thousand stings of a jellyfish, pain pricked at him, bristling against his face and mouth and nose. He sobbed into the quiet. The steady sounds of the coals buzzed beneath his anguish. The stench of blackened bread filled the room. And he curled up on the stone floor wishing for death.

59 MERYEM'S HOME

Lord, help him.

Nothing else came. Just the three-word prayer. Then sadness.

The pressure in my throat and chest felt like it might kill me if I didn't let it out. *I need to get home.* The city flickered by like a filmstrip. Shops and restaurants gave way to homes stacked haphazardly on one another, leaning this way and that, like they might collapse any minute.

Is this my fault? Have I done something to hurt Murat?

Then an idea came, making me even more anxious to get back to the orphanage. I marched through the gates and headed straight down the path to Murat's home, hoping Meryem was there. When I arrived, all the kids were home from school, filling the house with noise.

I knocked on the open front door. Meryem stepped out, rubbing her hands on a dish towel. I took in her traditional Turkish attire. Somehow the picture comforted me. So many memories involved Turkish women wearing *şalvar* 'baggy pants' with the crotch near the knees, T-shirt tops, and head-scarves. I inhaled a deep breath hoping to calm things inside.

"Meryem, you look busy."

She surveyed the activity, then said, "Yes, but can I help with something?"

"I need to talk to you. If you can't talk right now I understand." Though inside I screamed for her to talk *now*.

She shook her head and then stepped back into the house, telling the older kids to get dinner started, then pulled the door closed behind her. She motioned for me to go sit on the wooden bench, just a log on its side.

"Is problems?" She bunched her eyebrows together. "Murat is *iyi*?"

"No, I don't think he is doing well."

Meryem looked toward the entrance of the property like she might see him if she tried hard enough. I reached for her hand and tugged at her to sit on the rough-hewn, wooden seat.

"Meryem, today I took lunch to Murat at *Ekmek Fabrikasi.*"

"Yes?" She squeezed my hand.

I pulled away and said, "He threw it, the lunch. He looked so angry. He scared me," I whispered, ashamed to say that about this woman's only child. "What do I do?"

Meryem bowed her head. I knew she understood the gravity of her over-protective son lashing out in that way.

She only said, "No, I do. I do." Then she rose and said, "Thank you, Ella. But this was my afraid. This was my afraid."

She turned and walked back into her home, closing the door behind her. Shutting me out.

I imagined a giant finger pointing at me. *This is all your fault. Why did you even come here? You have done no good. Only harm.*

Tears burned my eyes and I pressed my hand to my mouth. I dragged myself only half of the way home and then bolted the rest.

Only harm. Only harm. Only harm.

And the call to prayer bellowed out, accusing me. Reminding me that I am nothing. Told me to quit. To go home.

But you've torn open the wound and there's no way to cover it now. ✦

60 THE DARK SPACE

With a sigh I reached for my jacket. Murat still hadn't returned home. Waiting made me feel like a bird in a cage. I knocked on Mustafa's door. Formerly June and Barry's. The substitution left me feeling emptier.

Mustafa opened it, looking like the typical baker, all roundness in the middle and plump cheeks, though the rosy part still lagged. The man needed more time to heal.

"Hi, Mustafa. Can I get you anything?" I limited my sentences to phrases I knew well in Turkish.

He grinned and said, "No, I am good. Where is Murat?"

I shook my head feeling defeated all over again. "I don't know." I didn't want to guilt the man by saying Murat probably worked late at the bakery.

I recalled Murat's face, all anger and sorrow. I had the profound feeling I was losing him. And that hurt more than I could process. I wished I'd held him at arm's length, a practice I perfected since Dad's death. Only Murat shattered 'arms length,' like a çay cup on cement.

"Is Murat okay?" Mustafa surprised me with his insight.

My insides tangled, like a Turkish puzzle ring no longer woven together in one band. Only a knotted pile with no cohesive pattern at all and no apparent way to fix it.

"Yes, he's good." Lying felt right. Another example of how things turned on end.

I left the man and stepped into the darkness.

Where are you? And how can I reach you? ✒

6 1 GRANDFATHER'S HOUSE

Murat stood in the center aisle of the blue worker's bus, his hand latched into the overhead grip. Today the closeness of so many sweaty bodies after a long day intensified his frustration. The bus hit a bump. The whole group lurched forward in sync, like a wave of apathetic souls allowing themselves to be shoved whichever way life might push.

Only Murat wanted to shove back. Murat watched the blur of traffic going past. The shoreline was nowhere in sight, just the drab monotony of a crowded city block, then dirt roads with smaller, more spread out homes of white limestone. The traditional Fiat was replaced by donkeys and horses with small vegetable buggies bouncing along.

The bus jostled along the back streets and dropped him off a few blocks from his Grandfather's. At this moment, Murat only wanted to talk to him. Maybe the old man could stroke his heart with wisdom or maybe the comfort of the old, familiar bond they shared, so long ago.

The tension knotting Murat's neck and fists made him feel almost afraid of his capability to vent the anger somewhere, anywhere. His actions earlier today proved he couldn't be trusted.

No, he was not like his father. At least he kept repeating that to himself over and over again. Even if at this moment striking someone sounded almost savory, he'd not surrender to violence.

I'm not like him. I'm not like him.

The words fell flat. Any comfort of a savior redeeming his brokenness bobbed, small and far off, like a fishing boat in the wide, cobalt Aegean.

The bus stopped. Murat shoved through the packed space to the door hissing open. Moments later he sat with his grandfather on the roof of his flat, an ice-cold Coca-Cola bottle in his hand.

"*Dede*. Everything feels hard and out of my control. Nothing makes sense. I'm so sick of not knowing about my past. I need answers. I found out something I pray is only a coincidence."

His grandfather's face shined bright and peachy in the orangey setting sun. As a Turk he leaned toward Aryan, light skin, bright blue eyes with his wavy white hair that once was platinum blond. Smile lines wrinkled the sides of his eyes. Creases on his forehead betrayed a hard life. The man nodded, not even attempting to provide any answers that weren't specifically asked for.

"*Dede,* please tell me about my father. About how he died. *Anne* said it was a car accident, but I don't believe her now." Murat leaned in, placed his elbows on his knees and stared hard at his grandfather.

"I cannot. Not if your *Anne* refuses."

Murat hung his head, looking at the rough pavement between his feet, opening and closing his clenched fists. Praying for peace that didn't come. *Lord, how can I bear this? How can I when my enemy hides? Invisible evil.*

"I feel like an explosion is waiting to happen, I am so full of anger."

Again the older man stayed silent, though he flinched at Murat's choice of words. *Can it be that my very own father killed Ella's father? How can such a cruel thing happen?*

Murat realized then that this anger could be harnessed. Power rides on the crest of such anger. But the cost was high—a pummeled shoreline, shells obliterated into nothing but sand. And that shoreline involved everyone he loved—his *Anne*, his grandfather, the children at the orphanage, and Ella. Murat rotated the cool glass bottle in his hands like a fortune-teller's crystal ball that could reflect answers.

"*Dede*, did my father kill an American?" He couldn't help it, sick of the hiding, the pretending.

The man hunched over. The words sucker punched his stomach. Without saying one word he nodded "yes," and moaned an eerie lament. The regretful wail sounded like the cry of a suicide bomber—awaiting redemption and death. ⤍

6 2 ELLA'S ROOM

A knock jarred me from my sleep. Three a.m. glowed on my clock. I dreamed of lying on the beach, the ocean encroaching. I couldn't move. Water rushed over my face. In between the ebb and flow of the waves, I gasped for oxygen.

I sat on the side of my bed still feeling the tug of the waves, then stumbled and pressed a hand to the door, opening it. Meryem stood there, tears dripping from her chin.

"What is it, Meryem?"

"Murat."

My stomach tightened. I struggled to breathe. "What happened?" A burnt street. An empty space where Dad's car was. Darkness.

"Murat not come home." I glanced at my clock, as if it would show a less concerning hour for Murat to still be gone.

Oh, God. I couldn't bear to consider the 'what ifs.' The last I saw Murat was at the bread shop more than sixteen hours ago—a man half-crazed.

An idea, a thin beam of light, broke through. "Meryem, maybe he got back late and didn't want to wake you and he's sleeping next door."

"No, I check this."

"You checked the room?"

She nodded and covered her face.

"Meryem, where else could he be?" I didn't want to know the answer.

"I don't know this."

I wrapped my arms around her frame that seemed smaller, like the worry shrank her a bit. I prayed, hoping God still heard me, despite all the damage I did by coming to Turkey.

God knew I hadn't shown up for the orphans. Not really. I knew that for sure now.

Soon Meryem left, saying she needed to get back to her house and the younger kids.

I spent the rest of the night praying like a mad woman. Praying Murat safely home. Fighting back the images of my street, littered with blood. ❧

63 THE COTTAGE

The next morning, Murat arrived home. I heard his shuffling in the entryway and snatched the door open and yelled, "Are you okay?" He only nodded, like he was sorry about it. Then he turned away, looking at his feet.

I grabbed the back of his shirt and said, "How could you just stay away all night? Don't you know there are people who love you and have been worried sick?" I hated the near scream of my voice. The tears flooding my words.

"Your mom was here last night, in the middle of the night, scared to death. I was up all night praying. What happened? Why didn't you come home?"

"Because I couldn't look at your face." Even as he said the words, he refused to look up. Murat paused, swallowing back tears. His Adam's apple bobbed like a fish tugging at a line, pulling it down, down, down. I reached for Murat's hand. He snatched it away.

"Murat, I forgive you for how you acted."

He swung his head back and forth, as if that meant nothing.

"Ella. When I tell you what I must, you won't want me." A tear crawled down his cheek and I wished I might wipe it away. "I stayed at my grandfather's house."

The air caught in my chest. I swallowed against the ache in my throat. "Please. This is torture. Just tell me."

"I researched. On your father's death."

"You what? Why?" My heart gained speed.

"I wanted to help. I thought maybe it would make you . . . more peaceful inside."

"But I told you not to."

"I know," Murat shouted, his tone heavy with regret. "I wish I'd listened. I wish I didn't know anything. It's so terrible."

"What, Murat? You're scaring me."

The drumbeat in my chest hurt. I breathed in slow and steady to calm it, only it didn't work.

"Ella. Your father died the same day my father died. Your father was killed by someone in *Dev Sol*."

"*Dev Sol*? How do you know about that?"

When Koray told only me, how could Murat know? And I didn't tell anyone else?

"A terrorist group."

"I know that. How do you know?"

"Is not important."

"So he was killed by *Dev Sol*. What does this have to do with *you*?" Anger drove my words out harder than I wanted. Murat looked ready to crumble.

I almost felt violated—he had no right to know anything about Dad. About that terrible day. The memory belonged to me, not him to step into like an actor on a stage. How could he stand there and act like my sweet father's death had anything at all to do with him?

"What?" I screamed, the quiet shattered like a jackhammer to my chest. "Have the courage to spit it out."

Murat's eyes looked darker than usual, as if trying to let light in. No soft, golden brown flecks, just a deep, hooded black.

"My father. He did it. He died the same day. He was part of this terrorist group, *Dev Sol*. He killed your father. *My* father." He pounded his chest so hard the sound echoed. "How can it be, Ella, that this man whose memory I've suffered for so long is the one? I've lived with the burden of what he did to my mother. How is it that now I must bear this? This knowing that he's also the cause of your terrible pain? I cannot make it right. I will never be able to fix this shame. He killed the father of the woman I love!"

Red splotches mottled the skin around his eyes. The veins in his neck stood out, fat and full of terror. He stood there, a man deranged by guilt.

I couldn't move. Couldn't fully take in what he confessed. How could such a thing be possible? What were the odds of arriving at the same place as my father's murderer's wife and son?

A memory smoked his face, pulling me away from him: My daddy held my hand and said how much my fingers looked like his, all knotted and intertwined.

As always the ghost image faded. I couldn't breath—the air blanketed and acrid.

"I . . . " I couldn't formulate a single word beyond that. Then I managed, "His name was Yenibay. That's not your last name."

"Anne changed back to her name before my *Baba*. She changed it when we moved here. I didn't know why before, but now . . ."

Get away from me. The hissing command smoothed the jagged edges. The words, a powerful surge of anger pulsating through my face and hands. *Forget forgiveness. What's the point? Hatred gives you back control.*

I needed to tell my father's killer how he ruined my life. I lunged forward and shoved Murat—hard. He staggered, but didn't fall.

I stared at the palms of my hands, not recognizing them. Murat didn't retaliate, but waited, head and shoulders bent, welcoming a good beating. Anything to absolve the guilt and burden.

I couldn't look at him anymore. I covered my face and sobbed so hard my stomach burned, my head pounded, and my ears rang.

Why, God? Why would you let this happen? What kind of sick joke is this?

Murat's arms wrapped around me and he prayed softly in Turkish. Then Murat spoke in sobbing gasps against my hair. "My Ella. I don't expect you to forget, but I beg you to forgive me. I carry this for my father since he died a coward, unable to face the punishment of what he did. Maybe God will help your heart heal again. I'm so sorry I didn't listen. Now you have to bear the pain all over again. I know when you look at me you will be reminded of your father's death. I pray only for your forgiveness."

"Murat. I'm . . . "

What, Ella? Didn't you come here to resolve this? Didn't you pretend, at least, that you forgave long ago?

I sucked in a shuttering breath then blew it out, slow and steady. A resolve struck me with such a rush of tingling power, I knew it must be straight from God.

I looked up at Murat, his face swollen with sadness. "I forgive your father, Murat. I don't blame you. You were only a child. I forgave your dad long ago, even when he had no name. No face. I

forgave the man who did that terrible thing. Well, maybe I didn't. But I choose to now. God will help me, like He always has."

So many of my words were what I wanted to believe about myself, rather than the truth. Saying them gave me hope they might become true.

The urge to kiss this broken man in front of me made me reach toward Murat—not a kiss of passion, but a kiss to press back the pain and usher in sweetness.

Given the desire to pull him in and push him away at the same time, my instability mocked. I made a choice. I wouldn't let the hurt cause me to hide from life anymore.

I touched the sides of his face and leaned in, pressed my lips to his, tasting the tears. "I love you, Murat." Words I knew to be truth.

Murat's voice sagged heavy with pain, a sob pushing out the words. "But how can you?"

"Because of Jesus." I kissed the place under his eyes. "That's how."

Murat acquiesced with a slow nod. "Is the only way because . . . " Murat shook his head then glanced at me his face red and his eyes so sad. "I love you too." ༄

6 4 MERYEM'S HOME

Ella walked into Meryem's home quietly, a strange look of peace made her face look smooth and younger, like a little girl. Meryem watched in silence. Murat already had spoken to his mother about what he discovered and she handled the news like she expected it.

Murat now understood why his mother tried to stop him from getting close to Ella. Tried to make her want to run home, using fear. So that the truth remained buried in the ground with his *Baba*. But they'd all learned truth had a way of finding its way through the hard-packed ground into the blue.

Meryem stepped forward, embracing both. Kissing each of their cheeks. Stroking their heads as if they were both small children needing the comfort of a mother.

"Are you well?" Worry lines marked Meryem's face as she looked from Ella to Murat, checking for cracks she might fill.

"We will be," Ella offered.

Murat sensed God's Spirit quieting them in the subdued evening, singing His comfort over them.

"I will tell you a story of when I was little child," Meryem said. Maybe to fill in the quiet like a dam leaking and plugged with rags to hold back a rush of water.

Murat listened, moving his gaze between his mom and Ella. He wondered if Ella could truly love him, despite everything. If her love might pull away, like the early morning tide, the shoreline exposing the water's presence with the wreckage left behind.

Not so with You, Lord. Your love is complete and perfect. Even in Your dying You forgave—extended to the enemies who nailed Your hands against unforgiving wood. Even then You still loved. Help us to love like You.

Meryem broke the quiet: "It was when I was twelve years old, so big in my eyes and full of myself. My *Anne* and *Baba* worked very, very hard at their pottery shop in Mersin, many day keep their doors open to midnight during tourist time. They so tired,

I remember noticing even then. They loved me. I was everything for them. No boy for keep the family name. My *Anne* was not able to have more children, because some woman's problem. So it was just us. *Baba* taught us how making the pottery, cook it so it make hard, and paint it. The pottery not need white paint because it had white already. Then with tiny black shape we paint, then fill in with blue. The blue small colors my *Anne* did most this. See?"

Meryem stood and walked to the small window above the kitchen sink, grabbing a potted plant. The trailing vine nestled in a globe-shaped pot, beautifully hand painted.

"I make this with my *Anne*."

Ella leaned in to examine the decorations filled in carefully with the cobalt blue, almost mosaic-like.

"I love it," Ella said.

Murat swallowed his tears seeing the red rimming Ella's eyes. *Help me, Lord. Help her.*

"Is especially beautiful because of my mom teach me. Make with me. I see her hand in this and *Baba*'s. So, my *Baba* decide we take family vacation, one whole week at sea. We can even stay in a hotel at *Kizkalesi*. It was years since we visit there. This was dream place because of the castle sitting out in the water. I remember get there and running around the hotel, up and down the stairs to beach, then back again. My parents laugh because they being happy to see me so happy, I think. The second day we were there, we decide take a small boat out to castle. It take a long time to get there, but we do it. I had some . . . "

At this point Meryem leaned in and asked Murat the word for "goggles." Murat whispered the answer.

Meryem began again. "Yes, I had some goggles. The water was calm so I was lay on my stomach and float, like *pide* bread, and look at the bottom of the ocean. It was not very deep there right near castle. I think it was long time ago small island, but now all land is under water so . . . I saw urchins. Black urchins. Really still and sharp. I dive and pick one off bottom. But it cut my finger little bit. I was mad because I want to look at it really close, you know? My *Baba*, he come near me and then asked what I did. He was float

just near me. I tell him about the urchin and that I want to hold it. He said that if I just grab it fast without think much, I will cut my hand many time. But if I be careful, good girl and put my hand under urchin, it sit quiet for me to look at and enjoy." She spread her hand up, flat, as if in worship.

Murat wished he remembered his grandparents, but like so much else, their faces were foggy, like bodies with smudged, erased heads.

"I was just think today about *Baba's* words. Maybe God wants us hold things we love more careful and not so tight. Maybe don't grab fast because of being scared. Wait for God's voice, then gentle take when time is right with soft hand. Is a better way, I think."

Murat considered his mom's message. That he held everything, especially Ella, too close, rather than clinging first to God. That had not worked.

No, only God's love held a person up, an almost invisible foundation, like a castle on the horizon surrounded with only ocean blue filling in the spaces as far as the eye can see. No more floating and bobbing along wherever the angry waves might choose.

I stared up at the minute cracks spreading here and there on the ceiling, like a roadmap. Only the roads all led in different directions and went nowhere.

The sun rose enough to allow a slant of light below the large window perched above my desk. The room hushed me with its dusty gray. Almost sad, like it waited for the full rays of the sun to break over that horizon, filling the space with smooth, yellow hope.

So much happened in a few days. I wished things might pause to process through it more. Or maybe not. It already hurt so much.

My thoughts screamed at me, though the room remained quiet. The image of Murat's father, slinking beneath the moonlight, planning and preparing for that moment . . . the following

morning his hand ended my father's life . . . made forgiveness a toy, snatched away by a mysterious child's hand.

When I pictured Murat's dad, I envisioned Murat himself. Though unfair, the connection couldn't be erased and glittered razor sharp. Blaming someone living rather than someone who never understood what his actions did to my life, forced Murat forward as the scapegoat.

I meant what I told Murat yesterday. But now, doubt seeped in like acid, gagging the song of a new beginning.

I squeezed my eyes shut against the stinging, the old ache pulled down warm tears toward my pillow.

Lord, take this pain away. It feels like I'm losing Dad all over again. ⚬

65 MERYEM'S HOME

"*Anne*?" Murat spoke to his mother's back. Meryem wore her usual outfit, bright, floral, loose harem-type pants with a T-shirt on top, and plastic sandals on dusty feet. Her hair, dark and straight, pulled back in a white head-scarf, peeked out the back.

"Son." Meryem turned, then leaned in to kiss her boy on both cheeks. "Did you sleep?"

Murat didn't miss the fact she hadn't asked "if he slept well," just whether he slept at all.

"Yes, a little." The pain of seeing Ella's face with a look of betrayal swam through the tears forming in his eyes. "Where are the little ones?" He cleared his throat and blinked the evidence of sadness away, not wanting to worry his mother further. Besides, he'd cried enough.

"Oh, outside. I needed them to give me some quiet. Yell, yell, yell. That's all they do. So, they are outside kicking the ball around."

"Good idea."

Before five a.m., Murat heard the loud "whispers" of his siblings and shushed them to be quiet. Exhaustion blanketed him. And his mother too. He knew how she prayed for him. And cried. Her muffled weeping nearly broke his heart in two. Now he understood her tears better.

She was a strong woman—maybe the strongest he knew. But some things couldn't be controlled inside. The tears freed a little of the pain somehow.

"I think I'll join them. Do you need help with these?" Murat pointed to the rest of the dishes on the counter.

"No, no." Meryem waved him off. "You go."

"Call if you need me."

Meryem turned to her son and blinked her eyes. She nodded her head, offering only a sad smile.

Murat turned quietly, but said before stepping outside, "He works everything together for good for those who love him and are

called according to His purpose . . . . In all these things we are more than conquerors. For I am convinced . . . " The last verse dangled.

Anne knew nothing could separate them from the love of God. She taught him those words from the Bible when forgiveness—sand tossed into the wind—seemed unattainable. She anchored him, helping him not to float out away from life to never return.

For I am convinced that neither death nor life, neither angels nor demons, neither the present nor the future, nor any powers, neither height nor depth, nor anything else in all creation, will be able to separate us from the love of God that is in Christ Jesus our Lord.

Not even the unthinkable—of carrying the blood of another man on his hands. At that, Murat stepped into the sunshine, the humid, salt air turning his skin instantly sticky.

To the Lord he added out loud, "I believe you. But I don't know how you'll work even this for good." ❧

66 THE LETTER

I tore open the letter with Mom's neat script and name in the top left corner. *Took you long enough to respond, Mom.*

I knew well enough how long mail took to get to and from the U.S. I emailed her three weeks prior telling her all I discovered.

She only responded with, "I put a letter in the mail. It doesn't feel right responding on the computer."

Her letter began without preamble.

> *"I'm finally telling you the truth. That's what I'm doing. I'm so sorry. I knew. I've known for a long time now. You see . . . I did some research of my own after your daddy's death and found out who they deemed responsible.*
>
> *I searched the Turkish newspaper, then turned to Koray for help, because I was so angry I needed a place to lay my hurt. I didn't just find out about Murat's father, Ella. I found out about Meryem and Murat, too. It didn't take long to feel burdened by their situation. I learned of the orphanage and what they did for battered women and I asked if maybe there could be a place for them."*

I swallowed over and over again, the letter shaking in my hands.

The obvious became clear. *This job was no divine appointment stumbled on by mom.*

I read the next lines thinking my heart might just burst and then I'd burst too. Then I'd be gone and the pain would be gone. Finally.

> *"I might have been wrong not telling you so many years ago. I've wondered that every day since I made contact with Meryem. I feared your little heart*

couldn't handle it. Every time your father was even mentioned by friends or family you ran to your room and sobbed. I thought if I told you it was just an accident, you wouldn't have to carry the weight of fear along with everything else.

How on earth do you tell a little girl someone intentionally killed her daddy? And for what? For nothing except to make some sort of horrendous point that we were the bad guys.

And more than that, how could I tell you I helped the family responsible? Even now I cannot imagine saying such a thing.

What if you found out as a little girl at a time when the grief of losing your dad nearly crippled you? Do you think you could have taken the truth, Ella?"

Was any person as they appeared? Could anyone be trusted to lay the truth out like grapes in the sunshine allowing them to sweeten over time? Rather than all this rotten hiding and mystery? No, that only produced one thing: pain.

"Ella, I'm so very sorry. I wanted to protect your heart. I don't pretend to think I've been perfect in this. I was totally unprepared to explain it all to you. I wasn't even prepared to handle it myself.

Please forgive me for hurting you. You must know by now your job was set up with hopes you might discover truth for yourself. I saw the discontentment, the not really living.

I thought this would allow you to start new. I hope I wasn't wrong. I have to tell you that Meryem was against it. She felt that you and Murat had been through too much already. That he might not recover should he learn the truth. You see, he didn't know any more than you did. He is a victim too, Ella. Remember that.

Meryem thought I needed to let things be and was very upset that I arranged for this whole thing. However, despite my earlier struggles, I knew it was time. At least for you, Ella."

Her words swirled like water through my mind. Was she wrong? What could a mother do, but try her best to love and protect her baby girl?

I knew my flaws. My tendency to make a complete mess of my life. To trade in mercy, forgiveness, and peace for resentment and hate.

I whispered into the quiet of my room. "I do forgive you, Mom."

The whole thing tangled, like seaweed wrapped tightly around a delicate shell. Pulling the feelings apart would be tedious and messy, and might even crush altogether the thin, white hull. ❧

67 THE FOYER

Sitting with Çiğdem planted happily on my lap in the cozy foyer of June and Barry's home softened the weighty ache in my chest.

Gray and heavy.

Working with the kids brought me joy, partly because of loving the process of teaching and watching the dawning of understanding. It also took my mind off all the disjointed imperfection of my life. Extending myself to the kids aided in the release of old hurts. Like releasing black crows into the sky in exchange for green.

Umut walked over, with the usual thumb plug in his mouth and reached for my hair, rubbing a curl between his small fingers. I smiled at him and extended one of the apples I brought to share with the kids, for bribery.

"Remember what you say, Umut?"

He nodded, unplugged, and made a smacking noise as the suction released, "I have it?"

"May I have it?" I corrected gently.

He grabbed the apple, then handed it back to me and giggled, the whole exercise clearly a big joke.

"You say it, Umut."

"May I have it?" He grinned at me.

"Yes, you may." I laughed then handed the apple to him and he shoved the fruit against his teeth and bit into it.

I wrapped up my teaching time with a song and prayer, then sent the children off to their respective homes. Murat stepped into the room.

Barely meeting my gaze, he said, "I just wanted to check on you."

To hide the pain Murat brought just being near me, I turned away, trying to keep myself busy. "It was a good day."

I glanced up quickly, then inspected my stack of drawing paper and crayons leaning to one side. Since finding out, Murat checked on me every day.

So humble and vulnerable.

Murat leaned in to gather the supplies spread throughout the space. "No," I brushed his hand aside, "I can do it." I had so far to go regarding my tangled feelings for Murat.

"Can I take you for *İskender* tonight?" Murat squinted at me all tentative.

"Um, no not tonight." I couldn't spend a whole evening alone looking at his face, trying to hide the brewing fear, anger, confusion, all of it. I pressed the stack to my chest trying to steady my hands. The shaking ushered from the depths of myself. Somewhere I couldn't reach or deal with.

Seeing Murat's concerned look, I touched the edge of his sleeve. "Maybe next weekend? I planned to go to Pinar's tonight and help there." The last part I added to ease my conscience.

I told him his father's involvement in my dad's death was not his fault, that I still wanted a relationship. Now I harbored such an urge to run and just get away from him. Was I fooling myself? All the anger and feelings of betrayal needed a place to land. Somehow, Murat in his need to take care of everything, was the easiest target.

"*Tamam.*" Murat spoke quietly, a load of defeat rested on such a small word. "Good-bye, Ella."

I watched his back, shoulders lowered, hands shoved deep into his pockets. *Lord. I need you to do something, because I'm messing this all up.*

I picked up the rest of my materials and headed to my room. ❧

68 ELLA'S ROOM

I need to be alone. Stepping into the silence of my room gave the ache space to breathe, almost come alive in my chest, pressing and clawing for release.

Kneeling in the center of the boxy space, the rough Turkish rug supplied by June, pressed into my knees, and I prayed. Never before had I dumped my heart out so completely and ended up facedown, sobs filling the quiet, begging Jesus to cut the pain out like surgery.

The daylight slipped away. When I looked up, the darkened room held the orange glow of a harvest moon melting through the window. A knock on the door startled me.

I stood, unsteady and worn out. Without even thinking about checking my appearance, I opened the door. I blinked against the light of the hallway, Murat's figure a dark silhouette against the brightness.

"Murat. Hello. I was just . . ."

How could I explain what I was doing? *Crying my eyes out, praying prostrate in the middle of the floor, begging God to help me not blame you for everything?*

"Did I wake you? Is only 9:00."

"You know, you keep asking me that." The small smile forming felt good. The chipping of an iceberg, cracking away from the depths of its frozen stronghold.

Murat's face looked so sad and serious. He rubbed his thumb beside my eye, his touch warming my face. I wrapped my hands around the back of his neck, the tears flowed again.

When would I ever compose myself again? As if I had no control at all. And did I ever, really? Still, these tears were different, like a relinquishing of demons, like a releasing. I prayed I didn't set my cages out to recapture them.

I allowed my hands to press against the back of Murat's neck and move up into his hair. I wanted to soak up the warmth there.

I wanted to be close to him, almost frantic thinking how I tried to sabotage the bond. Trying to lose someone I loved—adding him to my victim's list.

Murat's rough cheek pressed against mine, and he managed to utter, "What's going on, Ella?"

I released a tight breath, then quickly stepped back. "I don't know." I dropped my hands to my sides. "One minute I'm crying and praying, the next I'm hopeful and holding on to you."

Murat stood still, waiting.

"I'm trying hard to remember about forgiveness. And to remember about where my peace comes from. But I'm so up and down."

Again Murat only waited. This time his knowing nod affirmed he experienced the same turbulence.

"I spent tonight praying." My cheeks reddened, realizing I never went to help Pinar and felt foolish for the lie. "I'm sorry I didn't tell you the truth earlier about helping Pinar. I did plan to go after I said it . . . "

Murat shook his head, like it didn't matter at all.

"I'm fine. At least for the next five minutes."

Murat squeezed my hand. "Good night then, Ella."

"Good night." I went from resisting him to wanting to draw him close, the distance now a frigid breeze off the sea. ✎

69 IZMIR, 2008

Winter brought rain and somehow with the rain, a slow eroding away of a rocky coastline of hurt. Murat became a new person, strength defined him. He stopped trying to be all things to all people.

Mustafa healed too and returned to his home, to running the bread shop. Barry's news filtered in with few victories marking his time away. The doctors removed a tumor leaving him blind in one eye. The loss seemed symbolic—like severed vision for the future of the orphanage, too.

June's letters pretended all was going as well. However, fissures of worry marked her words, slanted her sentences, keeping them short and factual. I walked the path to Meryem's house and poked my head in.

"Murat?"

A blue-orange flame danced beneath a large pot of something. The place smelled like memories. Meryem shuffled in holding one of her little boys whose head snuggled on her shoulder.

"Ella, *canim*." With the term of endearment, she leaned in and kissed my cheeks. "Murat is work on the van."

I stepped toward her little one. "Is he feeling okay?"

"No, he has hot head." She pressed her free hand to his red cheek.

"Poor little guy." I rubbed my fingers through his hair.

"Is cold wet weather to do this."

I tugged my jacket around me feeling cold with the mere mention of the rain. Non-stop for a week nearly made me, and the squirmy kids in my morning class, want to pack up and move to the dry eastern Anatolia region.

"Do you need me to get him some medicine? I have to go out anyway. I wanted to let Murat know."

"Yes. Is good for him. Medicine for the hot and the cough."

I left the house, walking around the side to where the van sat like a squatting dog. Murat's legs stuck out from underneath. I

must have been distracted on my way in, walking right by him. I kneeled and tipped my head upside down, my hair swinging in a tangled drape. "Hi there."

Murat grinned with a smear of grease across his chin. "Ella." He said my name with such gentleness I nearly melted into a blob.

"The kids drew cards for Barry. We talked about all of his favorite things. I wanted to head out and buy Barry's treats today so I could send a package soon. It takes so long for anything to make it back to the States."

"*Tamam.* I need a break. This van is old and tired and needs a nap." He chuckled at his joke. "I'll clean myself and come get you."

"Good. I need to drop by and check on Pinar anyway."

"*Tamam.*" His face tipped to the side to see me better.

I avoided checking him out fully. *Nobody likes a pervert.*

Murat showed up later looking like a man ready for a date wearing dark jeans, a fitted, button-down shirt, and dark gray blazer. I cleared my throat since it seemed an entire flock of birds roosted there. When I tried to talk, I only squawked a little. "You look beautiful," I said before the birds stopped me.

He laughed, low and manly. "This is good?"

"Definitely." My face burned a little. I pretended the exchange left me unfazed. Murat's cologne drifted in my direction as we walked through the orphanage's front gate and stepped out onto the subdued street. The sun sat like a fat genie on the horizon. Murat strolled, casual and slow, toward the main part of town.

"Is okay to walk?"

I nodded. The birds were back.

"You're not cold?"

I shook my head apparently unable to answer basic questions.

"Oh." *Thank you, Jesus, for an assignment.* "Your mom needs medicine for Adem."

"Hmm." His voice buzzed and rumbled in my chest. "This store up there will have medicine."

"Good."

Again silence. An actual flock of birds swooped in, landing on a sagging phone line and watched me like a jury. *Great. I can't*

escape them. I resisted the urge to peg one with a rock and send the group of judgers on their way. Besides, I saw the movie *The Birds* and knew what happened.

"Maybe we can get a coffee first."

I managed to nod again, wondering if Murat liked the quieter version of me. All talk of romance stalled after the revelation about Murat's dad two million years ago.

But things changed in me. I wanted to reach for Murat's hand, or ask him to marry me—whichever came first. Only I knew he held back out of respect—probably thinking such a thing could never be. So I shooed that possibility away, too.

Murat allowed me to enter a dimly lit coffee shop ahead of him. He pulled out a chair. I sat and ran my hands flat across the white clothed table.

"Can you tell me what's in these?" I pointed at the list of options on the menu, dropped off by a grinning waiter.

He pulled his chair closer to mine and pointed. "This one, *salep*, is thick milk. Is hot with cinnamon. Or you can have this one, with some milk, coffee and Baileys. Is good too." I chose the latter, needing to loosen up a bit.

After ordering for both of us, Murat said, "Barry is not good."

"No." The truth couldn't be smoothed out with extra words.

Murat embraced my hand under both of his on the table. I knew it was for comfort only. But still, the act made my heart race.

"What will happen to the orphanage if something happens to him, Murat?" Two months ago I wouldn't have dared voice the question knowing Murat would move heaven and earth to solve that problem. It felt nice to air my worries without adding to them because of his savior complex kicking in.

His answer assured me he stayed on solid ground away from lakes and trying to walk on water. "I don't know this, Ella."

The drinks arrived. I let go of Murat's hands and wrapped my own around the thick, white porcelain mug. Sweet foam topped the coffee. I soaked in the warmth from the cup and inhaled the malty, caramel flavor from the Baileys. I sipped the vanilla sweet liquid,

the drink going down a little too easy. When the aftertaste kicked my butt, I set it on the table.

"This is good," I said all profound and deep.

"Yes. Is my favorite." Murat took a drink wetting his upper lip with foam. I leaned in and wiped it with my thumb, then snatched my hand back when he stared at me not saying anything.

"Sorry."

We finished our drinks, sufficiently warmed up, and stepped out into the cooling evening. I listened for the ocean, but only heard traffic.

After several stops we headed home with the needed supplies. Medicine for Adem and all sorts of goodies for Barry. Çay cups and saucers, lemon cologne, Turkish delight, and strong coffee.

"Would it be too much trouble to walk over to the beach and get some sand?"

"Sure. Is no trouble." We walked several blocks to the boardwalk lining the beach. I knelt, suddenly wondering what to put the sand in.

I looked over at Murat. He already found an empty, glass Coca-Cola bottle and walked over to the ink-black water.

He rinsed the embossed, fluted bottle, then moved toward me, his outline silhouetted against the slate-blue sky.

What do I say? What do I say?

I wanted to grab him and kiss him and tell him things like fathers murdering fathers shouldn't stand between two people in love. But that would make me forward.

What if he saw no way for us? Then the awkwardness would return. So I said the next logical thing. "Thanks for the bottle."

We ambled back to the orphanage, our hands holding bags with tea cups and sand in bottles. And a little regret. Everything, but each other. ✤

70 THE MEETING

I called a meeting with the mothers at the orphanage. With Murat. *What else can I do, but tell them?* The email came in the middle of the night after a doctor's appointment stateside.

Everyone sat, tight and sober in the front entry of the house. I cleared my throat for too long. *They know.* I could see from their expressions.

"I received news from June."

Quiet hung sober in the muggy air.

"The doctor said Barry might not be able to return to Izmir. His cancer has advanced. He might need ongoing treatment if he doesn't . . ." I studied Murat hoping to soak up strength. His pale face and wet eyes caused pain to fill my throat. *I can't do this.*

"If the treatments even work," I revised.

Murat leaned forward from his place on the floor, running his hands over the Turkish rug, tracing the pattern. "We cannot let this place close, even if Barry does not return. We need to pray for a new person to come if that happens."

All the women nodded and glanced around. Meryem spoke up, "Will June come back to orphanage if Barry does not?"

"I don't know. She didn't say. I think they're just figuring things out, one step at a time."

Pinar rocked lightly beside me, so small it could be missed. I recognized that body posture. I hoped it didn't exist anymore—but new beginnings were fragile as a robin's delicate egg shell. And sometimes old habits were hard to break.

I reached over and touched her hand, steadying the movement. I spoke with conviction, even though I was ready to join Pinar. "Barry and June wouldn't want everything they started to end. This is God's work which goes on and on. It can't be stopped because bodies are sick or things are hard." The warmth of Pinar's hand soaked into mine. Osmosis of shared strength. Or maybe weakness. Either way, having her near made me stronger. ❧

71 THE ORPHANAGE

Time filtered by, like light through glass. Moments of dull and shiny bright, flickering one after the other. Somehow we managed to survive the winter and the spring. Like a book tossed on the beach, the wind lifting the pages and rushing to the end, we stepped into the summer, hoping for new answers.

The fifteenth of June arrived with hot, salty wind. An influx of gulls reminded me that like so many things, the school year was ending. With the older kids out of school, the schedule would be different.

I wondered what it would feel like having tweens and teens join in my daily meetings with the children. June mentioned the idea in one of her emails, to include them so they practiced their conversation skills throughout the break.

With so many different age levels, I still hadn't figured out how to make the class work. I lifted my box of materials and headed to my room to drop them off, when Murat walked toward me.

"*Merhaba.*" He leaned in to kiss both of my cheeks, then lifted the load from my hands.

"*Merhaba.*" I rubbed my sweaty palms on the sides of my jeans while walking beside Murat.

"Here's my idea," Murat said. "Maybe I help you with your class this summer. I was thinking it might be difficult to teach the old and young together. Maybe I can help."

The wind lifted the loose tendrils of my hair in one big gust as I opened the front door of the house and stepped inside. The open windows and open front door created a tunnel of warm, sticky air.

"Could you?" I peered at Murat. "I'd love your help. I was just wondering how I'd work it out."

"*Evet.* Yes. I can help. I already talked to Mustafa. He said I can work early, because I don't need to take the kids to school. Then I'll be at the new teaching time for the summer. I can come for class. *Sorun değil.* No problem."

I smiled at the very Turkish "no problem," then touched Murat's arm. "That would be wonderful, thank you for asking."

Murat's expression took on a mischievous grin. "So, I need to plan with the teacher. Is important, yes?"

"Hmm . . . I think I'll just plan myself and then tell you about it."

"No. This isn't the best way. I will come with fresh cigarette *börek* and Coca Cola. This will help us think."

"Oooh. I forgot all about *börek*. That's phyllo dough stuffed with feta?"

He nodded, lifting his eyebrows. Clearly he knew I wouldn't say no.

"So you're bribing me? That's not very nice, Murat." I raised an eyebrow. "If you promise to focus, we'll try it out. I usually plan for the following week on Friday evening."

"*Tamam*. I will come then on Friday?"

"Friday it is."

"No problem." Murat looked as though he just won a prize.

"But first, Murat. Will you take me to buy a rug?"

Murat hesitated. "Yes, but why?"

"Well, I've always wanted to pick one out that suits me just right. It might seem strange to you. I think each rug tells a story and has a personality of its own. I have some savings and think I'm ready to go look. I know a great rug dude, you know." I grinned at Murat.

"You do? Okay then, Turkish woman, I will take you today to buy this rug. Good?"

"Good. I'll just run and grab my things." ✎

7 2 THE RUG SHOP

"The alley, right?" Murat smiled over at me from the driver's seat.

"Right."

Murat navigated like a bull on the narrow streets of Pamplona, practically elbowing and shoving the other drivers aside.

I sighed, closed my eyes, and imagined being read my last rites.

We arrived alive at Nergiz's old rug shop, the one where I spent countless Saturday afternoons with my parents, talking, drinking *çay,* and watching as the young helper rolled out rug after rug. We entered the shop. The smell of moth balls and the darkness of the windowless room created a cool cove away from the street's dust and heat.

The young man I met almost a year prior greeted us. Again I noticed the resemblance he bore to Nergiz. His years of service as a little boy rolling rugs out one after the other, faithful nephew to the older man, paid off. The shop would most likely pass to another faithful family member one day.

"*Merhaba. Nasilsinez.*"

"*Eyem. Sen nasilsin?*" I responded with an "I'm well, how are you?"

"*Iyi. Iyi.*"

Murat shook the gentleman's hand and stepped back giving me the lead.

As if seeing the deference Murat gave, the man turned and asked, "How can I help you, *Madame?*"

"Yes. I don't know if you remember me. I visited about a year ago. I knew Nergiz. My mother and father used to come here when I was little and I remember you rolling out the rugs for him."

I wanted to establish the long history to make a connection, hoping to get the best deal on the rug I wanted to buy. There was a reason the street was called "Rip Off Alley" by the Americans. An inexperienced buyer would not get the deals an insider received.

"Yes, I remember this now." The man offered a friendly grin, his teeth bright white against his tanned skin. "Welcome back to Nergiz's rug shop. I am Yusuf. Your name is . . . I forget."

"I'm Ella and this is Murat."

"Welcome." The man repeated, clearly comfortable with his role as salesman. "How can I help you?"

"I thought it would be nice to look at some of your rugs."

"Great. We will do it. Would you like to sit?" Yusuf signaled to a worn wooden, backless bench lining the far wall.

"Yes, thanks." Since entering the shop, Murat hadn't said a word. I figured he wanted to give me space to shop.

Yusuf leaned out of the open front door and whistled.

"Why are you being strange?" I asked Murat.

He shook his head looking ticked off before he said, "He looked at your hand."

"What do you mean?"

"Your hand. For a wedding ring." Murat's face resembled a small boy not getting his way.

"What? How did you notice that?"

At that very moment, Yusuf stepped back in and began his age-old routine of rolling out rugs, listening for the detail the customer liked, then matching it in another rug with more of the colors or patterns sought. Feeling slightly tense about Murat's antagonistic silence, I overcompensated with conversation.

A young boy entered carrying *çay* cups on a copper platter. *Thank God.*

"Ahh, help yourself, please." Yusuf urged us to serve ourselves before continuing with the parade of bright-colored rugs.

I leaned over to touch the tight-patterned piece he rolled out and asked, "Is this machine made?"

"No, is made by my friend, Ibrahim. He makes rugs for fifty years. Very beautiful. This is called *Uşak kilim.*"

I fell in love, kneeling down to run my fingers over the smooth surface. The rug looked like art—an ancient Roman tiled floor, scrolled designs framing the larger emblems in the center, knotted expertly together. Being handmade and a larger, room-sized

piece, I doubted I could afford it. The soft azure against sand-colored caramel reminded me of our visits to the Mediterranean—at times the ocean swallowing up the solid ground.

This is the rug.

In a tentative voice, trying hard not to appear too eager, I ventured, "How much?"

And the negotiating back and forth began. Still the price remained out of my range. Yusuf hit his rock bottom price, and I stood to go, trying not to behave like a spoiled child. "*Teşekkür ederim.* Thank you. You've been very kind."

"Please." The man stepped forward to make one last offer.

I shook my head 'no.'

Yusuf added, "This good price."

"Yes. It's a good price. But I can't afford it. Thank you so much for your time."

With a sigh, Murat stepped forward and began speaking to the man in Turkish. I couldn't follow their fast-paced conversation, though a few numbers dotted the back and forth.

Murat stuck out his hand and shook the store owner's, a grin on the faces of both men. Then Yusuf rolled up the rug in question into a tight coil, and tied it in place with burlap thread.

Murat leaned in to my ear and said, "*Madame*, you have a rug. He said he'll sell it to you for half the last price."

I threw my arms around his neck, planting a kiss on his cheek. "But how? How did you convince him?"

"I told him you have many American friends who will want to come to his store to buy rugs, if he gives you a good deal."

"How did you know what I could afford?"

"I didn't. I just know what *I* can afford."

"Say what?"

"This is my gift to you, Ella."

"No. You can't. It's too much. This was my idea. I've been planning this. I'd never have asked had I known you'd . . . "

"Please. I want to. It would make me happy. Please say this is okay." Murat held both of my hands as if proposing, his brow pushed together with pleading.

How can I say 'yes?'

Even at half the price of the man's lowest number, the gift cost Murat hundreds of dollars. But before I could say anything else Murat hefted the rug roll on his shoulder and carried it out of the store, loading it into the back of the van.

Yusuf shook my hand, clearly happy with the sale and the prospects it brought. "Enjoy this rug, *Madame*. It will make nice in your home once you get married. This man has much love for you to buy this."

The whole transaction blurred in the end. Somehow I found myself in the front of the van. Murat pulled in front of a car onto the dusty road. The man he cut off honked. Murat extended his arm out of the driver's side window.

A salty breeze whipped my hair around and tickled my face. I didn't mind. Somehow the rug felt like a promise of a future together.

Perhaps Yusuf was right. I let myself hope. *Maybe one day this beautiful carpet will grace the floor of our home.* &

73 THE BEACH

To celebrate the end of the school year, Meryem and I planned a picnic on the beach with all the families. Each housemother prepared a basket full of cheese, bread, olives, *börek*, and sliced tomatoes. Cherry juice in box cartons were packed. As a treat, I purchased baklava at a local *pastanesi*.

Meryem laid on her side looking very much like an ancient Greek woman with her beaded head-scarf and billowy pants. Feeling uncomfortable sporting a bathing suit around the teenage boys who'd soon be my students, I dressed in my favorite white blouse and flowy. Underneath I wore my plain black Speedo, in case I was convinced to take a swim.

To avoid kicking sand into the feast, Murat played ball with the boys further up the beach. Popping an olive into her mouth, Pinar smiled as she squinted into the sun sinking below the line of dark blue water.

"You look happy," I commented in Turkish.

"I am, Ella. I really am." Pinar's smile shone vibrant against her reddened face.

Umut squealed as he dug in the sand and covered his legs.

"You like him, yes?" Pinar grinned at me.

"Yes, I really do."

Pinar acted momentarily confused seeing me watching her son, then said a little too loudly, "No, Murat. You like Murat."

Heat pricked at my face. And not just from the intense sun. I looked at Pinar who laughed out loud, clearly amused she figured things out.

"What?" I glanced around, realizing all the women sat still, all ears perked forward like cats. Meryem sat amongst them. She smiled as she gave me a sidelong look and tore off bread with her teeth. Then she looked toward Murat who never looked so good.

His skin almost glowed in the sunshine. His powerful legs, those of a Greek god, sprinted across the sand. Sweat made his face and

arms look glossy. He blended into the landscape while at the same time defining it.

Nope, I don't like him at all.

"Pinar. I will not answer that question." Pinar looked as though she held back a flood of laughter. In a moment the entire group of women exploded with cackles, making the content of the discussion clear to any person who might wander by.

Just then Murat jogged in, out of breath, with a small smile touching the corners of his eyes. He panted as he asked in Turkish for a drink of *vişne suyu.* Then he scanned the circle of women, shook his head, wiped his cherry-red, stained lips with the back of his arm, turned and dashed off toward the waiting little boys.

I let out a too-loud breath which only served to bring on another round of obnoxious laughter. I stood, nodded at the group, and walked toward Çiğdem who dug in the sand closer to the shoreline. I knelt beside the girl. The soft sand gave way beneath me.

"What are you doing?"

Çiğdem squinted up, a look of concentration on her face. "I make house. See?" She pointed a damp, sand-coated hand to the first "building," which was in fact just a pile of sand.

"May I help?" I waited a moment, even though I knew what her answer would be.

"*Evet.* Yes. Help."

I ran back to the pile of women and grabbed the plastic tub that held the drinks. Now empty, the container made a perfect base on which to build.

"Here." I pulled the tub to the water line, the tide rinsing over my feet then retreating, making me feel as though it beckoned me to come in and soak. I tucked the saturated hem of my skirt, now caked with sand, into my waistband giving the appearance of wearing Turkish *şalvar* pants.

Filling the tub halfway, I dragged it back. Seeing my plan, Çiğdem shoveled in the sand with the Frisbee she used to clear the area for her masterpiece. Soon we finished packing the tub with

the damp sand, and several of the other kids joined us. Murat approached, too, having lost his team to the activity.

"Can I help you?" Murat smiled as he leaned down to turn the tub on its side before flopping it over, then pulling it up gently. The result brought a collective gasp of excitement from the kids. A moment later each child dug out roadways and small doors and windows. I watched as Murat sat back and took it all in, a blush of sunburn touching his nose and cheeks.

One child carved a face in the side of the building. "Who is this?" I pointed.

"Atatürk," the boy said with a proud grin, then leaned in to add a scratched out frame.

"Oh, good. That's important." I smiled, ruffling my fingers through the boy's curly, black hair. I knew all about the revered former President of Turkey. The people saw him as the one to transform their country into a nation of which they could be proud. He believed in separation of church and state and modernized the landscape of their nation, making it a contender in the international community.

I glanced up and caught Murat watching me. He nodded his head and blinked his eyes, showing me he approved of my reaction.

He smiled, then asked, "So what were the women talking about today, hmm?"

I couldn't help but grin back. "That, sir, is none of your business." I stared at the hoard of women, wondering if they were commentating on our interaction.

Instead the scene proved to be comical: eight women, mostly quite round, lying flat on their backs in the sand, brown feet pointing straight up to the sunshine, a quilt of floral pants, brown skin, and white beaded head-scarves against rosy, pink cheeks, each face split in the middle by a smile. ❧

74 IZMIR, 1990

Always gruff, all sharp edges—Ali. Life had cut away all the soft parts, leaving only angles, no smooth curves any longer. Meryem tightened her black head-scarf that managed to slip too-low on her hair.

Ali wouldn't approve.

He agreed to her wearing only the lighter covering when she worked at home. However, standing on the roof hanging laundry, possibly in view of passers-by, might press his patience. Still, the noonday heat required it.

She snapped Murat's small shirt in the wind, then pressed it to her nose. Such a kind boy, her son. He lifted her spirits like nobody else had the power to do. Perhaps why Ali took him away so often.

Another punishment.

School let out weeks ago, and so far every day, they were gone, leaving her alone to wonder and wait. The wind angling off the ocean loosened the knots in her chest.

The *Öğle,* the noonday call to prayer, radiated like waves pressing in, overlapping. *"Allahu ekber."* She gazed out over the apartments, seeing the minarets jutting in a scatter to the west.

And the sound reminded her of Murat's face this very morning, full of turmoil. She tried to let him know he needn't choose sides. Her love held no conditions, unlike his father's.

Meryem leaned in and touched his small nose, still baby-like at age eight. "You are my gift, son. Go, have time with your father. I will be busy here with laundry and cleaning, anyway."

Looking unsure, he hugged her around the middle, her heart a ball of love and anguish. *What do you do all day, husband? Especially now with my son?*

The powerlessness gripped her, filled her chest with such a weight it threatened to knock her over. Whenever Meryem asked, Ali only yelled that it didn't concern her and wasn't it a father's right to train his son?

Privately when she pressed Murat for answers, he said they worked on cars. His father taught him to fix them, hook things together the right way.

Then why did the knowledge bring no comfort?

Perhaps there was selfishness in her, after all. Perhaps she hated her son to love his Dad, because his dad had no love for her. Or maybe she needed Murat all to herself, because he was the best thing in her dreary life.

Her days sagged in mute existence. How many chores does a woman who lives mostly alone have? No, she spent so many days looking out over the city, all glittery against the sea, pretending to be someone else.

Despite the inconsistent income, Ali insisted Meryem not work as she had before. With Izmir Air Force Base so near, Americans always needed maids. She could easily find a job, but she stayed home instead. Once Murat was born, Ali took that escape from her.

The man made no sense. It all boiled down to pride. She knew if she brought in more income than her husband, her face would be the receiving end of that shame.

Meryem rubbed a damp hand across the back of her neck. *So hot.* Out on the rooftop the sun bounced and radiated like an incubator.

But that's what made it the perfect spot for drying clothes. Perhaps the perfect spot for a woman needing to air out her sorrows, too. ∽

75 IZMIR, 2008

The summer, a swift ocean breeze, moved past them quickly. The new school year started in two weeks. Murat welcomed it, even while begrudging the loss of his teaching time with Ella. They made a good team. Murat felt the first stirrings of knowing God's purpose for his life besides bread maker and van driver.

Murat sensed some sort of social work lay in his future—his life connected him to the hurt in a way that many would never hope to boast of. The key of forgiveness unlocked his heart to the possibility.

Forgiving his father. But more than that, forgiving himself.

The change was so freeing—all the truth laid out in the sun and washed clean. Until that day, he hadn't known the peace that went deep down, shaken into the space he didn't realize existed.

Things with Ella would never be what he hoped. That remained a hook that didn't fully come free. Some things were just too complicated. Their friendship remained. Murat knew a future together was a dream he had to release as well. And he tried. Still, the pain lingered knowing they'd never be together in the way he wanted.

Instead, Murat determined to focus on preparing for a different future. He needed to talk to Mustafa. It would be difficult, but necessary. With the training he needed to begin, there was little time to make bread.

Murat stepped into *Ekmek Fabrikasi*, the place so familiar it felt like home. His heart picked up its pace. A physical pain radiated through his chest as he walked toward the glow of the oven area. Murat paused and sucked in a deep breath to quell the ache. Being sure didn't make what he must say easier.

"Mustafa." Murat ducked into the heat where the man pulled a wooden paddle lined with golden loaves of bread out of the oven. "Mustafa. Good morning."

Mustafa shoved the bread off the paddle onto the long table to

cool, then wiped his glistening brow with his arm before extending a beefy hand to Murat. The two embraced like father and son. Mustafa stepped back to look at Murat as he let out a thick exhale. "Good morning, Murat. What brings you by on a Saturday morning?"

Murat shoved his hands into his pockets and looked at his feet. *How can I do it? Mustafa depends on me. What can I say to make things less painful?*

"Mustafa, I have decided I'm meant to do something different with my life." Murat began without delay—faster was better. "It has only recently become clear to me what that is. I believe God is calling me to help battered women and children. Yes, this is one thing the orphanage offers. But what about the many women and children we turn away? There's only so much room. I hope to create a ministry to help these dear ones find jobs, get counseling, and have a safe place to go to receive help. I haven't figured it all out yet, But . . . "

Murat realized he rambled. He wanted to spit the words out before he broke down. Taking in a deep breath he began again. "Mustafa. You're the father I never had. I love you. I hope you'll understand that it is with a pained heart that I ask you to release me from my work here, so I might focus all my attentions on this new venture."

Mustafa turned away from Murat momentarily, as if gaining strength from the warmth of the ovens, from the caramel-colored loaves lining the long table to the side. This place was Mustafa's whole life—his entire purpose.

Murat wondered how it might feel to be alone, completely alone, in the one thing you cared about most. Even now he saw no other bride for himself than Ella—and she was lost to him. The lonely ache of walking his future alone, too, throbbed like the flames licking inside the wood-burning oven.

Mustafa turned slowly then pulled Murat quickly into a hug. Silence hung in the heat of the room along with the unspoken release of the old, in the hopes something new might take root.

"Yes. I will release you from this work, Murat. I will do it. My

heart breaks to think that my son will not take this place as my gift. This was my plan. You are the son I have always wanted. When I am too old to do this anymore, I wanted to give my business to you. But then, perhaps this is not the way it was meant to turn out. Maybe my nephews would be interested in an old man's meager fortune." Again Mustafa turned away.

Murat stepped toward him. "I cannot think of a better gift. Perhaps you're right. This will not be the best way. Your generosity humbles me, friend. How can I repay you for all these years of teaching me, caring for me, and allowing me to be a part of your life?"

Mustafa wiped tears away with his floured apron, leaving a creamy-white smudge below his eyes. "No, it is you who I must thank. These few years have been the best in a long time. And that is because of you." Mustafa slapped his hands together, the flour floating away in a cloud. "We must toast this wonderful thing you will be doing. I am proud of you, son. No more selfish tears from me. You will stay for dinner with this old man. I want to hear all about your dreams."

Murat struggled to maintain control of his emotions. "I will. It would be my honor. I'll be staying in Izmir, so you won't be rid of me so easily. We must plan a weekly meal together. How does that sound?"

"Yes. Sounds perfect. Come back with your beautiful Ella and we will have a feast here in the shop. I will go get wine."

Murat stopped short. "Mustafa. I'm not sure that . . . " Determined to spare his friend the pain of knowing, he had not told Mustafa of all the news of the past few months. But now he felt like a liar. "Let's just have it be us two this time. I will tell you the whole story over dinner."

Mustafa eyed Murat contemplating whether to push the issue or not. "Then 7 p.m. you will come here. And I will get some *Efes Pilsen* instead. Beer is better anyway for just us men, yes? We will have a father-son dinner alone."

Alone.

Yes, but not really. Not when it came down to it. ❧

76 THE DECISION

Murat hunched over the roses growing like a wild jungle in the center of the circle in front of June and Barry's bungalow. His shoulder blades flexed as he snipped the scraggly branches to tame the beauty.

I walked up beside him and waited until he looked up. When he did, his smile filtered into my ever-weakening resolve.

It can never be, Ella, and you know it.

"Do you have a minute to talk?"

"Sure. Yes. Let's sit." Murat gestured to a log bench on the side of the yard, the spot shaded by a towering Russian elm. The pungent, sweet fragrance it emitted hung in the thick, salty air.

I plopped on the soft grass and smoothed the many folds in my long skirt, then glanced at Murat who sat on the bench waiting for me to begin.

His completeness startled me. Never before had he appeared so settled—the stormy sea that always used to rage in his eyes now calm. Where before he was controlling and driven, now he was almost restful—not resigned, but at peace with not manipulating the outcome by sheer force. I liked this version of him even more. Definitely not helpful with "us" being too complicated to pursue.

Let him go, Ella. I wanted to throttle my internal advisor. She never took any chances. *She'll most likely die single.*

Needing relief from the heat and needing to jar my thoughts to the present and away from winding impossible roads, I twisted my heavy curls and tied the whole mess in a knot, then said, "Murat, I wanted to tell you I've decided to commit to two more years here. I wasn't sure for a while if I would but . . . "

I paused, wondering myself why the decision was natural. "I feel it's the right thing to do." I glanced toward the entrance of the orphanage, the road I arrived on was so different now. "I just wanted you to know."

Murat chewed softly on the inside of his cheek. He remained

silent. Different emotions scampered across his face, a tumble of sea glass over unyielding rock.

So much transpired between us. How was it possible we met only one year ago?

My insecurity and doubt and treading water left me. And I threw myself into the kids' education, into helping Pinar. Forgiveness—real forgiveness—changed me. That forgiveness didn't just heal the recipient, but the giver too.

Letting go of anger and the need for retribution opened a new corridor I hadn't realized even existed. The women and children here needed that message of how release revitalizes a broken heart. *Maybe I can be a part of that in a more tangible way now.*

Murat grasped my hand before nodding his head and blinking his eyes. He rubbed a thumb over my knuckle and stared at it before letting go, then leapt up like he needed to get away from me.

I stood up too and walked out of the yard, away from Murat, so alone. I turned away, refusing to dwell on what couldn't be.

Time to start over. New. For the millionth time, I told myself. My past no longer overshadowed my future.

He makes all things new.

But still, whenever I imagined life without Murat, the old ache returned.

I straightened the curtains in my room draped over a tree branch Murat found on the property and shellacked to serve as a rod. The reminder of his consideration stung.

Everywhere I turned, I felt the nudge to see his core—the layer tied up with my father's murderer, completely gone. What remained was a man I envisioned a life with.

"What do you want from me, God?" My words, like pennies clattering in a tin can, pinging against the sides.

All noise.

I sat with a thump on the floor, more baby than big girl, and ran my hands back and forth across the thick wool of the beautiful Turkish rug: yet another reminder of Murat's thoughtfulness and love.

Maybe I should give it back. Wasn't this a promise? One I'm not able to live up to?

Suddenly the room felt as though it squeezed against me, keeping me from drawing a full breath. The walls seemed on sliders, careening toward me. I stood and shoved flip-flops on my feet before pushing the door open, leaving the turbulent memories behind.

Only they straggled behind like tangling seaweed around my ankles—and there was no outrunning the suffocating reminders. ✍

77 THE ORPHANAGE

Murat's gift as leader to their group fit into place, like a foundation piece clicking into a long abandoned spot—every woman and child at ease and comforted. He asked me ahead of time if I minded him preaching in Turkish, me being the only native English speaker of the group this day.

I appreciated his consideration. My Turkish still lagged in many ways, but I understood most of what he shared and wondered if it had more to do with knowing him so well.

My mind flicked back to the email from June this morning. Three months of the most aggressive chemo, and then a follow-up to see if the cancer held on.

I studied the children of all ages, sitting around on blankets, listening, fidgeting, and I wondered about their future. About the future of this place should Barry die.

As always, my gaze landed back on Murat, his strong profile and dark hair curling near his ears. Seeing his smile even from the side brought one to my face. I needed to see him content and happy. In the midst of all the disappointment and concerns, he was at peace.

Like a fog burned off by the sun's light, the burden he carried for most of the year vanished. Seeing those things in him only made him more attractive. I swallowed against the pain in my throat, the grip, a sudden stranglehold.

Meryem stooped toward me, a plate of assorted desserts just inches from her chin. I couldn't help but smile remembering how I was caught staring at Meryem's son more than a year ago in almost this very spot.

But that was a thousand years ago—before I knew.

"Take some, please." Meryem waved the plate to encourage me not to hold back. Turkish hospitality required happy acceptance, no coy American, "No, thank you, I'm happy with my salad" allowed.

I snatched two powdered-sugar-laden pieces of rose petal Turkish delight. "*Teşekkür ederim*, Meryem."

With that Meryem leaned even closer, almost spilling the entire plate to pinch my cheeks with her free hand. She confided in Turkish, "I spent so many years trying to control everything."

She squeezed her eyes shut, then nodded, and returned her intense gaze to me, "But no more. All we can do is take care of what we have been given. What is right in front of us. If we think, think, think and never live, we die in our hearts. Live, Ella."

Before I could respond, Meryem moved with her platter full of treats, to the little girls giggling on the rug beside me.

Murat looked my way. He didn't turn away quickly, so I wondered what he observed in my expression.

Fear?

Horror?

Longing?

I had no idea what he saw, because I had no idea how I felt.

A question reached his eyes and I waved like an idiot. Embarrassed, I lowered my eyes and stared at the rug. This ongoing struggle wore me out.

All I could do was pray God would make things easier in time. My request felt flat—devoid of life. Maybe what Meryem warned me against.

A dense sea of dark, swarming schools confused the matter, keeping a cool, blue crystal ocean of possibilities out of reach. ✺

78 PINAR'S HOME

Sunday afternoon, Pinar and I sat watching the children run and play in front of her home. The oldest two girls lay on the blanket beside us. Umut spun in circles arms outstretched, like a top. Once that bored him, he pegged rocks at invisible targets on trees. The boy then dashed into the brush and gathered a handful of long lilac stems. He returned to toss a pile at Pinar.

Pinar's face changed. She smiled at her son, all pride and joy. Umut displayed the benefits of his mom's transformation. I even scolded him on occasion during class, because he had trouble pulling his attention away from the adventures he played out in his mind.

Most recently he grabbed the ball I often used for word games, then pegged it at little Çiğdem's face. He hadn't done it to be mean, only in an attempt to knock off the mosquito that landed on her nose.

"Ella. I no ever tell you of my mother." Pinar turned to me, her face serious now.

"You don't have to, Pinar."

"No, I tell you." She began again this time in Turkish. "She was such an angry person. Always yelling and hitting. And, always, she had a boyfriend. Well, not always boyfriends. So many men . . ." Pinar's voice trailed off.

She pulled up a handful of grass, sprinkling the green blades on her bare feet. "I wanted to make her happy. She always looked so tired. I went to her boyfriend's house to surprise her with bread and other food. So she wouldn't have to cook. See? But when I got there, she was so mad. She grabbed the bread and threw it in my face."

A clear stream of tears streaked Pinar's cheeks. "She screamed she didn't need bread. She needed money. But had none. Then she told me I would marry Cem, her boyfriend. He didn't want her anymore, she said."

Pinar squeezed her eyes shut and sucked in a deep breath. "She said then she would be taken care of. Money wouldn't be a problem again. So I did. And after one year I had Umut."

She finished the terrible story in English, "I just a baby, thirteen years. My *Anne* only live only six month after I married. She never see my son."

Sorrow doesn't expire.

I saw well enough the waves of pain, repeating and washing too, over and over again—for Pinar's childhood years, a time when she should have worried about her hair, or studied for a math test. No wonder she had nothing to offer when she arrived. No wonder the anger.

How can people be so cruel to one another?

How can a child be used and manipulated by a parent in such a dark way? The horror struck me like a slap in the face, the realization.

How could I look at Pinar as a new creation, letting go of the pitiful person she once was, completely forgetting her dark past and somehow hold Murat responsible for what his father did? I did that by keeping Murat at a distance, by seeing him as different, lesser, and off limits. My eyes burned thinking about how I allowed the blame to fall on a little boy, only a little older than Umut, for grown-up decisions.

"Thank you for telling me, Pinar." I pressed my fingers to my eyes, blocking out the light, stars forming.

God, I'm so sorry. I'm a fake and a liar.

Pinar reached for my hands and wrapped them in hers. "I say because maybe you don't know why I so bad when you meet me." Then she stroked my hair and said, "I love like you soon."

I leaned in, the choke of tears making the words come out strange and muffled. "You already do, Pinar. You already do." ❧

7 9 THE NAIL

Murat stood out front June and Barry's home staring up at Ella's window. The rotted framing needed to be ripped off and replaced, as did the molding on the larger front window off the main entryway. The sea air ate away at wood. Murat wondered if the place would have done better had it been built more like the other homes around the property, with stucco, rather than as a more traditional American-style cottage.

He positioned the low stepladder below Ella's window and stepped up. Using a crow bar, Murat slipped the thin end between the house and window frame and pulled back, the piece loosened and swung on a rusty nail. Murat lifted it off and flung it to the ground beneath him.

Therapeutic and predictable, manual labor focused him. His plans spiraled like a whirlpool, such a long way around before getting to the center. He checked into an apprenticeship with a local agency whose efforts to aid asylum seekers gained international recognition. Though the focus was somewhat different than his would ultimately be, the experience could prove invaluable in learning local resources and finding out how to tap into them.

Just this morning he called to tell them he could only commit to one morning a week. With Barry and June gone, too much needed to be done. Progress would be slow with so little time invested at the agency.

Murat pried another board loose when he spotted Ella. She entered her room with a towel wrapped around her hair and carrying another over her arm. Too startled to speak or indicate his presence, Murat stepped back, forgetting he stood on a ladder, not the ground. He tumbled backward landing on a piece the window trim he just discarded. Instantly, the pain of something sharp pierced his backside.

Scrambling to stand up despite the sting, Murat noticed he landed on a rusted nail jutting out of the wood. He wanted to inspect the wound, but couldn't see it. He only felt the warmth of blood soaking the back of his shorts.

"Are you hurt?" Ella leaned out of her window looking at him, her wet curls carelessly dangling over the frame and her brow knit with concern.

"Yes, I think is okay. I fell on this." Murat stood and kicked the piece of wood on the ground. "I'm fine. I'll just go change."

Ella said slowly, "Are you sure? I must have startled you, I'm so sorry. I forgot you said you'd work on the windows today."

"No problem. I'll be back in a minute." Murat turned to jog home. His backside ached and he hoped the nail hadn't gone in too deep.

"Murat, wait."

Ella disappeared from the window and a moment later ran out the front door.

"You're bleeding. The whole back of your shorts is covered in blood. You need to have it checked."

"I'll just go change."

Ella shook her head, looking very determined and stubborn. Murat couldn't help but smile.

"Stop it, Murat. It's not funny. I'm serious."

"*Tamam*. You can walk me to my home. *Anne* will check," Murat grinned at her and added, "unless you want to."

Ella's eyes widened and she shook her head, completely missing his teasing tone. "No, your mom would know better if you need stitches."

With a chuckle Murat turned and hobbled toward home. The nail must have gone in deep, because with every step a searing pain stabbed his leg. How frustrating when he had so much to accomplish around the grounds today. One mother needed her toilet fixed. Another complained about a leak under the kitchen sink.

Murat called into his home before entering. His mom ran out with a grin on her face that faded quickly when she saw how her son walked.

"What happened?" Meryem eyed Ella, as if Murat were incapable of answering.

"He fell on some wood that he . . . " Ella opened her mouth, then asked. "What did happen to your . . . you know?"

"I fell on some wood with nails. It must have stuck into my . . . " Murat decided it would be less humiliating to finish in Turkish. He gauged Ella's reaction. Thankfully, she appeared more concerned than amused.

"Son, inside. Let's see." His mom always took on a bossy tone whenever she deemed a situation needing immediate action. Obviously, a soft word took much too long.

"*Tamam*. Inside."

Ella stopped just outside the door. "I'll wait here. Tell me if there's anything you need."

A few minutes later with the wound cleaned with a sharp antiseptic and bandaged, Murat emerged to find Ella sitting on the front step, her chin resting on her hands. She turned when he came out and jumped up.

"Is fine. *Anne* knows all about caring for cuts. She cleaned it and now is all good." He wouldn't admit it still hurt.

Ella opened her mouth, then closed it, then finally got out, "You don't need stitches?"

"No, it was deep, but not long." He hoped it wouldn't get infected though.

"Have you had a tetanus shot?"

"No. I am used to Turkish dirt."

"That's not the point. You could get really sick. Even die if the nail had tetanus on it."

Murat laughed at her. "I was making a joke. I did have a shot a few years ago. June made me. Ella, this is fine. I promise."

"Well, okay then." Ella still appeared lost as she ambled toward her home. She turned and added, "Then there's nothing you need?"

Murat's next words tumbled out like dolphins on a swift wave, unstoppable. "Yes, Ella. I need *you*."

Ella's expression changed, unsure and vulnerable, as if frightened to even respond. Her eyes filled with tears. Still she

didn't say anything, she just stood there looking at him, like she wondered what could possibly come next after such a declaration.

Murat couldn't help it. He moved quickly toward her, closing the terrible space that stretched her away from him. The space that gaped like an open grave. He paused a moment before pulling her into him.

"I'm sorry. I didn't mean to say that. I understand I cannot have you, Ella. But I wish I could. I wish it every minute I'm with you and every minute I'm away from you. I'm trying to let you go. Trying to trust God in this. I cannot seem to do it. Forgive me for pushing this. I know how you feel." Murat dropped his hands to his sides, wishing he didn't have to let her go—feeling cold all of a sudden, despite the heat of the day.

Ella shook her head, her eyes wet and the skin around them splotchy and pink. "No, you don't know how I feel. I feel . . . " Ella wiped her eyes with her fingertips.

She touched Murat's face so tenderly he could hardly stand still. He wanted so badly to grab her and kiss the wetness that dampened her dark lashes, to kiss her parted lips as she searched for the right words. He compelled himself to hold back. She didn't belong to him and never would. His throat burned as he swallowed against tears.

Lord, I can't do this anymore.

Ella looked into his eyes as she moved her hands to clasp his. Murat allowed himself to enjoy the warmth of them pressed softly there. Soon the cool emptiness would torture him. He was determined to enjoy this brief moment.

Then finally she spoke. "I feel as though my life will be so empty without you. I want to know you'll be with me through whatever comes next. I don't want to imagine, for one more day, a future without you, Murat." Ella cried, struggling to push the words out. "I want to be with you. Is that possible after everything? Can we be together?"

All the weight fell on one word: can. Her almost purple eyes searched his, looking for the answer to her question.

She wants me, despite everything.

Now Murat knew what to do. He placed his hands gently on both sides of her face and pulled her into him and kissed her, tasting her tears.

Looking into her eyes he said, "Yes, my Ella. Anything is possible for God, remember?"

She only nodded before leaning into him. "I remember." Her lips moved against his face. He felt the heat of her breath. "Don't let me forget again, okay?" She pushed back only enough so their eyes could meet.

"*Tamam*. I will spend all my life helping us both remember."

She squinted at him, eyebrows lowered. "What do you mean, Murat?"

"I want you to marry me, Ella. Is it possible you will say 'yes?'"

"Yes."

"Yes, is possible?"

She laughed. "Yes, to marrying you."

A movement caused Murat to turn. His mom stood just outside the house, hands pressed together in front of her chest, and laughing as shiny tears streamed over her round, rosy cheeks.

"*Anne*, are you spying?"

"Yes, son. I am. What do you think?"

"Aren't you sorry?"

"No, son. I am not." She giggled before running on her short legs toward them both, hands out in the anticipation of an embrace. Both of them moved in her direction, and pulled her in.

Thank you, God. He took the sin and wounds they bore and transformed their purpose into something new.

Filthy brown water, flushed out by clear blue. ☙

80 MERYEM'S HOME

"What is happened in that head, Ella?" Meryem reached into the center of the table and snatched a piece of baklava. We talked about wedding plans in Meryem's home.

My head hurt. That's what happened. "Just wondering about Barry. I wish he could do the ceremony."

"Hmm. Yes. I wish too. Did you talk to Mama?" Meryem's familiarity with my mom still startled me, but they were old, dear friends.

"Yes. Called her right away. I woke my Mom up."

Meryem snatched the pad of paper she carried around with her constantly and jotted something down in Turkish.

Already I knew to let Meryem take the lead. Besides, I had no clue how to plan a Turkish wedding. I nearly cried when Mom sent her simple ivory, A-line dress with a high waist, hand-stitched with minuscule piles of all-white daisies. The pictures of typical Turkish gowns I saw so far would bury me in ruffles. Not me. At all.

Murat leaned over my shoulder and planted a kiss warm on my cheek before grabbing a piece of the dessert.

Meryem smacked him over the head with her notepad and scolded him. "You stop, Murat. You kiss too much these days. The wedding day will feel far away if you kiss, hug too much."

She tweaked my cheek and said, "I'm sorry, Ella. My son does not know how to control himself."

Well, that's not embarrassing at all. "I'm tired anyway. I'm going to head home. Night, Meryem."

"You can call me *Anne*. Please. It make happy my head."

I leaned in and kissed Meryem on both cheeks. "All right then. Good-night, *Anne*."

Meryem grinned, tears glistening in her hazel eyes. "My daughter." She pulled my face in again and kissed me full on the mouth. Knowing this to be a normal sign of affection, I tried to appear nonchalant to the unexpected planting.

Murat smirked, obviously seeing my discomfort.

"Do you want to walk a little, Ella?"

"Sure."

All the wedding planning wore on my nerves and brought an unexpected sadness.

"Is all of this okay, my Ella? You look tired."

I swallowed the sigh I planned on letting out, long and mournful. "No, everything is fine."

"You don't seem the same these few days." Murat reached for my hand in the darkness and I soaked in his warmth. The evenings grew somewhat cooler, although the humidity remained high. Temperatures rarely dropped below 65 degrees at night.

I stopped and turned to face Murat, his features lit softly by the full moon hanging low. "I guess I'm just ready to be married is all. Planning everything is a little overwhelming." I didn't want to hurt Murat. However, I needed to tell the truth. "I wish Dad could be here to give me away."

Murat stopped and held me for the longest time. "Me too."

I began walking again, needing to push forward past the moment.

"I feel the same about the plans. I didn't know is this hard. Just one day and it takes months of talking. I'm sorry my *Anne* is a little . . . " Murat searched for the right word in English. Instead he left the word out and continued. "She has prayed for this moment for years and is very happy. I hope she's not too much for you."

I looked at my hands wrapped up with Murat's. In the darkness they were indistinguishable.

Where does he end and I begin? Is that how marriage will be?

All of the drama leading up to this knitting us together was like a *kilim* rug. The thick, wool-spun threads wrapped tight in lines and patterns. The change of colors looked endless, the entire piece woven with one, continuous strand.

"Murat, I love your mom and thank God I'll have such a dear mother-in-law. I have to admit, though, there are moments when I want to scream and run away from 'the list.'"

Murat pulled me into him and I pressed my face against his shoulder. "Can I tell you my secret dream?" He mumbled this into my hair.

"Yes."

"I dream of taking the list and setting it on fire."

He pulled back, his face so serious. Then he grinned. Proud and unashamed.

"I can't believe you just said that." I started to laugh.

"See, we're already acting like a husband and wife. We think the same." Murat pulled me toward him, his hands warming my lower back.

He leaned in for a kiss when I pushed back. "Your mom is right about one thing though, Murat. You better stop all the kissing. We need to save that for after the wedding. *Tamam?*"

Murat groaned. "But this helps me with wedding plans. Not so boring."

"True, but still. Cut it out, okay?"

"*Tamam.* I'll try." He brushed the end of my nose with his finger, apparently the next logical way to show love and affection with kissing removed. "I've wanted to have you for so long that now I have trouble letting you go. I will do it though. I give my words."

"You mean your word?"

"*Evet.* Yes. This is what I meant. See, you make me not be able to speak English anymore." Murat pushed his hands through his thick, black hair. "How about I pray the wedding comes fast."

"Good idea. Very fast is my prayer." I took hold of Murat's hand again and we continued to walk, the only sound now being the sound of our footsteps crunching on the gravel path.

Later, after I listened from my window to Murat's footsteps all the way back to his home, a memory filtered in. On the patio of our apartment in Izmir only a few months before Dad died, we sat and talked, hand in hand. He was always a question asker. He leaned in, his face close to mine, and smiled. "Ella, what kind of man do you think God has for you to marry?"

Being seven and very sure and comfortable with our discussions I answered, "Hmm . . . handsome and nice and Turkish."

Dad laughed and said, "What? Not handsome and nice and just like you, Daddy?"

"Well, yah, that's the handsome and nice part."

"And what about this Turkish thing? Why is that important to you?"

"Don't know." I didn't tell him the little boy I played soccer with on the street one day seemed the perfect match for me. Nice, with a good smile. Just the right height. Besides, his hair was dark like Daddy's.

"Well, if anyone would know, it would be you," he said.

"Yah, that's true."

"Well, at Turkish weddings do the dads still walk their girls down the aisle?" Dad turned in his chair to be closer.

"I'm not so sure." I squeezed his hand. "I can check on that." We sat there in the quiet for a while. Then I said, "But even if they don't, we'll do that, all right Daddy?"

"All right."

I forgot the memory until now. I turned the crank to close the bedroom window, but still the salt breeze and fragrant Russian elm slipped in.

All of the past danced with the newness of the present and the future. I needed to say good-bye, once and for all. No more hanging on with an iron grip. I knew what I needed to do.

I'll meet you there, Dad. ❧

8 1 PINAR'S HOME

"Pinar?" I stepped into the relative darkness of the small home, the heat of the sun unable to soak into the cool of the cement structure. Not seeing her, I went back outside and walked around the side of the house and found Pinar pinning up laundry, a long line of small T-shirts followed by medium-sized girls' dresses, and several wide-legged, Turkish floral pants Pinar's size.

"Ella." Pinar waved, but continued her work, her face red in the blister of the rays. The spot made for a great clothes drying space, but provided no shade for the one doing the work.

I grabbed a damp pair of boy's underpants and pinned it up.

"How are you doing?" I glanced at Pinar out of the corner of my eye.

"Good. I good. Kids crazy, but . . . good, too." Pinar turned only her head to flash a wry grin. "Umut yesterday throw all cloth on floor. I start again."

"He's a healthy boy with a lot of energy. Maybe you should have made him help you wash them again, so he sees the work he made for you."

"Yes. Is good. I do next time. You teach me good."

In minutes we completed hanging the pile and walked, arms linked, toward the cool of the home. Inside Pinar opened the refrigerator and pulled out a box of Orange Fanta and filled two glasses.

"Sit." Pinar pointed toward the low table. "No stand. Sit."

I gulped the bubbly drink. Pinar slipped her head-scarf off for a moment, wiped the sweat from her forehead with both hands, then refastened the scarf.

"It's a hot day for October." I wrapped both hands around the coolness of the glass.

Content to not move or even speak, Pinar nodded.

"I need to ask you something."

She looked at me and waited.

"I want you to be my maid of honor in my wedding." I realized that made no sense to Pinar by her blank expression. I tried again, this time in Turkish, explaining as best I could. The young woman became such a part of my life over the last year and a half and I could see no better person for the job.

Pinar smiled, looking somewhat shy, then nodded her head as she blinked her eyes. Satisfied with her very Turkish 'yes,' I leaned in and hugged her. The small room where we sat a sacred place—a life transformation took place in this spot, slow but sure.

"What I wear?" Pinar looked at her shabby T-shirt and flowered *şalvar*.

"I'm going to buy you something special. *Tamam?*"

"No."

"Please. It would be my honor. Will you please let me?"

Pinar gazed out the front door streaming in the rays of the hot sun. Tears stood in her eyes before she turned to me and nodded again, then blinked, a 'yes' to more than just the wedding plan, but to a new beginning. ❧

82 IZMIR, 2008

I hadn't wanted to mislead Murat. This wasn't something I could do with his eyes on me. It wasn't a complete lie—I wanted to walk the shopping strip to pick up a few things—but that was just the preamble to the real place I needed to visit. I was going home.

It's time.

I stepped from the curb and sprinted across the busy street. Taxis honked and slowed in hopes I needed a ride. I flicked my chin up and clicked my tongue to let the drivers know I wasn't interested. The smell of exhaust turned my stomach, then *ekmek* soothed the feeling.

I walked with confidence on the dirty sidewalk. So many of my afternoons here used to find me walking hand-in-hand with Dad. Often we went to the corner to buy ice cream, Dad asking me questions as we walked. I loved how he cared so much about all the things tumbling around in my mind, making me feel grown up, and truly known by him.

I slowed as I passed the ice cream store. The same as fifteen years ago: just a simple storefront with cardboard cylinders full of different colored *Maraş Dondurma*. I smiled recalling the chewy texture of the dessert—nothing like American ice cream—served in golf-ball-sized scoops on a sugar cone. I passed the store and turned the corner toward our old home.

Maybe I'll get some after. For old time's sake.

Just a few blocks more. 210 Gaziosmanpaşa, the apartment we lived in when I was small and thought nothing could change the peace and sunshine.

The gray, three-story building stood surrounded by a high iron fence. I stepped toward the gate, wrapping my hands around the bars and peering between them to the garden in front of the apartment.

Bright pink peonies bloomed all along the front of the property. How different their color from my mood. Seeing the place where

I stood watching the road that horrible morning made me feel as though I might be sick.

The spot, a time capsule trapped in the moment of Dad's death. An ache swept over me, not just for him, but for me. For the little girl whose carefree days ended in one terrifying moment. Tears pooled in my eyes as I remembered how things changed—every security I ever knew vanished with my father.

I let myself recall the details of that morning as if it happened only moments ago—as though seared into my mind with a branding iron. Mom baked cookies. I remembered how the smell swept through the house. I watched Mom shove several cookies into a baggie, then into my lunch sack. As always, she leaned over to write a little love note on a napkin and placed that inside too.

"All set?" Mom stepped forward and kissed me on the head, handing me the lunch bag.

I gripped the dry, crinkly paper in my hand. "Yep, thanks Mom. I better go out. Dad's ready."

"No, you don't want to keep the Colonel waiting," Mom said with a grin on her face.

At that, I walked out the front door, yelling my 'good-bye' behind me, and dashed down the two flights of stairs out the front door of the apartment complex. Daddy climbed into the driver's seat and turned his head to smile at me. He lowered his head a moment to turn the ignition key, then his eyes shot up to me when it only clicked. All he managed to do was scream my name.

The rest went in slow motion. The bright light of the explosion flared from beneath the car, searing against the blue morning until nothing was left of Daddy. The blast threw me backward. I scrambled forward when a hubcap, black and smoking still, hit the metal fence and bounced off the cement in front of me.

My ears rang, drilling into my brain, burning, stuffed with cotton. I looked around frantically like he might be lying nearby. Only pieces of the car remained, the shell—black and empty as a cave.

Across the street a young boy screamed, black-faced and bloody, hunched over a man lying on the road, staring at the sky. His hands covered his ears as he sobbed hysterically.

What happened to him? Why haven't I wondered until now?

Standing in front of the apartment, the memory was almost surreal so many years later. But I needed this. Being here still gave that feeling of something missing. Some piece not there.

Stepping through the gate, I brushed fingers over the bright blooms, and walked slowly to the spot where I stood that morning, turning to face the street.

Then I saw him. He stood in the road where Dad's car sat before it exploded. His face white as a corpse. His lips whispering something as he stared at my face.

"Murat?" I walked toward him. I felt jarred between two worlds.

"I'm sorry, I followed you," he whispered. "I was worried and was just . . . " Incapable of finishing his sentence, a moment later he began again, "I did not know . . . I did not remember. I was just a small boy." He said it like he defended himself. He shook his head back and forth.

"What are you talking about, Murat? I don't understand."

"It can't be. It just can't be." Murat's eyes begged me to understand.

I couldn't. I'd never seen him like this, not even when he discovered his dad's connection to my own. Where were the dark dancing eyes I grew to love? Where was the peace?

"I remember now. I made myself forget. I remember now. Being here again . . . oh, God, how can this be? How can this be?" Murat sobbed, and dropped to his knees on the street pulling his hands through his dark hair as if trying to rip it out. "Jesus, help me."

In the background a man yelled about prayer from a minaret. Then another and another and another.

"What is it? You're scaring me." I knelt beside him, the asphalt digging into my knees. I touched his shoulder, then grabbed his face between my hands, and forced him to look at me. "You can tell me, whatever it is. I know your father did this. We've been through that already."

"No. It will never be okay. I know that now. I wanted God to help me move on. Now I know why I couldn't all the way. I couldn't, because I knew deep down God must hate me. I don't deserve His forgiveness. I deserve only death."

Murat stood and turned away from me and stalked back and forth on the pavement like a madman.

I reached for him. He pushed my hands away.

"What is it you remembered, Murat?"

"It was him. It was you that morning. You were standing there and I saw you. You looked so small and then I knew what was happening. Before that I just thought we were destroying property, getting the attention of those who refused to listen. I was wrong. Now he's dead, your father, because of me!"

Despite trying to be confident for Murat, my voice dropped to a hoarse whisper, "How? How could you have seen me? Why on earth would you be there that day? How were you responsible, Murat? Tell me."

His eyes bore into mine like razors. "I remember now. I did it. He made me do it."

Tears peeled down his face. Red splotches dotted his neck. "I wired the bomb to the ignition. He taught me for so long. I never understood until that day what I was doing. I thought I was a part of something important. That's what he said. He said it was for Allah. So I did it. But it was all a terrible lie. I remember seeing your dad walk out and get in the car. It was too late. I saw you walk out, just as it happened. I ran to stop him. To stop you from coming closer. My father grabbed me away, pushing me back with his body."

My stomach coiled like a basket full of snakes.

Murat sobbed as he finished. "After that day, I saw you over and over in my mind until I couldn't anymore. Everything disappeared, except the pain. It was always there. Now I remember. Now I know why. I'm so very sorry. I am the cause of all of your suffering!"

I stepped away from Murat, even as he tried to scramble toward me. "No," I whispered, "It can't be. How can that be? Why would

you do such a thing?" My voice rose. "He was my dad. I was right there to watch him die!"

The guard stationed at the apartment stepped out of the building and walked toward us. He started shouting at Murat in Turkish, waving him off like a fly.

Murat's face contorted in pain. He turned and vomited on the sidewalk.

I couldn't stay. I had to run away from him, from the terrible pain.

How can it possibly hurt more?

I heard Murat calling my name, like he stood at the end of a long tunnel. I bolted, tears burning my face as I cried like a little girl losing her daddy all over again. ✎

83   THE ORPHANAGE

Murat called out to Ella. She refused to listen. She was lost to him forever. Nothing he could have imagined, nothing could have prepared him for the truth.

He shoved it as far back into the darkness as he could manage until forgetfulness brought some semblance of reprieve from the pain and guilt. Then life began again.

They were ushered into this place of new beginnings fifteen years ago . . . were told of a God whose forgiveness knew no bounds and he believed it. But that was only because he hadn't remembered his role.

His mother, too, pretended the kids brought into her small home on the orphanage were truly hers, instead of the son who she could barely look at for almost a year.

Murat remembered now.

The ache never went away. The story changed in his mind until he no longer remembered at all. The vision of working on her father's car pushed forward, reminding him of its acid truth. He learned how to wire a bomb to a car's ignition system.

The old desire for vengeance surged across his chest, streamed through his arms, and tingled in his fingers. Murat took a taxi home only half-aware of his surroundings, determining to dig out answers from his mother's mouth.

No more pretending she could be proud of him. No more lying about hope. Nothing mattered anymore. He murdered an innocent man. His blood could never be removed.

"*Anne*." The word sounded like a curse word. Murat fought to remain calm. "I know it. I know it all. You lied to me. You made me think I was a good boy. That you were proud of me."

Murat ran through the small kitchen into Meryem's room as he screamed. He found her tucking one of his so-called brothers into bed. Without saying a word, she kissed the little boy's small head and smoothed back his hair.

She walked toward Murat, out the bedroom door, and closed it quietly behind her. Turning, Meryem said, "You are not the boy your dad tried to make you into."

"I am. I am a murderer. You let me believe . . . " Murat's voice broke. Suddenly it made sense. "This is why you tried to scare Ella away. I thought it was because of *Baba*. No. It was because of me!"

Tears filled her eyes and she nodded, defeated. He didn't know what to say. What had his mother done wrong?

Nothing, but love him despite how detestable he was. Nothing, but try to protect him, despite her flawed methods. Nothing, but living a life of make-believe where murder and violence and fear didn't exist.

"You knew I forgot it and you let me," he said through clenched teeth.

Meryem didn't look away. Murat noticed she was prepared for this moment, her face so set. Her feet spread enough to show determination.

"You are a new creation. I would not torment you by reminding you of the terrible past we both endured. You were just as much a victim as Ella's father. Your dad tricked you, Murat. Don't you see that? He knew what you believed, that it was just a small thing to teach a lesson. That nobody would get hurt. He knew. He let you go there. All in his cowardice. Your father never once stood up to injustice like a man. No, only in secret. Only in beating a fearful woman. Only in using a child to do his dirty work. When you pushed the truth away, I saw it as a blessing at first, you were able to move on. Finally, you laughed and began to act like a child should. You are nothing like him, Murat. He lived like a coward and died like a coward."

"He grabbed me that day. He died on the street. He saved me."

Meryem let her tears fall now, all strength gone. "This one thing I will always be grateful to him for."

"You knew the truth and let me believe the lie I told myself."

Meryem moved within inches of Murat's face and said slowly, deliberately, "And I would do it again."

Murat couldn't look at her. All his anger and confusion left

him limp, without any fight. "What happened to Grandma and Grandpa?"

Meryem covered her mouth and smothered a sob. "He wired his car earlier that day after pulling it in front of my father's store window. It exploded killing them, too, Murat. Don't you see? This is all my fault. I married him so we wouldn't starve. *Baba* tried to warn me not to do it. I was stubborn. So, they are gone, because of me."

She coughed out the words through her tears. "And you suffered more than any boy should have to. All because of me." She turned away from him and hunched over, like she couldn't stay upright.

Murat could hardly stand now. "Why? Why would he do this?"

"It was his last revenge against me for my rebellion. I confronted him. You remember that day. I learned the poisonous ideas he put in your head and told him to stop. The next day it all happened. He wanted to have the last word."

"And he did." Defeat swarmed like killer bees, a humming, stinging pain.

"No, he did not, son. Our *Lord* does. He always has the last word. As big and frightening as your father was to you, still is to you, our God is still bigger. As terrible and painful the guilt is, His forgiveness is still bigger. You cannot forget the redemption, Murat. Or your father *will* win. And the life you have been given, the new start will be worthless. Don't let him have it, Murat. He cannot win." Her staccato words pounded his chest.

Murat turned his back and strode out the door, out into the muted light, out past the entrance where fifteen years ago he and his mother were embraced without question.

Where they welcomed a murderer into their lives, like it was the most natural thing to do. ✎

8 4 THE BEACH

I sat on the beach glaring into the sparkling deep blue flooding the horizon. The sand wasn't soft—it became cement. And the pain, like the waves, ebbed and flowed in turns.

One moment I reasoned it away, reminding myself about forgiveness, about what I already forgave—so many times. And besides, Murat was just a boy doing his father's bidding. Then an image sliced in like a sinister smile of Murat crawling under Daddy's car and connecting wires that sparked the explosion—and in my mind, I saw him watching, the blaze flickering in his dark eyes making him appear so different, so evil.

Help me, Lord. I'm drowning!

No other well-formed prayer came. Just loss.

The waves moved close enough to wash my feet in the cool Aegean water, as if Jesus himself ministered to me. I hunched over my knees, hugging them against my chest. I lowered my head, the waves wetting my skirt and pulling its length out, then in.

I could let the agony take me, down, down, cradled in the sea.

Sinking slowly beneath the surface, light giving way to darkness, until the darkness overtook.

Silence.

Silence from my thoughts.

Silence from the pain of loving Murat.

Silence from the tugging to forgive the unforgivable. It would all be over and I'd be free.

A memory pressed in like a note in an open palm. Mom said when it felt too painful, to draw pictures, let out the hurt in color. I reached into the sand, raking fingers through silky, pulverized shell.

Is that how it works, God?

Softening comes after a battering against rocks until who we are becomes something else entirely? Something that doesn't cut any longer?

No, we always have the capacity to inflict pain on one another.

My first instinct wasn't to comfort Murat, but to escape, to leave him behind until he melted into the darkness, to leave him so heartsick he might not survive.

I'm no different then.

I picked up a handful of sand and watched it sift through my fingers and blow like a spirit out toward the water.

An image rose up like a cross erected and shoved into packed dirt.

Jesus.

Hanging there bloodied and broken and whispering, "Forgive them, they know not what they do."

But that's not me. I've never been that person.

If He did it, if He forgave his killers, how much more should I forgive a little boy of eight, manipulated to be a part of something he didn't even understand? Seeing Murat as a child transformed the hurt into pity. That gave way to compassion and the agony fell away in a huge lump.

I sat there for hours. Quiet swirled like a spirit off the sea. Something inside me changed. I listened to the gentling of God's voice in the insistent waves.

I waited, thinking it couldn't be real. How can I not hate him? And I knew.

Because it made no sense. And God's love didn't either.

I rose, the retreating wave pulled the sand beneath my feet, shifting me, sucking me out into nothingness.

I moved away from its lure and back toward home, the chill of the ocean lifting with each step. ❧

8 5 THE ORPHANAGE

I walked through the entrance of the orphanage, the gate slammed too loud as I closed it. Someone left it open for me.

Murat.

An act of kindness in the middle of his agony. I walked only a few steps before I spotted him, slumped against a tree, asleep. I approached quietly hurting for the little boy there. I knelt in front of him. He remained still, a sad look covering his features, knotting his brow in a tight pucker.

Sleep doesn't even allow escape from agony.

My fingertips touched his face and brushed under his eye, heartbroken to find it damp, making his lashes even darker than usual.

Murat's eyes fluttered open. He lurched forward and grabbed me, a rim of tears a constant, threatening to drown him too.

Sobs wracked his frame as he burrowed his face against my chest. No words, just the sound of complete brokenness.

Tears streaked my face as I stroked his hair feeling the silkiness between my fingers, hoping he knew of my love in this small act. Hoping he sensed I no longer tried to escape the sight of him, the feel of him. He relaxed against me like a child begging for reconciliation. I had no words, just choking tears. I hoped he understood.

What can I say to make him see?

I knew any words spoken could not relay the peace only God gave, like the golden fingers of the sun reaching through my window more than a year ago.

So I spoke the words from the book of Jeremiah, words committed to memory as a child. *"For I know the plans I have for you,' declares the Lord, 'plans to prosper you and not to harm you, plans to give you a hope and a future.'"* I waited, wanting him to really hear me. "God wants us both to have a future and a hope, Murat. He died for that."

Murat slowly raised his face to meet my eyes, still smudged with tears.

"I love you, Murat. And I forgive you, even though you didn't understand. You were just a little boy. I still give that to you, because I know you need it." My throat ached as I spoke, the hurt hanging there.

"Do you still love me? After everything?" Murat asked.

I couldn't say anything else. I reached for his face and pressed my mouth to his. Things like death and mistakes and stolen childhood couldn't reclaim the land. It was ours, the future.

Old demons were put in their place. Like rocks hurled out into the black water. Buried to a place where no one alive could find them again. ✷

86 KIZKALESI, 2009

Leaning over the railing of the boat, the translucent blue water lapped and sprayed upward. For the past week, we travelled the coastline on a private boat, just the captain, Murat and I, each day finding new harbors to explore.

Today we stopped at *Kizkalesi* to visit the castle sitting out in the water, the one from Meryem's childhood vacation. I considered for the hundredth time our incredible love story.

Only you, Lord.

Despite dire predictions, Barry's cancer scans showed no remnants after the chemo. He returned—a weaker man than before, a patch over one eye and hair snowy white—with joy more evident than ever. And an even greater depth of gratefulness, if that was possible. Barry performed our wedding ceremony.

Murat came up behind wrapping me in his arms—leaning into my neck and nuzzling. "Good morning, my bride." This he murmured against my skin, making it tingle.

"Good morning," I said as my husband continued to kiss near my ear. "I'm looking forward to going to the castle."

"No, let's just stay on the boat all day."

"Murat, you planned this whole trip for us, but seem very uninterested in the sites."

"Yes, is true. I admit it." The man was not in the least apologetic.

"Don't you want to explore?"

"Yes."

"The castle, I mean."

"Oh, yes, I guess it will be interesting." Murat pulled back just slightly to look out at the water, his cheek rough against mine. He hadn't bothered to shave and looked rugged and sexy.

Murat's dark skin appeared almost like milk chocolate from our days of resting in the sunshine while the small boat bobbed on the reflecting water.

Our wedding day was one of dreams.

Mom flew in and she and Meryem reunited after fifteen years. They held hands just crying and laughing. Mom walked me down the aisle. "For Daddy," she whispered against my ear.

And it seemed he was there, linking hands with us, smiling on his girl who married a Turk—as she predicted. Murat stood with his grandfather, both grinning and wiping tears—a new beginning for several generations.

Murat and I decided to live in our own home at the orphanage, taking in adoptive kids ourselves when the time was right. He continued to pursue his dream to work with displaced women and children on a wider scale. I taught the kids at the orphanage where my heart remained.

I leaned in to Murat and said, only a little bossy, "Go get dressed."

"Do I have to?" Murat tried to claim another kiss.

This man's definitely a lover. "Please. I've always wanted to go inside the castle."

"*Tamam.* I'll do it." But instead of going to get ready he moved behind me, pulling me back against his warm chest. "Do you know this story? Of the castle?" His words resonated against my skin.

"No."

"A king was told by a fortune teller that a poisonous snake would kill his only daughter."

I shivered. Murat rubbed his hands up and down the sides of my arms.

"So the father built the castle on the island to try to protect her. But as was the fear, a poisonous snake was brought to the girl in a basket full of fruit and she died. It couldn't be stopped."

"Well, that's a terrible story."

Murat chuckled and said, "Is just a story. Probably not true."

I looked toward the shoreline, pale gold with lime-washed buildings etched against the periwinkle blue sky. And just east, another castle perched like a dove on a jut of land. Maybe the king's home before he tried to hide away and protect his beloved daughter.

This place felt like a full circle. The little girl in me

finally released the fear that kept me hidden, separate—as if I could actually avoid pain by cloistering myself from everything, especially love—a girl in a tomb surrounded by an ocean-sized moat.

Murat spoke against my ear, "What's going on in my wife's brain, hmm?"

"I'm just grateful. Grateful to finally be living."

He wrapped his arms in an 'X' across my stomach. "I love you, my Ella."

"I love you too."

Silence—not emptiness—swirled in the wind and hooked over the waves.

"Ready for what's next?" I asked looking at the castle floating on the glittering waves of the Mediterranean waters.

"Always." ⁓

⟶ ΛBOUT THE ΛUTHOR ⟶

Holly, a military-brat-who-never-lived-anyplace-for-very-long, turned local after marrying her born-and-reared-in-Colorado husband. Together they enjoy home schooling and trying to keep five kids alive. Culture shock was Holly's childhood, moving from Taiwan to Norway to England to Turkey to Germany and back to Turkey. Holly established a love for travel, for different people, for outdoor cafes, and for castles sitting in the middle of the sea. ✎

Connect with Holly:
URL: www.hollyyoderdeherrera.wordpress.com/theorphanmakerssin/home
Facebook: www.facebook.com/AuthorHollyYoderDeherrera/

—◦ ᴀCKNOWLEDGEMENTS ◦—

I'd like to thank my mom and dad for providing me a life of travel-adventure and for their willing sacrifice for the U.S. Air Force—because of their love for our family, and for our great country and all its freedoms.

To the Turkish people who I adore—your culture of love and beauty and hospitality are a part of me.

To my two writing groups—one at 9,600 feet above sea level, the other just slightly below that—who provided regular, honest feedback and never stopped cheering me on.

To Kathi MacIver who taught me so much and believed in my storytelling.

To Natalia Brothers who said, "Did you start the story in the right place?" and her many other honest insights, causing me to begin a painful but necessary re-write, one of many, of this novel.

To Debbie Allen, my one-woman promoter, who is the reason this whole thing got rolling.

To my first readers who willingly read through this story, offering constructive feedback and encouragement.

To Scoti Domeij, my editor, who is so artistic and concerned about the details, always trying to make the end product honest, authentic, and well-thought-out.

To my dear friends and family who have been my biggest fans along the way—especially my awesome husband who insisted I write when I thought I should get a real job, and who spent countless hours brainstorming the plot with me.

And especially to Jesus, my Lord and Savior, who says that nothing can separate me from His love. I'm so grateful for that truth. All praise and honor and glory to *Him*! ☞

A CONVERSATION WITH HOLLY DEHERRERA

1. How did you decide on the setting of Turkey for your novel? How did you research Turkey in order to set such vivid scenes for your readers? What people or events in your life sparked the ideas for the characters and plot line of this book?

As a 'military brat,' I spent many of my growing up years over seas, living in Turkey a few years in elementary school, and then again during my high school years. I fell in love with the people and the place and still consider those years some of my fondest memories. Some of the events of the story are based loosely on my experiences in Turkey, including, sadly, knowing a man who was killed in a car bombing in Ankara, the capital city, during the Gulf War.

2. What people or events in your life sparked the ideas for the characters and plot line of this book?

My favorite character is Meryem. She's based on our maid, Anur, who became like part of our family when I was in the 2nd, 3rd and 4th grades in Adana, Turkey. I recall vivid memories of:

bumping along in a bus to her home;

sitting on the rooftop and seeing the whole city from there;

peeling potatoes for dinner and being scolded by her for cutting the peels too thick;

sitting on the floor of her mostly unfurnished home and using sign language and choppy sentences to communicate;

hearing her wheezy laugh;

and even seeing her wedding photos with her abusive, alcoholic husband's face poked out of each picture.

Aynur was all love and life and round-faced, flower-panted beauty. And I adored her.

3. Why is forgiveness so important to you as a writer and person? What sparked the idea to write an entire novel with the underlying theme of forgiveness?

Setting the story in Turkey brought to mind memories I'd forgotten, namely the death of an acquaintance by a car bombing, with whom I sang a duet in a play. As an adult, I discovered how peace and forgiveness are intimately knitted together.

My deepest struggles have been when conversations, situations, and past hurts play again and again in my mind. The root is a lack of forgiveness. I know that freedom from those barbs can bring deep, abiding peace—even when the other party never apologizes.

Offering unconditional love, like Christ, through the act of forgiveness, frees us from a sort of bondage. But I've also found that forgiveness is a conscious, daily choice. The universal struggle to forgive others isn't possible without God's supernatural love. As I began remembering and planning so many years ago, forgiveness flowed naturally from the story line. ᴥ

—꙰ GLOSSARY ꙰—

Afiyet olsun: Bon appétit, which means "Enjoy your meal."
Allahu akbar/Allahu ekber: An Arabic, Islamic liturgical proclamation that literally means, "God is greater" or "God is [the] greatest." *Allahu ekber* is Turkish for *Allahu akbar,* which is Arabic.
Anne: Mom
Baba: Father
Börek: A pastry made of baked flaky, phyllo dough filled with cheese, vegetables, or meat
Canim: Darling, my dear
Çay: Turkish tea
Çaydanlık: A small teapot brewer
Çeşme Seyahat: Cesme Travel, a trade name for a bus transportation company
Çok fena: very bad
Çok güzel: very good
Dede: Grandfather
Dev Sol: Considered a terrorist group by Turkey, the European Union and the United States, *Dev Sol* is virulently anti-United States, anti-NATO, and anti the Turkish state.
Dolmuş: bus
Domates: tomatoes

Döner kebab: A type of kebab made with meat cooked on a vertical rotisserie.

Eczane: pharmacy

Efendi: A term of respect and honor that means 'master.'

Ekmek: Raised bread (similar to French bread)

Efes Pilsen: The number one Mediterranean Pilsener beer brewed by Anadolu Efes, a brewery in Istanbul.

Ekmek Fabrikasi: Bread Factory

Evet: I do or yes.

Eyem: I'm well.

Eyem. Sen nasilsin?: I'm well, how are you?

Ezan: Prayer is the second of the Five Pillars of Islam and is performed five times a day by adult Muslims. In Turkey, the *ezan* (call to prayer) is chanted six times daily by *muezzin*, a man who calls the Muslims to prayer from a minaret. Below are the calls for prayer in both Turkish and Arabic.

1. Early Morning Prayer: *İmsak/Fajr*: The *Fajr* prayer is offered before sunrise. It's the first of the five obligatory daily prayers recited by practicing Muslims. *Fajr* means 'dawn' in the Arabic language.

2. The Noon Prayer: *Öğle/Dhuhr or Zuhr*: The second prayer starts midday when the sun passes the zenith. *Zuhr* means 'noon prayer.'

3. The Mid-afternoon Prayer: *İkindi/Asr*: The third prayer is said when the shadows cast by objects are equal to their height.

4. The Sunset Prayer: *Akşam/Maghrib*: The *Maghrib* prayer is the fourth of the five daily prayers and said when the sun disappears below the horizon.

5. The Evening prayer: *Yatsı/Isha*: The fifth prayer is said when the red glow on the horizon disappears.

Güvenli Bölge: Safe Haven

Hayir: No

Hiç problem değil: No problem.

İskender: A Turkish kebab dish made with flatbread, sliced lamb and tomato sauce

Iyi: good

İyi misin: Are you okay?

Iyiyim: I'm fine.

Kaç para: How much?

Kapali: closed

Kilim: A pileless, flat woven rug

Kizkalesi: Means 'Maiden's Castle,' the name of a village 150 meters from a crusader castle floating offshore on a tiny Turkish island.

Limon: lemon

Lira (plural *lire*): The basic monetary unit of Turkey

Merhaba: Hello

Madame: A respectful title or form of address used to a woman

Maraş Dondurma: A chewy Turkish ice cream that stays cold for a long period of time

Nasilsinez?: How are you?

Otogar: bus station

Pastanesi: bakery and snack shop

Pide: pita bread. *Pide* is Turkish, pita is Greek.

Tamam: okay

Tunali Sokak: Tunali Street

Sahan: A two-handled skillet for frying eggs

Salep: Hot thick milk with cinnamon

Salvar: Turkish şalvar are baggy pants with a dropped crotch.

Sarımsak: garlic

Sen nasilsin: How are you?

Seyahat: travel

Simit: A type of bagel with black sesame seeds

"Simitçi. Simitçi. Taze gevrek!": This is the call of the *simit* sellers yelling about their fresh, crisp Turkish bagels.

Soğan: onion

Sorun değil: No problem.

Su: water

Taksi: taxi

Teşekkür ederim: Thank you

Tost: smooshed-cheese sandwiches

Tuz: salt

Uşak kilim: A rug made in the city of Uşak, Turkey from a particular type of silky wool, using a family of designs within a soft-toned, color palette

Vişne suyu: A popular tart and sweet sour cherry nectar drink

Yok: No ≈

⟶ HOLLY'S UPCOMING BOOKS ⟵

The Root Cellar Mysteries for Ages 7-9

The Root Cellar Mystery: Late one night, Poppy and her cousin Sadie, two Old Order Mennonite girls, spot an elderly woman snooping around the root cellar. While seeking to unravel her mysterious behavior, Poppy helps out at her aunt's bed and breakfast where the suspicious guest stays. Can Poppy and Sadie discover what this stranger is up to?

The Key in the Wall Mystery: Poppy and Sadie find another mystery while cleaning out the guest house at Sadie's mom's bed and breakfast. They discover a key hidden inside the wall. If they discover what the key opens, will they find treasure or only more questions?

The Covered Bridge Mystery: Poppy and Sadie feel it's their duty to find the thief stashing items at the covered bridge. Can the girls discover the identity of the person responsible for stealing from their *Mammi* and *Grossdaadi*, while ensuring the safety of their grandparents?

For Middle School and High Schoolers

Unleash the Pen! Writing Outside the Lines: A Tween & Teen Multi-Genre Writing Curriculum: This creative writing curriculum allows your student to dive deeply into a subject while experimenting with a wide variety of writing genres and unique writing assignments. From writing a eulogy, to a wanted poster, leap into this fun writing adventure. ≈

CHAPTERS 1-12

1. Insecurities and unresolved issues from the past rise to the surface for Ella and Murat, like tea leaves in a steaming cup of *çay*. How do Murat and Ella's struggles with their pasts sabotage their lives on a daily basis?

2. Like cutting into an old wound with a *döner kebab* skewer and drizzling on lemon, can you pinpoint any painful roadblocks that hinder you from accomplishing any daily tasks?

3. Discuss the balance between caution and fear. What is the dividing line between the two? How can you tell where one ends and the other begins?

4. What unresolved mourning from a traumatic or painful event makes you feel like a leaf shoved down river?

5. Meryem takes matters into her own hands, choosing to marry someone for the financial stability versus heeding her father's warning, essentially out of fear of the alternative. Do you think she's justified in her decision? Why or why not?

6. Are there times when you allow concern for the outcome to guide your decisions, versus relying on your fundamental beliefs or convictions? If so, how does surrendering to anxiety versus confidence in God or your spiritual beliefs affect the outcome? ◌◌

CHAPTERS 13-33

1. Ella wondered: *How open have I made my small home? How open have I made my heart? Do I ever prepare for a possible guest who might need me? Or am I solely in the business of protecting myself? Doing things on my terms, with all the proper buffers in place?* What buffer in your life shields you from offering hospitality and distances you from developing closer relationships?

2. How did Ella's independence and desire to be in control put her safety at risk? When are times when you resist help?

3. Murat's secondhand faith struggles to believe his mother's wise words to release the hurt and fear from his past. The ghosts of the old, ugly past still maintained a stronghold in the present. How

did that stronghold complicate Murat's life? What strongholds in your life complicate your life and relationships?

4. As a young woman, Meryem's father warns her to slow down and be careful. What does her heart desire *more*, causing her to ignore his wisdom? Have you ever felt a nudging to use caution or go slower with a decision or an action? Did you listen to wise advice? If not, what was the outcome of that choice?

5. Releasing the past, like birds in search of an olive branch, takes faith. How does releasing the past free you to imagine and embrace new beginnings?

6. What roadblocks do Ella and Murat perceive standing in the way of their relationship with each other? What roadblocks do you erect that blind you from seeing the blessings in front of you?

7. What is the difference between true hope and wishful thinking? In what is each rooted? ❧

CHAPTERS 34-55

1. *İskender,* a dish that represents Turkey to Ella, drives her desire to learn how to make it. What recipes trigger memories for you, and why?

2. On their first official date, Murat takes Ella to the ocean. Why is that symbolic?

3. Ella finding out her father's murderer was dead, deeply disappointed her. Have you ever struggled to forgive someone who wasn't sorry or, at least, never apologized? From what does forgiveness free the wounded forgiver?

4. How well does Murat trying to control everything work out?

5. What do you attempt to control in your own life? In what ways does the need for control add stress to your life?

6. Ella faces a stalker and decides she needs to go home. However, Ella is forced to ignore her own concerns and defers to the greater need at the orphanage. Tell about a time you laid down your problems to help someone else in greater need? If so, how did that help you? ❧

CHAPTERS 56-68

1. *Dede,* Murat's grandfather, abandoned Murat and Meryem, blaming them unfairly for Murat's father's sins. How did *Dede's* actions affect Meryem and Murat's social status and financial security? What are some things you could do each week to reach out and help someone overwhelmed by circumstances and struggling just to survive?

2. How does blaming another person shut down communication and reconciliation? When devastated by someone's life-altering actions, have you ever blamed someone else unfairly? If so, what could you have done differently?

3. When Murat finds out about his father's involvement in the death of Ella's Dad, he takes the burden of blame on himself. Jesus did the same for every person, but what is the difference? How did Jesus's example bring freedom and Murat's bring oppression?

4. In what ways does Murat punish himself for his past? What ways do you punish yourself for regrets from your past?

5. Both Meryem and Ella's mom cover up the full truth of the past. What do you think about their choices to hide some of what happened?

6. Is there ever a good time for secrets? When and how is it appropriate to share a secret that might cause someone pain? ◈

CHAPTERS 69-86

1. How did Ella struggle in her efforts to reach out and connect with Pinar, who was abused and closed down?

2. Discuss ways to support someone who's struggling, or hurting, or abused who appears resistant to help.

3. Ella buys several things that are special because of what they represent, like the market fabric, lemon cologne, and the Turkish rug. What objects in your home represent something special or someone you cherish?

4. Why is Murat a better leader when he quits trying to be a savior to all?

5. When Murat recalls that he wired the bomb that killed Ella's father, Meryem tells him, "You cannot forget redemption, Murat, or your father will win." What does that mean?

6. What does the legend of *Kizkalesi* Castle have in common with Ella's story?

7. How do you hide away from life due to past hurts and current fears—bigger obstacles, insecurities—which thwart you from moving through mourning or toward healing?

8. What can you do to reclaim life from the losses or hurts in your life? ❧

⸺ PHOTO CREDITS ⸺

Border and Cover Design: 16th Century Islamic pottery in the Metropolitan Museum of Art. Tile with saz leaf, tulips, and hyacinth flowers from İznik, Turkey.

Source/Photographer:
Marie-Lan Nguyen (2011).

‐⚬ RECOMMENDED RESOURCES ⚬‐

"The future is meant for those who are willing to let go of the worst parts of the past."—Corey Taylor

The following organizations deal with the issues addressed in this book. They provide referrals for those who want to seek help and for those who want to help the abused or orphans in a practical way.[1]

The Tragedy Assistance Program for Survivors: www.taps.org

The Tragedy Assistance Program for Survivors (TAPS) offers compassionate care to those grieving the death of a loved one who served in our Armed Forces. Since 1994, TAPS provides comfort and hope 24 hours a day, 7 days a week through a national peer support network and connection to grief resources, all at no cost to surviving families and loved ones. TAPS has assisted over 50,000 surviving family members, casualty officers, and caregivers.

TAPS serves ALL survivors: adult children, children, ex-spouses, extended family, friends and battle buddies, grandparents, parents, siblings, widows/widowers/widowed and significant others through survivor grief seminars, suicide survivor grief seminars, retreats, expeditions, 'inner warrior' events and an online community. The TAPS Military and Veteran Caregiver Network provides pre- and post-9/11 era military and veteran caregivers with peer support and partners to reduce their isolation and increase their sense of connectedness, engagement, hopefulness, wellness, and their knowledge and skills.

800 Phone Number: If you just need someone to talk to, please call TAPS any time at 1.800.959.TAPS (8277). The TAPS survivor care team can also tell you about services and programs you might find helpful.

Facebook: www.facebook.com/TAPS4America

Twitter: www.twitter.com/TAPS4America

---

1. Blackside Publishing (BP) is not responsible for, and expressly disclaims all liability for, damages of any kind arising out of use, reference to, or reliance on any of recommended resources. The referrals are provided "as is" without any representations or warranties, expressed, or implied. Referrals are provided solely for information and BP encourages you to contact them directly.

YouTube: www.youtube.com/supporttaps
Address: National Headquarters. 3033 Wilson Boulevard, Suite 630, Arlington, VA 22201

The Warrior's Journey: www.thewarriorsjourney.org

Warriors hold to a set of guiding principles that shape their worldview and characterize their community. Each branch of service offers its own focus, but all hold to core truths about the value of defending the constitution and honoring the legacy of those who served before them. The Warrior's Journey is an online resource for the military community offering trusted content relating to the mission, vision, challenges, and ethos of the warrior. Offering insight, perspective, and support, The Warrior's Journey empowers and equips warriors and their families to find wholeness in everyday life.

GriefShare: www.griefshare.org

GriefShare provides materials to help churches facilitate grief recovery support meetings, and assists individuals to connect with these local groups. Thousands of GriefShare grief recovery support groups meet throughout the US, Canada, and in over 10 countries.
Facebook: www.facebook.com/griefshare/
YouTube: www.youtube.com/user/GriefShare
Twitter: www.twitter.com/griefcaring
Address: P.O. Box 1739, Wake Forest, NC 27588
Phone: 800-395-5755

The National Domestic Abuse Hotline: www.thehotline.org

Operating around the clock, seven days a week, confidential and free of cost, the National Domestic Violence Hotline provides lifesaving tools and immediate support to enable victims to find safety and live lives free of abuse. Callers to The Hotline at 1-800-799-SAFE (7233) can expect highly trained, experienced advocates to offer compassionate support, crisis intervention information, and referral services in over 170 languages. Visitors to this site can find information about domestic violence, safety planning, local resources, and ways to support the organization.

Open Hearts Ministry: www.ohmin.org

Life is a path marked by hurt, hope and struggles. Open Hearts comes alongside those who've been abused to help them find wholeness. Open Hearts trains you to engage people along that journey in deeper and healthier ways. Through a safe and confidential group process, their curriculum leads you through your own stories of pain, disappointment and abuse, equipping you to share the care you receive with others. Open Hearts teaches how to share and listen honestly and practice good self-care. Seeking to love like Jesus, with empathy and forgiveness Open Hearts helps create authentic community where people are heard, loved and healed together.

Address: 5340 Holiday Terrace, Suite 9 Kalamazoo, MI 49009
Phone: 269-383-3597

Childhelp National Child Abuse Hotline: www.childhelp.org/hotline

The Childhelp National Child Abuse Hotline 1-800-4-A-CHILD (1-800-422-4453) is dedicated to the prevention of child abuse. Serving the United States, its territories, and Canada, the hotline is staffed 24 hours a day, 7 days a week with professional crisis counselors who, through interpreters, can provide assistance in over 170 languages. The hotline offers crisis intervention, information, literature, and referrals to thousands of emergency, social service, and support resources. All calls are confidential.

Prevent Child Abuse America: www.preventchildabuse.org

This non-profit organization works with local, state, and national groups to promote healthy parenting and community involvement as effective strategies for preventing child abuse.

Address: 228 South Wabash Avenue, 10th Floor, Chicago, IL 60604
Phone: 800-244-5373

Children's HopeChest: www.hopechest.org

Children's HopeChest releases the potential of orphaned and vulnerable children and their communities through partnerships that cultivate holistic transformation and sustainability. Children's HopeChest engages churches and other Christian communities in long-term partnerships that:

Addresses the complex causes of poverty, including material, spiritual, emotional, social, economic, and educational needs.

Tends to the child's holistic needs for survival, community, education, and employment.

Transforms the lives of children through a focus on sustainability, independence, and long-term self-sufficiency.

Children's HopeChest partners primarily with churches, but also businesses and other Christian communities including online groups, book clubs, bloggers, and other small groups. Sponsoring communities form deep, meaningful relationships with the orphaned and vulnerable children served by Children's HopeChest, which in turn offers positive self-worth and hope for the future.

Compassion International: www.compassion.com

The hallmark of Compassion's work is one-to-one child sponsorship. Children are welcome to participate in a Compassion-assisted, child development center regardless of their faith. Compassion International, a Christian child development organization, is dedicated to delivering children from economic, physical, social and spiritual poverty, enabling them to become responsible, fulfilled Christian adults. To sponsor a child, log onto www.compassion.com/sponsor_a_child/default.htm. **Phone:** 800-336-7676, Monday - Friday, 7 a.m.—5:30 p.m. MST

Teen Mission Trips

CRU.org: www.cru.org/train-and-grow/leadership-training/sending-your-team/serving-at-an-orphanage-on-summer-project.html

Teaching Overseas

Association of Christian Schools International: www.careers.acsi.org/jobseeker/search/results/

—∽ RECOMMENDED READING ∽—

The Hiding Place and Amazing Love: True Stories of the Power of Forgiveness, Corrie ten Boom

Orphanology: Awakening Gospel-Centered Adoption and Orphan Care, Tony Merida and Rick Morton

Silent Tears: A Journey of Hope in a Chinese Orphanage, Kay Bratt

Dangerous Surrender: What Happens When You Say Yes to God, Kay Warren

Three Names of Me, Mary Cummings, Age Range: 8-13 years, Grade Level: 3-8

Adopted for Life: The Priority of Adoption for Christian Families and Churches, Russell D. Moore

The Connected Child: Bring Hope and Healing to Your Adoptive Family, Karyn Purvis, David Cross, and Wendy Lyons

There Is No Me Without You: One Woman's Odyssey to Rescue Africa's Children, Melissa Fay Greene

Fields of the Fatherless: Discover the Joy of Compassionate Living, Tom Davis

The One Factor: How One Changes Everything, Doug Sauders

Triumph Over Terror

Are you searching for comfort and wondering, "Where is God?" amidst terror and turmoil?

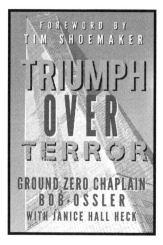

The day that changed the world—September 11, 2001—propelled America into the long war, the Global War on Terror. Like many Americans who serve our country, Chaplain Bob Ossler donned his firefighter turn-out gear, boarded a plane, and made his way to Manhattan to help in any way possible. He was escorted onto the smoldering, quaking heap, dubbed "The Pile." Entering into the Gates of Hell—the crematorium and morgue for nearly 3000 beloved souls—an electrifying chill of horror shot through him.

Trained as a professional first responder, Ossler served five tours of duty during the cleanup at Ground Zero after 9/11. Bob's eyewitness vignettes recount the questions, fears, struggles, and sacrifices of the families and workers overwhelmed by despair. Chaplain Ossler conducted over 300 mini-memorials for the fragmentary remains carried off the Pile. He comforted the mourners, the frightened, and the heartbroken laborers sifting through millions of tons of carnage for the remains of their friends, the unknown dead—and their faith.

From the broken fragments of glass, steel, and men, Chaplain Ossler's mosaic of God's grace unveils the outpouring of generosity, heroism, and unity from people who stepped up to do "something." Ossler honors the ultimate sacrifice and bravery of first responders who rush toward terror to save lives.

Chaplain Ossler chronicles the best of humanity—acts of courage and goodness in the midst of chaos, personal tragedy and unimaginable devastation. As terrorist attacks continue to assault humanity, Ossler reveals how your spirit can triumph over terror's reign, and how you can help others suffering from trauma and loss.

Authors: Ground Zero Chaplain Bob Ossler with Janice Hall Heck
Foreword: Tim Shoemaker
Published: August, 2016
Available in both paperback and e-book.

A Soldier to Santiago:
Finding Peace on the Warrior Path

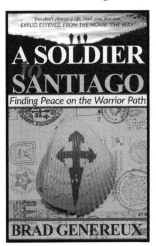

"I gave the best years of my life to a cause—to a belief that proved false. I loved living on the edge. The thrill of standing the watch. Rushing into harm's way on behalf of my country. For over 22 years and with pride, I represented America by wearing the cloth of the nation. When my service was all over? Life had passed me by and . . . I fit in— nowhere."—Senior Chief Petty Officer Brad Genereux.

Is forgiveness and peace within the grasp of those who spent their lives pursuing the next mission on behalf of their country? Brad Genereux traces two parallel journeys—one through the inferno of war in Afghanistan, and the other through the healing purgatory of the Camino de Santiago. Juxtaposed between a combat zone and The Way of Saint James, experience two adventures and the two lives of one man. Willing to sacrifice his life to aid the Afghanis, Brad's candid account chronicles the challenges to carry out missions while operating under a complex chain of command, Afghani corruption, and deadly sabotage by the Taliban.

After Genereux retired from the military, he faced the arduous pursuit to assimilate into civilian life and to make sense of the unexpected deaths of three family members. Brad revisits dark demons imprisoning his spirit and the healing peace unlocked on The Way of Saint James. This book shadows the reflections of a war-hardened man devoid of identity and purpose and his search for answers, hope, and himself on a 769-kilometer trek over the Pyrenees and across northern Spain.

Are you searching for peace and purpose? Are you suffering from isolation, hypervigilance, nightmares, or insomnia? Experience the camaraderie of warriors deployed to the battlefield and the *esprit de corps* of Camino peregrinos as they triumph over the inner battles of the spirit.

Author: Brad Genereux
Foreword: Heather A. Warfield, Ph.D.
Afterword: Dr. Christine Bridges Esser
Available in both paperback and e-book.
Brad leads other veterans on the Spanish path to peace in the Spring and Fall. If you're interested in trekking the Santiago de Camino, connect with Brad:
Email: bgenereux@mail.com
Facebook: www.facebook.com/brad.gener.1
Instagram: www.instagram.com/bradgenereux/

The Ghosts of Babylon

The haunting poetry of The Ghosts of Babylon is as near to the crucible of war as you can get without wearing Kevlar and camouflage.

Every war triggers the question—what's war like? *The Ghosts of Babylon* offers eyewitness accounts of warriors who lost their innocence dueling in the sands of the Iraqi inferno or fighting in the chilling Afghan mountains or on the khaki-colored plains. Wounds enshrouded under the bandages of headlines and sound bites will never bridge the gap between soldier and civilian.

Only a soldier poet lays bare the honor and horror. Only a veteran reveals the physical and mental battles waged by the warrior caste. Only the war poet distills the emotions of those who tasted bravery and terror, love and vengeance, life and death. Based on the experiences of a U.S. Army Ranger turned private security contractor, these powerful poems capture the essence of Jonathan Baxter's twelve military and civilian deployments.

Jonathan reveals the contradictory nature of deployment in a war zone—exhilaration, monotony, ugliness, and occasional beauty. From ancient times to present day, war poetry telegraphs a dispatch across the ages about the universal experiences of war—brotherhood and bereavement, duty and disillusionment, and heroism and horror. No history mirrors the brutal realities and emotions of armed conflict than the shock of war erupting from the warrior poet's pen.

Jonathan resurrects the ghosts and gods of soldiers past. His poignant memorial to fallen brothers transmits the shadowy presence and ultimate sacrifices of the coffined to the fortunate un-coffined. *The Ghosts of Babylon* strips away the cultural varnish of the 'enemy,' painting the bitter irony of every day lives caught in the crosshairs of terror, chaos, and death. From moving to startling to soulful, these masterpieces provoke you to think about the truths and consequences of those who risk their lives on the frontline of freedom—for you, their friends, and our country.

Author: Jonathan Baxter
Foreword: Leo Jenkins
Available in paperback.

Made in the USA
Middletown, DE
03 March 2019